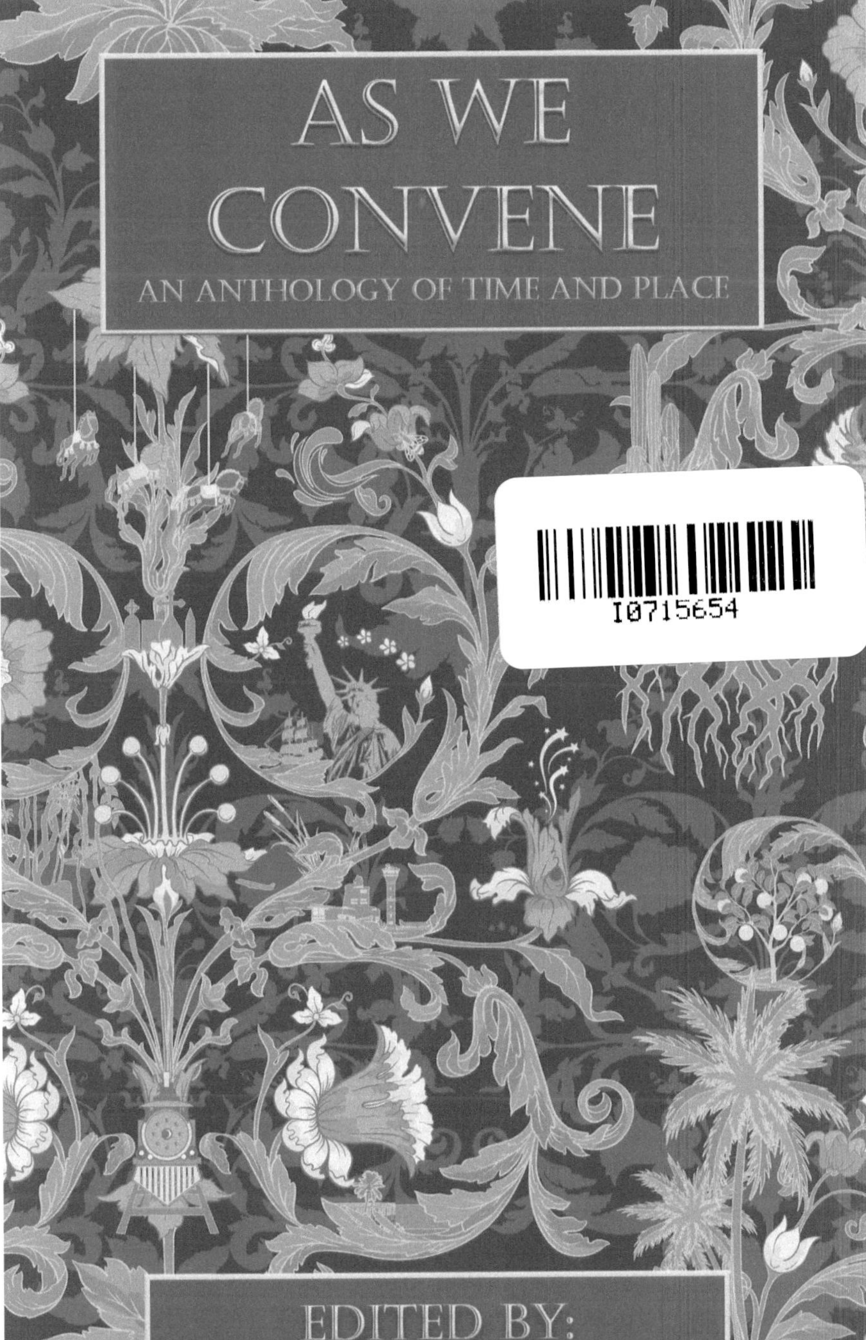
AS WE
CONVENE
AN ANTHOLOGY OF TIME AND PLACE
EDITED BY:
LAUREN T. DAVILA

As We Convene
An Anthology of Time and Place

Edited by Lauren Davila

Featuring Stories by:

Casie Bazay   Amanda Bender   Shelli Cornelison
Emily Gray   Elizabeth Holden   Sara Kapadia
Jennifer Kaul   Alexandra Z. Lazar
C.M. Leyva   K. Psych   Nico Vazquez
Gerardo J. Mercado   Mary Winsor   Angela Sanchez
J. Ophelia Vazquez

CONTENTS

Foreword
By Lauren Davila

I didn't travel outside of the United States until I was in college studying abroad. For a semester, I had a chance to explore all of the history and romanticism that Florence, Italy had to offer. Sure, maybe I wasn't *really* prepared for all of the art and architecture I was seeing, but in some ways I was. All of the historical fiction novels I had read on the Medicis and the Renaissance had prepared me for the archways and cobblestone streets and lush gardens. In some ways, fiction allowed me to travel in ways I couldn't physically, up to that point.

I will say, it wasn't just historical cities across the world I had explored though. Through fiction, I had a chance examine locations that became home to me without even stepping foot across their imaginary borders — especially fantasy worlds.

I was able to wander around haunted, misty, Yorkshire moors with star-crossed lovers.

I sat next to a little, brown girl who looked like my nana on a stoop on Mango Street.

I danced around the floral covered lanes of Avonlea with a group of tight-knit friends.

I crawled right behind the Pevensie children to a land of snow and talking creatures.

In all of the ways that mattered, these locations, these locales, became part of the very fabric of my being. They shaped who I was and made me a "world traveler" before I ever had the privilege of loading onto a plane.

This collection was compiled with the idea that, in many ways, location can be the most lasting experience to a reader in a piece of fiction. In the stories in this anthology, the setting is just as important as the characters or pacing or plot twists. My hope is that you will explore settings and locales very different from your own. That you will have a chance to see yourself or those you know in these extraordinary tales. That you will find yourself feeling like you need a nap — the one you take after a long day of exploring a new city.

Thank you to all of the contributors for trusting me with your words. Now, to all of you excited travelers, enjoy your trip through time and place. Take a few pictures and send a postcard back to yourself if you'd like.

A Note on Trigger Warnings

Some stories in this collection have trigger warnings. We have done our best to identify relevant trigger warnings. They are listed below and precede each story.

Combined Trigger Warnings: Descriptions of suicide and murder, alcoholism, grief, violence, references to off-page domestic violence and sexual assault, child brides, death, corpses, contagions, gore, mentions of parental death, diaspora, colonization and slavery, themes of classism.

The Grand Canyon Historical Society

Mary Winsor

I have been waiting in the parking lot outside my birthplace since dawn. Locals believe this site is haunted — not an uncommon origin story. But rumored ghosts and restless spirits are less interesting than — or perhaps owing to — the building's location in a tiny village at the edge of the Grand Canyon. The once-upon-a-time clinic's reputation is earned in part by the virtually unchanging population growth of the village; there are right around zero births each year, while recorded deaths are upwards of 12 or 13 annually (or, in some years, as much as ten times that number for airplane or helicopter crashes). And it is rumored many more deaths occurred in the earlier iterations of the building itself than are accounted for in its "official" history. Traveling against cosmic traffic, I made my entrance twenty-five years ago in this place where exit is more anticipated and less surprising.

Rain pelts the roof of the pickup and washes down the windshield in sheets, creating an impressionist view of the log building in the distance. It is easy to imagine the past lives of this structure: first, decades ago, it was temporary quarters for the mule drivers who led tourists down the canyon trails; then it was a storage shed for grain and alfalfa to feed said mules; next, a post office where park employees cashed their paychecks and sent letters home to New Hampshire or Texas or wherever the mostly-young work crews called home; then a two-room clinic. In this small clinic, my mother pushed me out of her body and into the waiting arms of the Canyon's only doctor, an exhausted and nervous-looking man whose photo hangs now in the reception hall of the latest repurposing and expansion of the pine log and adobe building — the Grand Canyon Historical Society.

This is my second visit to the GCHS in hopes of retrieving records from the "Archives," a dusty storage room that, the office manager told me, was once the L&D room of the old clinic. Where I was born, copiers and fax machines, old computers and stacks of old National Park leaflets have gone to die.

I need a history. The future, including a family of my own, feels impossible until I know more about the family I came from. My boyfriend Julius has told me he understands this. I'm hoping he understands it enough for both of us.

But I am reluctant to go inside. The embarrassment of my visit last year to the GCHS will forever be married to the smells of dust and old electronics and the stink of sweat and vomit. Before I could even really get started on my research that day, I vomited in the Archives room, then in the hallway, and again in the lobby. Shirley, a volunteer receptionist who was probably wishing she hadn't retired from teaching middle school in Flagstaff, ran in my wake, holding a small trash can in a futile attempt to contain the mess. When I finally collapsed on a chair in the lobby, Shirley called Tina to come pick me up. That first attempt at researching the GCHS archives was thwarted by a debilitating case of flu, we later guessed, that landed me in bed for a week. It was the only time I had ever contemplated my own death — at first because I was afraid I would die, and later, in the violent throes of the illness, because I feared I wouldn't.

But I should've known better. Forget old age, ordinary sickness, or boring disease; around here, death is dramatic, almost instant. There are no long goodbyes. Death is the result of freak accidents or suicidal leaps, unforgiving stupidity or inescapable sadness. People die publicly in moments of astonishing carelessness as they strike a pose on a crumbling rock face just beyond the guard rails of a tourist lookout point. Or they drown in the bottom of the Canyon, seduced by deep, pristine waters famously still and calm one moment, wildly unnavigable in the next. Some leap from what they believe is the canyon's edge, the point beyond which brief flight and nothingness await. Their footprints reveal a careful choreography, even if the jumpers leave behind no letter or text or social media post. For the unluckiest of souls, attempts at emancipation from sorrow are thwarted by a dark ledge, a hidden crag in the face of the canyon maybe twenty or thirty feet down, where their broken bodies lay undiscovered for days, weeks, even years. And like any place where two or more humans convene over time, the Canyon has its murder stories, rumors of people being pushed to their deaths by jilted lovers or greedy business partners. At the Canyon and on the river that courses through it, death is dramatic, foolish, reckless, even willful.

Then, there are people who, like my parents, simply vanish. Tina knows better than anyone that I have mixed feelings about my birthplace. The grandeur of the canyon itself sometimes only intensifies the grief and curiosity I feel about parents. Of course Tina knows this — she raised me. She tells me, every chance she gets, that she took me in and brought me up right.

It was in the cards, she says.

Contemplating another foray into the Society's heaps of useless records — this time without Tina's knowledge, I am overcome with shame. It was Tina who picked me up from the GCHS when Shirley called to tell her I was sick. Tina who nursed me through that awful flu. Tina who drove me back to grad school in Tucson a week later.

And Tina has stuck by me through all the hard days in my life. I feel treasonous and a little selfish, sneaking back home this way

— not even giving her enough notice to take time off work for a quick breakfast or dinner together.

When the rain lets up, I decide not to search the archives. Instead, I will drive to the rim and hike a few miles, clear my head. Then I will go straight to Tina's place. And I'll try to explain, for the two-hundredth time, that I need to know. I will tell her, again, my curiosity is natural. That I'm not trying to hurt her by, as she puts it, "digging up bones."

I want to jump out of the truck and slam the door hard enough for Tina to hear it inside the trailer. And then I want to hear her shout as she does when surprise and delight collide at the black-jack table or in her daily horoscope: "What in the world? Can you believe it?" I want to leap up the steps of the sagging porch and run my hand along the railing worn so smooth by the canyon's radical weather that I can no longer read my name carved there.

But I am transfixed by the million-dollar view from Tina's property. The rim of the canyon is ablaze with ocotillo and sage blossoms in shades of red, yellow, and purple. All of it is rendered brighter under the cover of storm clouds gathering in the distance; the intense colors of this landscape are best viewed in half-light.

I left this view and the Canyon for the first time in 2005, right after my seventeenth birthday. Tina said, "Summer babies are so hard to buy for," and pressed a small *Western Savings* passbook into my hands. "Your folks didn't have much to leave you, honey, but I've been saving. And anyway, I came to the Canyon with my own money." The name on the inside flap of the passbook, above the balance of "$85,000," was mine: Lucia Anne Carter. "You have to go to college," Tina said. "Or else what is all this for?"

We had packed my clothes and books into two suitcases I didn't even know Tina owned, and I boarded the twilight Grey-hound bus to Tucson. I cried for most of the nearly ten hours of that ride; I thought I was mourning Tina, the only home I had known. But it was the first time I had grieved, in body and mind, the parents I never knew. And I was finally allowing myself to be angry about their seemingly capricious disappearance.

There is something about a road trip, with all your life in a Greyhound rearview, that brings all the troubled cards to the top of the deck. By the time the bus arrived at Ronstadt station in Tucson, I had no more tears left. I spent the next six years studying biology and taking a few botany classes, a logical extension of my childhood spent at the Canyon, despite Tina always urging me to study rocks. "Geology is where the mysteries are solved, honey." But I'd had more than enough mystery in my life.

I am about to go inside the house, when I feel Tina's hand on my shoulder. She has always been able to get the drop on me.

"Hey, you," she says. "Been calling your name. Didn't mean to startle you."

She hugs me hard, and there seems to be a little less of her than in our last embrace over a year ago. Tina's lifelong practice of yoga and a mostly plant-based diet from which she departs only once a year for a steak at the El Tovar have served her well. Her only other indulgence now is coloring her hair a shade or two darker than her once-natural blonde, refusing to surrender to the gray that would otherwise sprout at her crown. Each time I visit, in these first moments of greeting I'm aware of small shifts, subtle changes that, added together, should mean Tina is finally aging. But then, in the next glance or word, I cannot see these signs at all. She is as timeless to me as this place where we became each other's family.

"It's good to be home. How are you, Tina?"

Our greetings are awkward after we've been apart for a while. At her insistence, I've always called Tina by her name, never *Mama* or *Mother* or *Mom*, except during a short period in second grade when Mr. Nez assigned us art projects as Mother's Day gifts. When we finally carried the clay pots and decoupaged hearts home, I imagined each of my classmates bringing their art to a "real" mother who received their gift — and them — in awe and adoration. So, for a while, I said the forbidden words. At night, after she had pulled the quilt to my chin and closed the door behind her, leaving me in darkness, I whispered *Thank you, Mother* or *Love you, Mama.* And this endearment, this title, almost escapes my lips now.

"I'm alright, Lucy," she tells me. "A better question is *how are you?* Come on inside. I've got supper. Took the night off."

Tina tends bar at the El Tovar lounge here at the Canyon, and deals cards at invitation-only poker games at the Lucky Luz, as she has since before I was born. She met my parents when she was their blackjack dealer at the Luz. She had shown them a map of the village trailer park where they ended up renting a single-wide. My parents were on a "hippy-dippy adventure," Tina had told me. "And they didn't have a care in the world."

A few years after my parents went missing, Tina sold my parents' camper. When I was nine years old, I began asking for mementos, letters, photos, clothing — anything they had once touched that I could hold in my hand. Tina told me all of their belongings and the contents of their rented trailer had been hauled to the Goodwill in Flagstaff. "Except for you, darlin, there's nothing left of your parents," she told me. "Bless them, they didn't have much." The camper is still parked on Tina's property, elevated on stacked railroad ties. But it has not really belonged to us in years; coveys of quail and a few chickens nest there now.

Tina has cooked her go-to meal of roasted vegetable fajitas. The onions, squash, and peppers are grown in her greenhouse — the "shed" as she calls it — that seems bigger every time I come home. She seasons everything with her own garlic, cumin, and chili powder, the way most people do around here. Except, unlike the cafes and cantinas we love, she never uses cilantro—Tina doesn't grow it or buy it, because we both think it tastes like soap. Over dinner, we talk until the sun has set and we realize we are sitting in near darkness. She brews mint tea and brings me a steaming cup. "With honey, just the way you like it."

She switches on a lamp beside the sofa strewn with books and magazines; index cards and grocery store receipts spill from the pages she wishes to revisit. Years ago, she converted my old bedroom into a study, but still works her crossword puzzles and does all her reading here on the cozy sectional. Her literary range says more about her than most anything else in her home: celebrity and tabloid magazines share space with literary journals and hefty novels, poetry collections, newspapers, gardening books, and a few geology texts.

She stacks her scattered library on the coffee table and motions for me to take a seat. In these first hours together, there is always some formality I find slightly unsettling, but the discomfort is eventually overcome as we fall into our habits and routines.

"What would you like to do while you're here, hon? How long are you staying?"

"I don't know," I say. I hate lying to her. "A week, maybe? Long enough to meet the new man in your life?"

"Oh, yeah, well — he's gone. Like all the rest. And you know me. I like my independence. And my solitude. And anyway, what about you, missy? What's up with that musician? Not a bad looking fella. And talented to boot. So, what gives?"

"We're taking it slow," I say, but my smile gives me away.

"Come. On."

"His name is Julius. Grew up in Chicago," I say.

"Julius? Such a serious name."

"His friends call him Juice. I call him Jay. Or Jules. Whatever you want to call him, I'm going with him to Chicago. Two weeks from yesterday."

"What? The Windy City?" Tina leans toward me, takes my arm as she does when she is excited to share. "Let me tell you some great clubs you should go to."

"I'm going there to meet his parents."

She leans back now. Goes quiet. She is far away. *Elvis has left the building* as she likes to say.

"Well, one of these days," I say, "you should be open to the idea, too, Tina. I don't want you to be alone."

She laughs at this. So hard it almost hurts my feelings. But I let it go. And when her laughter has turned to heavy sighs, I change the subject.

"Just want to hang out with you, if you're free. Maybe we could hike a little. And I'd like to visit the GCHS."

"I knew it." She looks up at the ceiling, smiles wide, and exhales deeply like she has been dealt a winning hand. I know all of her tells. "Research, am I right? You're back at it?"

"Well, not really," I say. I can't stop myself from running my hand through my hair. My fingers worry my red curls, one of the features Tina says I share with my mother. When I was a kid, Tina always complained that my hair needed cutting or taming.

"Uh, uh. You've started again," she says. She knows my tells, too.

I'm not sure why I don't want her to know I've begun — or rather, resumed — researching my parents, except I don't want her to worry for me. As a child, I was determined to retrace their last hours. My investigation, documented in notebooks Tina stores in my old room, sent my twelve-year-old self reeling into what we now call, with almost no irony, my "nervous break-it-down." She drew me back from that emotional ledge with lots of talking, dancing, long hikes in the canyon, and with late-night brownies and old movies — Marilyn Monroe films are her favorites. Tina is still told, at least once a week, she could be Marilyn's double.

"It's okay, Luce," she says. "It'll be different this time. Better. And nowadays I have more time to help."

I take her hand, but say nothing.

"If you want," she says. "Up to you, darlin'. Only I wouldn't go to the Society in the morning. Start at the park library, is what

I'd do. They have some new database or some such in there now. That's your best bet."

"Thanks," I say. "Really, Tina, thank you."

She hugs me hard, kisses me goodnight, and disappears into the darkness of her bedroom at the end of the hall. I succumb to the combination of exhaustion and sheer relief, and settle into Tina's comfortable sofa.

I wake to a quiet house. Tina has slipped an extra pillow under my head and drawn one of her patchwork quilts over me. Sunlight slices through the gaps in the heavy curtains over the trailer windows. I love sunrise here, and it is unusual for Tina to let me sleep through it.

It's still too early to call Julius. He'll be sleeping after a wedding gig in the Foothills; he says his band is only rehearsing for our wedding one day. It's a good thing, what we have. So good it scares me. I will call him tonight after Tina goes to bed.

I swig lukewarm coffee from a chipped ceramic mug, then quickly shower and dress. When I step outside, the August heat feels good on my damp head. The recent rain has brought with it a little humidity, and the air is heavy with the scents of juniper and ponderosa pine. Tina bought this small acreage, this little piece of heaven, as she calls it, a few months after the state of Arizona said she could raise me. I grew up discovering every inch of these ten acres adjacent to the National Park near the south rim of the Canyon.

Tina's green Volkswagen Beetle is not parked in its usual spot beside the trailer. But she wouldn't have gone any farther than the village for groceries or maybe to the post office — not while I am home for a visit.

I scan the property Tina insists on keeping as natural as she can: no fences, no gravel, no water wasted on lawn or non-indigenous plants. The pines and piñons are taller and fuller, of course, and there is a bit more scrub grass near the road. The mesquites had a hard season or two; they are fewer in number now on the west side of the property. The place is mostly unchanged, except for the "shed." And I wonder who has helped Tina expand her greenhouse; the extension is likely home to dozens more new plants and growing pots. I have to take a look inside.

Right away, I'm that kid again — helping Tina thumb little seedlings into pots, re-planting sprouts into still bigger pots. I always loved turning the soil in growing beds built from a bathtub and a couple of old water troughs Tina found in Flagstaff.

Her greenhouse garden is as practical as it is beautiful; flowers and small trees whose only job was to be proud and colorful grow alongside herbs and vegetables and medicinal plants. I walk along the flagstone paths between the rows of plants, touching each one and breathing in deeply the greenhouse air that always amazed me as a kid — sweet-smelling, somehow cool enough in summer and warm enough in winter to not be oppressively humid, and so energizing, almost restorative. I used to hide in here after a rough day on the school bus or when another little friend had moved away from the village — transient workers and park employees don't tend to stick around more than a couple of seasons. And Tina would find me hiding between the stock tanks of heirloom tomatoes and baby peach trees. She would bring me a cup of tea or cocoa, and then sit down beside me. Neither of us said much. And then she would offer me a hand, pull me to my feet, and guide me out of the shed.

The garden is bigger now. Tina is growing squash, a few varieties of peppers, a couple different kinds of melon, and some root vegetables—new varieties of potatoes and some turnips, maybe. On one side of the new "wing" of the greenhouse, clumps of fat, black-purple berries hang from vines staked up with wire and strips of old t-shirt. This is a triumph; Tina always struggled with berry vines and bushes. I pick a few berries, and hold them up in a toast Tina; then come tears that have no source other than the sweet-and-tart, juicy goodness that fills my mouth. I am so happy for Tina. Berries, here in the high desert, and on a thin budget, too. On the opposite side of the new addition, three growing beds in direct sunlight are devoted to flowers: Phlox and Blazing Stars and Lupines and Dalmatian Bellflowers, each their own dazzling purple, and together a radiance that calms and soothes.

In still another section, Tina's stalwart little families of herbs have grown in number and variety. Their combined powerful fragrance would be unmistakable even if the little plants were not: mint, thyme, rosemary, basil, oregano — the kitchen essentials. And Tina has even managed to coax ginger and turmeric from the carefully mixed soil in nearby pots. With the help of strategically placed shade sails and mounds of the rich soil Tina has learned to balance — acidic soil for some plant babies, and alkaline for others, there are a few different growing seasons simultaneously occurring in the shed. She has installed a new watering system; she no longer needs to drag hoses and heft buckets, apparently. And she has poured sand between the flagstones; they have settled a bit, and the tidy, narrow pathways are smoother.

From the looks of things, Tina has been working double shifts at the El Tovar or standing a few more card games than usual. And her energy can't be what it once was. The least I can do for her while I'm home is prune some of the plants, pull the few brave and tiny weeds that somehow manage a start in Tina's beds, and snap off a few buds that have lived their last.

I retrace my steps to the "old" part of the greenhouse, to Tina's worktable near the entrance. Tina's gardening gloves, worn and permanently shaped to her hands, are ready to work. Gardening tools (to be used only for the purposes for which they were engineered, she always told me), buckets and pots filled with soil or fertilizer cover the table. And resting atop back issues of Gardens Illustrated and Arizona Highways is the current issue of The Old Farmer's Almanac. "Everything under the sun, including the moon," is the 2012 tagline. "Weather forecasts, planting tables, and Zodiac secrets."

On a wall shelf beside the worktable is the clay pot I gave Tina in second grade. The exterior of the pot is blue – Cobalt, Mr. Nez told me, with cottony-looking clouds like those that hover above the canyon in early summer. Glitter-glue letters encircle the pot like a label, the one word I was forbidden to speak: "Mom." The day I gave the pot to Tina, she read the word and smiled at me. She did not correct me or tell me she was only Tina to me; instead, she kissed the pot, and said "Thank you, baby." Then she placed it on the shelf where it still sits. The only other thing on that shelf is her transistor radio tuned to a classical music station that every few years goes broke and leaves the airwaves. (Plants are especially responsive to string quartets, Tina says, but public radio stations thrive only with listener donations.)

Out of habit, I open the small drawer underneath the tabletop and find only what I expect: a few seed packets, some loose change, pieces of sandstone or crystal that never found their way into the windowsills or planters, and the small photo album Tina kept out here for me when I was a kid. "So, you can look at them whenever you want, in privacy, if that's what you need. These are yours, kiddo." There are exactly thirteen photos of my infant self in various dispositions: fussing in Tina's arms even as she beams at the camera, asleep in my crib (even in the 80's, you'd think they would've known not to let a baby sleep on her belly), in a bouncy chair set on a quilt spread over pine needles — "not far from here, honey," Tina has told me, or asleep on her couch, sandwiched between thick, avocado-green, rough-upholstered cushions Tina replaced when I was ten years old.

I flip to the last cellophane sleeve of the tiny album, to the only existing photo of my parents and me, a Polaroid taken on the day they were last seen. Tina photographed us standing beside my parents' camper in the forest somewhere near Jacob Lake. My father is holding me in one arm like a football, his giant, almost gaudy, silver belt buckle glinting in the sun, his free arm draped around my mother. My mother embraces us both, and the two of them smile like, well, like they don't have a care in the world. The sun is at their backs; they don't squint or bother to shade their faces. They look directly into Tina's lens.

Time has muted the colors in this photo. My mother's wispy curls, caught by the breeze and seeming to rise as if in answer to static in the air, are less bright, less red in the photo now. And maybe I only imagined it growing up, but my father's eyes, once soft and doe-brown in the Polaroid, are only another dark detail, no more than a shadow. This photo was the only inspiration for the soundtrack of endearments and conversations I invented for us — *baby girl sweetie-pie sugar-baby sweetheart time for bed everything will be okay what do you want for your birthday.*

Only one word comes to mind when I think of them now: missing. I no longer torment myself with false memories. My father's cologne: Obsession, I told myself in junior high — he wore Obsession. Or my mother's favorite music: she loved U2, I just knew it, and she thought Kirk Whalum was the best jazz saxophonist who ever brought a horn to his lips. I have stopped attempting to reproduce the dizzying thrill of my father holding me high above his head and laughing at me as he squinted into the sun, or the way my mother's freckled hands slathered way too much baby lotion on me after a bath. These ever-dimming moments were all borrowed or imagined anyway, pieced together from photographs or conjured from stories that were never mine.

All I really have left of my parents are the details I was told by the bartender who took me in when they disappeared. Tina, whose features, habits, and gestures are easily recalled as needed on any bright day or on any dumb and sad one, is the only mother I have ever known. I return the photo album to its place in the drawer and, like every time before, decide not to take it with me.

Tina's heavy canvas gardening apron is draped over the yellow utility chair we bought twenty years ago at a yard sale in Holbrook during one of our trips to the Petrified Forest. I pull the apron over my head and tie it in front, like she taught me. The cell phone I carry in my back pocket (not what a lady should do, according to Tina) fits perfectly in the front pocket of the apron.

There is more music stored on this little device than Tina could listen to in a year; I should insist on installing some speakers out here for her. I pull on the gloves that seem poised for work. The pruning shears feel good in my hand and, for the moment, everything makes sense. I will work quickly and then head to the GCHS.

All the occupants of the greenhouse are healthy from root to bloom, and I marvel at Tina's ability to render perennial every plant in her care; they will all grow and thrive forever, it seems. I make my way through the shed, tending to each bed, to each little row and bunch of vegetables and herbs, then to the vines where I cannot resist a few more berries. I save the flower beds for last.

I carefully trim the cloud of purple, one bed at a time. Tina will want the Phlox in the middle of each bed to stand a little taller than the rest. But the shorter flowers, planted in a ring around the taller, need direct sunlight, too. Tina's careful planning here is apparent. The little Bellflowers are thriving. But I spot a few weeds taking root at the center of the bed — opportunist little suckers that grow with very little sunlight or encouragement. I pluck up one such weed, and am dismayed at the purple blossom in my glove. This is no weed, but neither is it a flower. When I part the closely bunched flowers and further inspect the bed, I find several rows of flowering herbs growing in the shadows of the great purple flowers: Belladonna, Lobelia, and Monkshood. A little intentional community all their own, carefully cultivated. All purple. All potentially harmful. Or deadly.

I am perplexed not by the fact that Tina would grow these herbs — in the right circumstances and at the right doses, they have proper and advantageous uses. But she hides them. They are camouflaged in taller, brighter flowers of similar hue, and even put down in what seems to be a slightly different mix of soil than is used in the rest of the bed. If Tina were standing beside me now, she would say, "Don't count your cards yet. You don't know what's what," her dealer parlance for *Don't jump to conclusions.*

But I remember this, too, and I would give up a full house or a straight flush not to remember it: "People only see what they want to see. You can throw down the Ace or the Queen of Hearts in plain sight, and still they don't see," she told me once. "They don't pay attention. Their eyes follow the cards they want, not the ones that are still in the deck."

Fun day in the shed is over.

It is easier than I would have imagined, compelling myself to look at the greenhouse not as an extension of someone I love, but as a laboratory or a library. I decide I will see everything with new eyes. I will catalogue and inventory. I will assess this place as a sum of its parts. And then see the parts.

I walk every inch of the greenhouse. I don't even know what I'm looking for, but I am led by some awareness as old as I am. Or at least as old as those photos in the drawer. I turn over empty buckets, check the small storage bin where Tina keeps a few tools and supplies. I even dig at the bases of the larger tanks and pots. Even the new water system is not safe from my suspicions; I crawl around on the floor of the greenhouse, following the snaking system of pipes and misters and valves. But each of these inspections is only a motion, only a way to delay. Because I know. Maybe I have always known. And the truth is, just as Tina says, hidden in plain sight.

The air in here is thick now, stifling. I'm nauseous. I walk back to the work table. I remove the gloves Tina wears to lovingly and carefully tend to all the life in this greenhouse. My hands are slick with sweat. I reach for the pot, and with both hands bring it down from the shelf. But the dusty film that covers the clay surface and the sweat on my hands combine for a calamity I should have seen coming. The pot slips from my hands, and falls to the flagstone floor of the greenhouse. Shards and chunks of clay are scattered at my feet. Glitter-gold winks up at me. But it's not the chunky, glue-y lettering made by a second grader that catches my eye. It's a buckle. A big, silver buckle with inlaid gold vines and etchings of a man on a horse. It's the buckle in the photo. My Dad's belt buckle.

The buckle is heavier than it looks, covers most of my hand. It's big even for a rodeo cowboy. Which he wasn't. No, this was bought for him as a gift, a souvenir of his time at the canyon. The kind of thing tourists love to take home to New Jersey or Ohio.

I have to get out of this damnable place. I'm sick of the vast and impassable. The mystical and the metaphysical. I will drive straight back to Tucson. But first, the reason I came back in the first place. I need to go to the Archives room at the GCHS.

The apron strings have somehow become knotted, and I can't untie them. Won't try to untie them. I take up the shears and snip the apron ties into little bits of curling canvas, pull the neck strap over my head, and drape the apron over the back of the chair. The mess on the floor can stay where it is. I feel no need to sweep up the past or the goddamn fragile vessel where Tina hid it.

I step outside and return the greenhouse key to its not-so-secret hiding place beneath the mat. I have to leave before Tina returns. I have never really understood why I didn't want her to accompany me to the library or to the county registrar's office or to the GCHS. Until today.

At the kitchen table, I scribble a note. *Back to Tucson. Bye.* No hearts or smiley-faces, no wishes or warmth. Some farewells shouldn't be fond.

I toss my backpack into the cab of my truck. As I pull away from Tina's, the skies open up again and rain fills the low spots on the road. By the time I arrive at the GCHS, lizards and toads are skittering across the surface of the water pooled in the parking lot, and a few rabbits nervously survey the perimeter.

The GCHS has undergone some renovations. On the east side of the building, a whole new set of offices, still empty, is a stark contrast to the rustic pine of the original structure. And, along with broken or outdated electronics, the old "Emergency"/L&D room is filled with boxes and boxes of the files state archivists insisted on keeping but never bothered to collate or curate.

Or at least that's what I saw the last time I was here. And I hope in the six months since, no one has decided to finally clean out the Archives room and haul off the junk. I was assured by the Arizona Department of Health Services that files and records from the old Canyon Clinic were not relocated or destroyed; these documents were still housed on site, they said, and the physician who abandoned the clinic over thirty years ago had signed an affidavit affirming the safe and secure storage of clinic files.

I am hopeful that a record of my birth is somewhere in those boxes. I want the original record, not the legal birth certificate Tina applied for on my behalf when I was a child. And if not my birth certificate, then perhaps the records of my mother's visits to the doctor who saw her through her pregnancy, the man who delivered me and then, apparently, disappeared himself. Tina has told me, many times, that my parents were traveling under aliases, that she never learned their real names. "I knew them as 'Ella' and 'Arthur,'" she said. "That's all. They had no connections to anyone, no one ever came looking for them. You're not going to learn anything more about people who were already hiding when they disappeared."

Maybe I was influenced by Tina's old movies and celebrity tell-alls, but I used to imagine a criminal past for my parents. I pretended they were fugitives. But, as Tina likes to remind me, you can run from the table, but that doesn't change the hand you've been dealt.

The Society's windows are still dark. The parking lot is empty except for my truck, and will likely remain so until Shirley unlocks around 9AM. So, I have an hour to read my notes, watch the rain, and think about what I will say to Society staff when they ask why I need access yet again to the "archives."

The rain has not slowed, and I glance up from my notes to catch a glimpse of a green Volkswagen easing onto the main road from the access alley at the back of the building. Tina is at the wheel, but she does not even glance my way. And I can't be sure, even as slow as she is driving in this rain, but I think the fuel door on the Beetle is open and the gas cap is off.

I start the truck, shift into drive and step down hard on the accelerator to follow her. My earlier impulse to leave, to avoid Tina altogether, has been supplanted by an overwhelming desire to scream at her. All these years, I have carefully planned every conversation about searching for my parents' disappearance or searching for their families, always so sensitive to Tina's feelings and respectful of her sacrifice. Always so grateful. But the talk I want to have now will be anything but tender and cautious, and it will begin with a barrage of questions.

I reach for my phone. Not in my shirt pocket, not in the seat beside me. And I know it's not in my backpack. The shed. I dropped it when I was crawling around in the goddamn shed.

As I turn the truck onto the main road, I glance up at my rearview mirror and see light in the great windows on the face of the GCHS; but it isn't the obnoxious overhead fluorescence, visible from outside even during the day. It is more like the most brilliant dawn I have ever seen, the fastest rising sun — too much for the cabin-turned-office space to hold.

And then I know.

Flames shatter two of the windows, curl up the eaves and shoot across the face of the building. My relief that no one is inside is followed by a wish I hear myself scream, *rain, rain, rain, goddamnit.*

And all I can think as I speed through the downpour to the Village fire station is, *Tina, what have you done.*

When I finally return to Tina's, her Beetle is parked beside the greenhouse. I slam the truck door and slog through the mud. She opens the door and waves me inside. Under other circumstances, my hesitation would earn me a scolding or a sarcastic quip. But her forehead is all stitched up in penitence or pain — these are the same expression on her face. And she says only, "Please."

The mess of broken clay and remnants of canvas has been swept into a little pile beside the table. Tina offers me a towel, like she has been waiting for me. "You're soaked," she says. She sets a fold-out chair in front of me. She sits across from me in the yellow chair.

"I can explain."

"How nice," I say. "Maybe you should practice on me. I'm sure the Village cops or park rangers will be here soon enough."

"Not unless you told them what you think you saw."

"What I *think* I saw? Are you kidding me right now? Are you fucking kidding me?"

She stares at me. I cannot read her face. Finally, she says, "No, I'm not fucking kidding you."

"I mean, of course I saw you, Tina. And you know I did. Besides, don't you think they have security cameras all over that old place? *Historical landmark of the State of Arizona and the Grand Canyon National Park?*"

"Nope, there are no cameras."

"I'm not even gonna ask why you know that. The point is, what the fuck, Tina? You burned down a building where people work. What if Shirley was inside? What if the custodians had shown up early?"

"No one, I mean no one, was there," she says. She places her hands on her knees and leans forward like she is bracing herself.

I stand and pass the towel over my wet head a few times before tossing it to the floor. When I step toward her, so close I can smell her Chanel No. 5, she doesn't even flinch. Her eyes are still locked on mine.

"You destroyed precious records. The history of that place. My history. My mother's and mine. Why would you do that to me?"

"Who says I destroyed them?"

She looks up at the ceiling of the greenhouse and exhales. And then I know — she is way ahead of me, as always. And she holds a royal flush.

"I think you were looking for these," she says. She turns around in her chair and, for a moment, rests her hands on the surface of her work table. With her back to me, I can only read her shoulders: she has wilted somehow. She slides out the drawer under the work table and retrieves my cell phone, then withdraws a short stack of envelopes and a couple of large, faded yellow folders. Tina turns to me and taps the metal fasteners of the top folder with her acrylic nails. She sets it all on the table. "But you should probably have some tea first."

There are two cups steaming on the table. And I marvel once again at what goes unseen, even in plain sight.

"I don't feel like tea," I say.

"Sure, you do. Come with me."

And, inexplicably, I do just that. I am perhaps only a few breaths away from the truth I have hunted my whole life. But I follow Tina to my old spot between the tomatoes and ever-struggling baby fruit trees. She takes a seat on the flagstone, not spilling a drop from either cup, and leans against the tank. She pats the ground next to herself, and again I surprise myself by accepting her invitation. When I am seated, she passes me a cup. And I am almost comforted by the scent of fresh chamomile, sweet and smoky and a little earthy.

"With honey, just how you like it," she says, and takes a sip of her tea. She closes her eyes and swallows. "Drink up, Lucy."

She is quiet when instead I set down my cup, sloshing tea onto the stone floor. But she smiles. We sit in silence for a few minutes in the waning daylight and listen to the rain pelt the greenhouse roof.

Tina rests her head on my shoulder. "I will tell you everything," she says. "It was in the cards, darling. It was all in the cards."

About Mary Winsor

Mary Winsor grew up in the Southwest, the setting for most of her stories and essays. Her writing includes a Notable Essay in Best American Essays 2023, and appears or is forthcoming in Cutleaf Journal, Threepenny Review, Northwest Review, Atticus Review, Blue Mesa Review, Ploughshares, and elsewhere. Mary is a 2020 graduate of the MFA program at George Mason University. She teaches English and Creative Writing at Salt Lake Community College.

Website: marywinsor.com

X x.com/MaryWinsor

The Patchwork Man

Angela Sanchez

Late afternoon on a Sunday in October and the temperature still clocks in near eighty degrees. Fall in Los Angeles should probably just be christened Summer Part II.

But at least I'm off to make some money for it. To be bringing in a paycheck at sixteen is more than most people at Piedmont High can say — and it's going toward *something*.

Caliban Street Station is a short three blocks up from where we live. I pass a locksmith who will replace any key with not a single question breathed, an empty lot where cars have been stopped to their final rest, and a discarded sofa that still somehow has evaded Los Angeles City ever picking it up.

This side of Amarillo Heights isn't "fixed" yet. But maybe the rent hike our landlord kicked us in the gut with last month is meant to change that. Of course, that also probably means shaking out people like me and my family as if we're some interchangeable parts.

But is my job actually stopping that or just delaying the inevitable?

I get to the top of the train station's platform and finish my water bottle, taking a seat on a bench. The bench is old, but the metal armrest added in the middle of it is new and coated in fresh, shiny paint. It's a silent and menacing *"Don't sleep on me."*

If my family and I got nowhere to go, where will we eventually sleep?

I turn away, try to focus on the tracks, maybe spot my train — instead I stare right into a creepy, freaky pair of yellow eyes. I don't mean like you-got-liver-problems yellow, more like the color of lion's eyes in my grandma's cobija: golden, mesmerizing, and lethal.

The owner smiles at me. "Hi."

I jump. This man with yellow eyes is just suddenly standing in front of me, leaning in and staring. Chills race up my back. His jawline is long and sharp. His nose curves out into a fine hook like my Uncle Noé's. There's a hint of a mustache underneath, like a kindergartener took a pencil and quickly scribbled it there. That plus his long, black hair make him young-ish, a late twenty-something, but there's this chilly vibe rolling off him. Like, it's Summer Part II and suddenly, it feels like it's actually a cold autumn day.

He clears his throat to repeat himself and I realize he must've spoken earlier.

"Are you done with that?" He points to the empty water bottle now crunched between my hands. Wordlessly, I hold it out. "Gracias."

He plucks the bottle out of my hands and tosses it into a canvas bag filled with more empty water bottles and soda cans. That's when I notice he's dressed like a total weirdo. His clothes are full-on patchwork. His shoes are both sandals, but one's a flip-flop and the other's a heavier one with straps and belts. His cut-off jeans are held up by suspenders over an old boyband shirt. Oddly enough, he doesn't smell the way he looks. I catch a whiff of sagebrush, prickly and fresh, like the hills around Amarillo Heights.

"Waiting for the train?" he asks.

Dude's still a weirdo, so I go, "Nothing else."

Please don't sit next to me, please don't sit next to me.

He plunks down right beside me on the bench. *Great.* The weird chilly feeling worsens, going from opening the fridge to standing in the freezer.

"Got any glue on you?"

Is he looking for something to huff? Where the hell's the train?

"I have some tape." I hold up the tiny, plastic dispenser I swiped from school because we ran out at home. Yeah, I'll say three Hail Marys and one Act of Contrition later. Right now, this dinky piece of stationery is helping me keep peace with a creeper.

He takes the tape, then rummages into the canvas bag. He pulls out a marionette. Dangling on strings wrapped around two slender wood blocks, the marionette spins and dances at his feet. It's the kind of puppet you can get at Olvera Street in downtown, ceramic head with traditional Mexican clothes. This one's a farmer, all in white with feet made of wood and a tiny sombrero.

But the puppet's right arm hangs limply at its side. The Patchwork Man picks up the loose string. It's too short to tie up, so he starts to tape it back to the control bars above it.

"So, you going to work?" the Patchwork Man says as he repairs the marionette.

"Yeah, it's still my first week." I realize I sound a little too proud, so I quickly add, "Why you wanna know anyway? You gonna be the next CSI of Amarillo Heights?"

He laughs. "Mi'ja, I can *see* the apron and cap you're holding. What's it say on there?"

"Persnickety. It's a coffee shop."

The man chuckles. "Sounds like one of the new businesses on Prospero Boulevard."

"Yeah, it is." And it replaced one of my mom's favorite bakeries. I wonder what the owner, Mr. Mando, is doing now.

"And you got hired there?" the Patchwork Man continues. "Well, good for you. You plan to work there for a while?"

I shrug. "My family needs the money, you know? It won't be my only job ever. Once I get to college and finish my degree, I'll have a better job. A *real* one, like an engineer."

He tests out the marionette. It twirls. He smirks. "And then what? You'll move out of the neighborhood, I'm guessing? Some-place nicer?"

"No!" The only reason I was taking this job was so my family could hang on to what we had. "Amarillo Heights is home. We ain't going nowhere."

For a moment, the Patchwork Man blinks wide and curious at me, like I've done something interesting. Then a big, curving smile stretches across his face.

"What?" I go.

The Patchwork Man laughs — a high, broken sound. "You're a survivor," he finally says. He smirks, eyes crinkling at the corners. "I respect that."

He hands me back the tape. I take it.

"Thanks, but you can keep the respect," I go.

I must not have too much of it myself if I'm working at a place like Persnickety to survive.

The train finally screeches up to my stop. I get on. Though I'm not putting on either the damn cap and apron 'til I'm actually inside the pinche coffee shop.

When I step out to the platform, the raised tiny tiles of a mosaic press through the thin soles of my sneakers. Like braille, I can tell without looking that the mosaic reads "Prospero Boulevard."

I always wondered with my little coffee shop job here, does that plug me into the system that rolled out the welcome mat for outsiders, like our landlord, to move into our neighborhood, buy up property, and jack-up the rent all around town? I'm not even sure if my mom would care. I think she's so glad that I have a job, forget that I'm supporting the whole food chain that's going to eat us up alive.

A bike lane that wasn't there before snakes alongside me as I make my way down Prospero, scanning the business storefronts. People line up in droves outside of what used to be a party supply store for brunch. The faded, patchy painting of Big Bird and Hello Kitty are still visible on the side. The old bowling alley is open again, but it's now sixty dollars for a lane. Is this what people mean when they say Amarillo Heights is "fixed"?

I pass a "help wanted" sign in a yoga studio's window. I should keep walking. I need to get to work. My body — with my dark skin and protective fat over my hips, nothing like the thin, pale bodies inside — reflects back at me in the glass window. The muscles in my legs bunch. I want to sprint all five blocks back to the train station, ride home to where I don't feel like such an outsider in my own neighborhood.

I get into Persnickety at five o'clock sharp. It's so weird this used to be Mando's Bakery, the place behind every birthday cake and celebration for my family and most others in Amarillo Heights. Straight-up gone and ghosted now. But the crowd doesn't let me linger on this for too long. The coffee shop is already filling up. It's Art Walk Night. People bustle in, some already hugging their first deals of the night — prints, posters, comic books, or a small jangling bag of new handcrafted jewelry. Not that I have time to look. Soon we're packed to standing room only.

"Glad you made it, Maria!" Brian calls to me. Tall and skinny with skin pale as cheesecake, my boss' hands are full with a tray of fresh pastries.

"Marcela!" I call back. It's only the first week. Brian's probably still getting used to me.

Then I hear the twang of a guitarist tuning his amp. From the sound of it we're probably the coffee shop closest to the art walk performance stage. The next couple hours are a whirlwind. No sooner do we bust out orders, a new wave of customers crashes into the coffee shop, storming the counter. Some folks come back and bring their friends. I don't get to practice pretty doodles in the latte foam tonight. Hell, I barely have time to breathe.

No clue how Jenny and Nate, the other two staff members, are so calm about it.

"I saw that there's a pub crawl going on tonight," Nate says as he blends a frappe.

I glance over. "What's that?"

"A booze fest," Jenny drones.

Nate waves a hand at her. "Don't make it sound so crass. It's a chance to explore. I got a weakness for IPAs. Now that I think about it, I can't remember the last time I had an exceptional hefeweizen."

"Nate," I go, "you talk about beer almost the way Brian talks about coffee." Beer in my family usually comes in a can, sometimes a bottle, and never has half the German words Nate rattles off.

Curling a few red hairs from his beard around a finger, Nate gazes longingly out the door. "Now that I think about it, Prospero is probably one of the best places to do a pub crawl. There's so many awesome bars that have opened up in the past year alone, like Quarter Horse on Avenue Fifty-seven."

Jenny tips her head in a ghost nod. "Or what about the one in the new bowling alley?"

"Mr. B's? Yeah, I been there."

Nate rambles on listing bars and I tune out. I can name most of the businesses those places used to be before someone had decided to make it rain liquor licenses in Amarillo Heights.

It's about nine when most of our rush finally trickles down, Nate stretches and calls to the back. "Brian! I'm out, man. Need myself a drink after today."

"Buddy, you earned it." Brian claps Nate on the back and waves him out to freedom.

I resist the urge to wimp out and say I got school in the morning. I have less than an hour to go. That's money on the table. Má toughs it out every day to keep a leaky roof over me and my sister. I haven't been on my feet for ten hours running between nitpicky customers yelling at me for how someone else cooked their eggs or woken up at four a.m. to be surrounded by deafening machinery and dust that turns my boogers and everything inside me black. I can manage a little longer in a comfy coffee shop.

I got it good, and I'm gonna get paid. People always get an energy boost when you add money into the mix. Look at Brian.

Adjusting his turquoise cap, Brian preens. "Guys, we're doing awesome tonight! We might be able to turn a real profit this month!"

Jenny yawns. "Yeah, maybe if every night were like this." She checks her phone. "Hey, I'm past due for a break."

Brian barely glances at the remaining customers in the shop. "Say no more! See you in fifteen." He turns to salute me. "Marcela and I got this, right?"

I blink, suppressing the urge to say something dumb like, "Aye, aye, capt'n." Brian's smile says he trusts me, sees me as one of the team. I know we are standing in the middle of what used to be Mando's Bakery, but for the first time since I set foot in Persnickety I feel like I belong here.

The second I think it, there's this recoil in my gut. Do I switch up sides that easy?

Once Jenny's out, Brian puts me in charge of "interfacing with clientele." While I bustle from the register to the barista, Brian hovers nearby, scratching away at spreadsheets on a clipboard, probably taking inventory.

"How do you feel about manning the front on your own?" he asks two customers later.

I slap my hands on the cool countertop, trying to take off some of the nervous sweat. "Pretty good."

Brian holds up his clipboard. "All right! I'll be in the back office running some numbers. Holler if you need anything."

"No problem. I got this!" I go.

The rush has eased up and I don't need to protect my fingers from getting bitten off by rabid customers anymore. Persnickety's indoor tables have only one couple making cow eyes at each other and mostly a bunch of abandoned cups and plates to clean up.

The front door swings open as six men bluster in. A real crowd. From the way they shove and joke with each other, they look like drinking buddies. No trimmed beards or blocky glasses, though. Collared shirts with loosened buttons and rolled up sleeves, dress slacks, a loose jacket over one shoulder — maybe an after-work group. They must be out for the pub crawl.

"Remind me why we're at a goddamn coffee shop and not Quarter Horse instead?" one of them whines.

"Because Justin wants his girly-ass latte," an older man shouts from the back.

Half the men laugh loud, deep, and stupid. A tall guy, looks like the youngest in the group, tries to shush them. Tall Guy slouches over toward the front. "My latte's what'll keep me awake to drive some of you shitheads home."

I get behind the register, guarding it like a goalie. My mission is clear: process their orders, prep them together, and get them the hell out of here. Clearly, this group wants to get on with their drinking. This could be quick.

"Hi, there," I call. "Can I help you?" I aim for Tall Guy since he stands closest. He hasn't turned around either, though, so it goes to their mini mob in general — which means my words are sucked into the vortex of their chatter. They get louder. The couple that's been seated in one corner stand up and tiptoe their way out. Damn.

I study the group as if maybe if I stare hard enough they'll notice me, remember why they're in a coffee shop and leave. That's when a bright red baseball cap catches my eye, the kind with the stupidest catch phrase imaginable stitched across. Maybe his voice only goes high-def because I'm paying attention, Asshat suddenly sounds louder than the rest of the group.

"Man, I almost shit my pants when you said we were going

out to Amarillo Heights tonight," he says, butchering my neighborhood's name to sound like an English word. "But looks like it's come a ways. The last time I was here was a few decades ago and the area was overrun with Mexicans."

A sharp, sudden pain — like static, or anger — jolts from my wrist through my fingertips. Maybe I shouldn't be surprised that an idiot with a red cap spurts shit like that. But I never heard anyone say it so casually, like breathing.

"Easy, Jeff." The man who speaks to Asshat has hair thinning up front and glasses that droop down his nose. His face flushes five types of red as he splutters hushes through nervous laughter. "You know you can't say stuff like that in granola-crunchy places like this."

Asshat Jeff mocks a scan of Persnickety. "What? Did I miss the safe space sign?"

Breathe, Marcela . . . screw it.

"Are you going to order anything?" I practically shout it.

Asshat snarls my way. "Hey, relax! We'll come over when we're ready."

They ignore me and yammer on, the volume increasing as they reminisce about a neighborhood they only know in late-night glimpses and news stories.

"Heard they had a major drug bust and that's what got them to clean up some."

"I still think they could step up the security around here a bit."

Jeff laughs a short, loud bark. "Can you imagine? Get enough cops around here and half the population would disappear back across the border."

My skin prickles. Asshat is some piece of work.

"Jeff," Droopy Glasses warns. "Ease up. I hear people actually live here now."

Wait, live here now? As in, me and my family didn't before?

The more I listen, the more I realize everyone else in the group is basically saying the same stuff as Asshat. The words just happen to be arranged differently. Hipsters talk like that, so do well-meaning people who don't know crap, and — at the end of it — they all sound like Jeff.

When I look up, Tall Guy finally takes the last couple steps up to the counter. "Okay, so that's a latte, two coffees, four croissants —"

"Hey, Shawn says he wants a coffee, too!" someone else chimes in.

"Okay, um, wait, that's four coffees . . ." Tall Guy drones.

"Three," I correct.

As if he doesn't believe me, Tall Guy twists over his shoulder to check with the group. "Shawn, Jeff, and who else wanted coffee?"

"Aw shit, here, I'll do it." Pulling up his belt buckle up to his saggy gut like he's about to do some man's work, Asshat struts his way up to the register.

"Step aside," he growls at Tall Guy, who jumps back two feet. Asshat leers at me. He whips out this big, yellow-toothed smile, not like he had joked that me and people who look like me in Amarillo Heights can be shipped off by La Migra tomorrow for no reason other than the bullshit in whatever sits under that red hat.

"Hey, sweetheart, we'll take three coffees," he says. "Make mine normal, though, none of that frothy shit."

I hear his order, crammed in with a tactless attempt to be "polite" or whatever you call it when a man thinks giving you an unsolicited syrupy nickname is flattering — but my hands don't move over the register. I don't feel like moving. Not for him. I notice the sign on the right over one of the tables. I read the first line aloud.

"We reserve the right to refuse service."

Asshat blinks at me, surprised I say anything else other than, "Coming right up!" Looking at the group, he's probably used to hearing the word yes a lot. "What's that, hon?"

I know that tone. It's the same way Má says, "What did you

say?" Not that she didn't hear you. You were simply being given a chance to correct yourself. *This guy isn't good enough to lick my mother's kitchen floor.*

"We reserve the right to refuse service," I repeat, stronger, firmer. Real talk: For a split second, I ten thousand percent *do* wonder if I might get my own ass fired over this. Asshat hasn't been an asshat to me directly. But Brian strikes me as the type of white person who has principles. Maybe not the type who would have walked behind MLK at Selma, but who would at least want to broadcast his support. More like the ones who tacked on safety pins to say they didn't vote an idiot into office or who would forego a straw to save plastic. If I really have to hedge my bets, Brian will probably back me before he serves a jerk like this.

"I think you should find another coffee shop," I say.

"Excuse me?" His voice pitches. "Do you want to say that again?"

Oh, he's going hard on Má's strategy.

"C'mon, Jeff, we'll look for a different place." Tall Guy tugs on the crook of his elbow. "You said you didn't even what to go here. Too trendy, remember?"

Jeff grunts, but his hands stay planted on our shiny countertop. He hangs on like it's a life preserve. I notice his watch — the fancy kind with three tiny faces on the main one — hangs heavy and expensive around his wrist. It isn't about the coffee anymore. It's about him making me do what he wants. Screw that.

"You're saying you won't serve me?" His voice booms, lips pull back, folded flesh around his neck stretches. "I want to speak to your supervisor. Get me your supervisor! Now!"

"I would like you to leave," I say. Props to me, I don't shout back. Don't have to really. Even the cronies Asshat walked in with have shut up.

But Asshat's already on a roll. He pulls out his wallet, slaps it on the counter and fishes out a twenty. "Look, I'm giving you money!" He waves it in my face. I step back, not just to keep the bill from brushing me but to resist from grabbing that twenty and smacking him with it.

"You're the one who obviously needs this job!" he shouts. "At least do the smart thing and take it!"

Brian bursts out from the back door. "Marcela, what's going . . ." He looks from me to Asshat. His eyes widen when he sees that cap. He spares one more glance at me, and I nod. He's got the whole story. But Brian is Brian. Smoothly, he asks, "Is something wrong, sir?"

"Yeah, something's wrong!" A stubby finger's jabbed in my direction. "*She's* refusing me service. You got some kind of prejudice thing going on here?"

I swear I almost laugh. In my Physiology Honors class last year, we covered how that's a common reaction to stress. Whenever your brain is beat down with so much tension you either got to laugh or cry. But this isn't done yet.

Brian will probably shuffle them out. Tell them to go to hell, in a Brian way, of course, so that hell sounds like a vacation. The door will slap Asshat on the way out and me and my boss will have a laugh over it. Brian is in my corner.

I step aside from the register, waiting for him to let them have it.

"I'm sorry to hear that." Brian punches a couple of keys on the register to reset it. "What can I get you?"

What. The. Fuck?

I gape at my boss. Jeff laughs, rough, ragged, and winning. It feels like he's laughing at me, like I'm the idiot, the dumbass who is so wholly, undisputedly in the wrong. My heart thuds in my chest, trying to jump up my throat. Asshat will *not* see me cry. He cheerfully rattles off the order, then turns to his buddies for theirs. Suddenly, everyone in the group wants a coffee or some kind of drink and pastry. It's as if they've won a battle and it's important to take the spoils.

Asshat grins at Brian with the same fake-news smile he gave

me. "Sorry about all the commotion here. I know I can get a little heated and lose my cool."

Now, most people might take this moment to go, "Yeah, you're a piece of human garbage. Get out of here. We have a sanitation code to keep trash to a minimum."

Brian instead mumbles three words I will hate for the rest of my life. "No, it's fine."

Fine? FINE? My fists are clenched so tight my nails bite into my palms. Keeping the anger in, everything feels ready to shatter and crumble — my bones, my brain, my soul. Brian caves to coddling Asshat the way the other guys in the group do. As if setting him off is somehow worse than telling him to piss off. Damn, Brian's no better than they are.

I want to say, "Why are you trying to make him feel better? I'm the one he yelled at!"

When the twenty is offered again — graciously slid across the counter this time — Brian shakes his head. "There's no charge."

Asshat waves his hand in the air and pushes the cash forward. "Nah, I can tell you're a decent guy." He angles his head my way. "Hope you educate your workers in the basics of business and needing to make ends meet."

"Thanks for your patience," is all Brian says. "We'll have your order out in a couple minutes." Grabbing a pair of tongs, he stuffs a brown bag full of Danishes and muffins. He passes the bag over to Asshat. "These are on the house, too."

Posing like a big damn hero, Asshat returns to his crowd of hooting Neanderthals. They shove a couple tables together and settle in. Somewhere in there is that ragged laugh. "Did you see how I handled that little punk?"

Every nerve-ending in my body feels fried. Exhaustion, like after you've puked your guts out from a bad stomach bug, sweeps over me.

"Brian," I say as he gets to setting out several disposable coffee cups. "I'm going to take my break."

"Can you help me fill this order first? Some of these guys got two drinks."

That's it. My customer service voice is done for the night. My patience is done.

I'm done.

"Brian, I don't want to fill the order of a single one of those racist assholes." The group is already lost in their own conversation again. We're behind the counter. Brian still snaps at me to keep it down.

He adds, "I'm not asking you to judge who walks in here, Marcela. I'm telling you to treat them like every other customer."

"You're saying you didn't notice that red baseball cap?" I only barely keep my voice down from going shrill. "I'm not judging, Brian. He's broadcasting!"

Arms stick-straight at his sides, Brian inhales slowly. His answer, when it comes, is short and terse. "Marcela, we're a coffee shop. We're not here for politics."

The skin under my eyes pinches. "The hell does that mean?"

"That means I'm asking you to be a professional, to do your *job*."

He hurls the last word like a gut punch. Maybe it's dumb, but I didn't pin Brian as the type of guy who could get angry — or get ugly.

I inhale slowly. My job. The thing Brian is paying me for. I glance at the crowd, guys who would never have set foot in Mando's Bakery. I think of my family and our home. And how I'm not telling them about the night I served white men who will never see any of us as people.

When I crush the lid over the last coffee cup, I move toward the back door before Brian can say anything else. "I'm taking my break."

"Thank you for your help, Marcela." He speaks in soft, even tones, then announces the orders are ready.

I don't stick around to see the group swarm up to collect their drinks. I don't say hey to Jenny as she comes back in or pause when she asks if something's wrong. There are no words left in me that aren't swallowed up with disappointment and disgust. I need *out*.

I should quit.

Out back, with the dumpsters and crickets, I take a deep breath. But it's not enough. My feet start moving me out of the parking lot. When I'm on the sidewalk, no more thinking. I run.

I hang a right on Prospero and book it. I don't stop when I bump into a craft jewelry table or barrel past a clamor of burnt-out band dudes tuning their amps. I run faster.

Peeling off Prospero, I wind my way down a dark street, racing past a locksmith and an overgrown, empty lot. Ahead, I see where the large flood lights loom over Prospero Station. Not even bothering with my metro card, I fly up the walkway and put my all into catching the train that races up to meet me at the platform. I make it on board right as the doors snap shut behind me.

Inside the train is too calm. How *can't* anyone else around me hear my hammering heartbeat? An old man with a small, metal pushcart dozes in his seat. In another row, a mom and her two small kids paw through their grocery bags, maybe searching for a snack. I wrap my fingers around the cold, metal pole in the center, sucking in and exhaling as much air as quickly as I can. My whole body hums on high alert.

I did it. I left my job. One text and I could tell Brian I quit.

So, why don't I feel better? My stomach lurches and sloshes with the stop and go of the train. Thankfully, the Caliban Station stop comes up fast. I can get out and go home — ideally without making a bigger fool of myself. As soon as we come up to my stop, I beeline for the old bench where the Patchwork Man sat this afternoon, and get to tearing off my Persnickety uniform — starting with the stupid, turquoise cap.

Forget this.

Running a hand through my bangs, I smooth out my loose, sweaty hair that's going all frizzy. The breeze in it feels good, cooling me down. I give the hat a kick toward the trash can. I don't need to work on Prospero. I can do something else. There are other options besides fake-ass, racist Persnickety.

Undoing the apron strings at my back, I unloop the rest of my uniform, tossing the apron the way of the Persnickety cap. Go home. Sleep. Deal with it in the morning. I start down the platform's stairs. I'm not expecting to get sprayed in the face.

"Ack!" I swipe my arm over the water in my eyes. "What the hell?"

It's the Patchwork Man. He crowds the stairs, one hand rests on the railing while a colorful water gun spins around a finger in his other.

That must be the crap he soaked me with.

As if he hears me, the Patchwork Man whirls the water gun around. Except instead of his usual flashing grin, he gives me a scowl. "So what happened?"

"Nothing. Move." I try to get around him, but he mirrors me, blocking the way.

"Really? Then how come you're not taking your uniform with you? Thought you liked this new job, don't y —"

"I don't need it. And whatever you need out of there, find somebody else. Gah!"

I get sprayed again. He waves the water gun mockingly, his taunting smile back in place. "That's for being disrespectful."

I growl and storm back up the steps. "Dude, get lost!" I plant myself on the platform's bench again.

the Patchwork Man follows, acts like he doesn't hear the anger in my voice. "Something happened at work."

His tone keeps it from being a question.

"None of your business," I go.

Leap-frogging over the bench, he takes a seat beside me, my apron clutched in one hand. "So, why are you throwing away your work clothes?"

I cross my arms and stand my ground. "I just don't want to go anymore. Okay?"

"That's hardly an explanation." Still crouching, the Patchwork Man stretches down and picks up the Persnickety cap I'd tossed. Shaking it twice, he delicately blows some of the dust off. "I thought you were doing this to help out your family."

"I was . . . I am. I'll figure out another way to do it." I don't know how sure I am about that. I am one-hundred percent on one thing. "Prospero's . . . all jacked up."

For a second, the Patchwork Man pauses, like he's really thinking about this. Then he laughs his broken, yippy cackle and goes, "You see coyotes around this neighborhood?"

Coyotes? The thing that ate my grandma's cat one summer? I gape at him. "The hell does that have to do with anything?"

"They're excellent survivors!" He spins the water gun. "They're not afraid of you. Not really. You can keep building, expanding — but the coyotes aren't running away. They'll simply figure out a way to live around you. *With* you, if needed." Yellow eyes twinkle at me. "I thought you were more like them — a survivor."

"Huh." I'm not too convinced. But if I quit Persnickety, I'll be back in square one: no job, no cash, and maybe no home to apply to college from. This was about survival, right? "Then do you need me to work at *that* place?"

In a flash, the Patchwork Man loops the apron over and around me and tosses the cap back on my head. "There you go!" he crows. Then, with a smirk that makes his yellow eyes glitter, he's up and starting toward the stairs down the platform.

"Hey!" I stand there, the apron undone but hanging around my neck. Behind me, I hear the throaty whistle of the approaching train headed to Prospero. Never did tell Brian I quit. I could still go back. Do I want to? "Hey, mister?"

He keeps walking.

Not sure why, but I chase after him. Like a little kid who's not sure what to do next, I reach out. I mean to grab his shirt, just give it a tug to get his attention. But I miss. I should be grabbing air. There isn't anything to see. Until I realize I actually catch on to *something*. It's prickly, but soft like . . . like a . . .

A tail?

I jerk away. And made the massive mistake of looking up. He's turned around all right. But it's not the usual guy at the train station who looks back at me. Where a man's face should be, a coyote's head cracks a lopsided grin. His big, conical ears flick forward and his long, pink tongue licks over his slender snout. The train's lights reflect off his eyes, making them glow a ghostly green. Somewhere in the background, I hear the water gun go *spritz, spritz.*

Then, like magic, the coyote head flickers, then it's gone completely, masked by a human face again. The Patchwork Man's angular face is back, but those creepy, creepy yellow eyes are all the same.

His mouth opens, flashing hard, white teeth. "Don't be late to work now."

I *bolt* into the last car, the door snapping shut behind me. One man looks up from his smartphone, and I realize how loudly I'm panting.

I'm on the train. My fingers clamp around the smooth, cool, metal framework of a seat I don't remember dropping into. The air inside is warm and stale, and the wheels outside go clack, clack, clack as we pull away from Caliban and closer to Prospero. Back to Persnickety. These are all real, solid things.

But . . .

I always peek in the middle of a slasher scene. I look out the window, out at the tracks, before the train picks up full speed. Sure enough, a skinny coyote with its bright, shiny eyes trots after the train. His tongue lolls out of his mouth in his fake chase, herding me back to Prospero — where I promised to survive. And from between those teeth in that big coyote grin, I swear I hear his broken laughter bouncing up and down the railroad tracks.

About Angela Sanchez

Angela M. Sánchez (they/she) is a Mexican American writer from Los Angeles. They were staffed on Disney Television Animation's upcoming series PRIMOS and have written on AppleTV+'s acclaimed STILLWATER, Nick Jr.'s RUBBLE & CREW, and over a dozen episodes for Moonbug's GECKO'S GARAGE. Angela is also a 2018 PEN America Emerging Voices Fellow and Las Musas alum. The Los Angeles Times has featured their picture book, *Scruffy and the Egg*, which tackles topics of family homelessness and single-parenthood. Angela's writing has appeared in the Los Angeles Review of Books, SOLRAD, LAist, Dictionary.com, and The Hechinger Report. They are currently co-editing the upcoming comics anthology, *From Cocinas to Lucha Libre Ringsides: Latinographix Stories of Sports, Food & Madness*, and have been interviewed for the New York Times, NBC News, LA Weekly, and La Opinión, among others. Angela can be found at angelamsanchez.com.

Alligator Queen

Emily Gray

**Trigger Warnings for references to off-page domestic violence and sexual assault*

Folks hate the swamp.

They don't understand the things that choose to live there, but what they don't realize is that the creatures that dwell in the swamp couldn't possibly live anywhere else — they have adapted to life in the mud. Some people don't think life in the mud is worth living, but I disagree.

Living on a smoothly-paved cul-de-sac in a cookie cutter house — that's easy. Not only surviving but thriving in the mud — that's a feat. That's something worth doing.

That very mud clings to my legs clear up to my knees, thick as tar. I pause to take a breath, rubbing at the trickle of sweat that runs down the side of my neck. My ratty sneakers slowly fill with wet, brackish slime that soaks through my socks. My feet ache. I can feel my pulse in the beds of my toenails.

The sun set ages ago, but it's still hot enough to liquify concrete. I clutch Dad's shotgun against my chest as I pause to listen for the sound of anyone following me.

It's unlikely — they're much slower than I am, and they don't know the land like I do. Dogs might be a problem, but I crossed enough creeks and put enough distance between us that I should have a good head start. For now, at least.

It's slow going, navigating around the knobby cypress knees and bouncing from dry patch to dry patch, trying to avoid the worst of the mud. But even in the dark, I've been out here enough times to walk it with my eyes closed. I can find my way to the chickee on memory alone, like a child stumbling their way into their parent's bed after waking from a nightmare.

I pick my way through the brush, passing the hollowed out remains of an ancient water oak. The sight of it stirs up old memories like a trolling motor stirs up the riverbed. Back when we were kids, my sister and I dubbed it the Fort. I should keep moving, but I can't resist ducking inside one last time. She'd want me to.

It's a tighter squeeze than it used to be. The space that used to fit both of us hardly fits my shoulders now. The earth and rot coat my tongue, worming their way into me until I'm convinced if I stay there long enough, maybe I'll rot away too. It sounds like a peaceful enough proposition. I could just sit here until this land takes me back, give myself over to the place I was born in and never really managed to find my way out of. My home left a mark on me from birth, a trailer trash stigmata, and it seems like a fitting end to just give myself back to it. Complete the life cycle.

No.

I force my eyes open and face the other little girl squeezed into the stump with me. She wears a crown of cattails and ferns. Instead of a rusty shotgun, she wields a sword hewn from a dry palmetto frond. Her sharp face is filthy, her sugar-spun hair thick with snarls. The knees of her jeans are worn thin enough to see milk-pale skin peeking through, and the smiling cartoon character on her t-shirt has warped and cracked under the strain of too many bouts with a washing machine. She stares back at me in the shadows, mud swiped under each eye like war paint. Her bony chest heaves as she points at me, dirt caking the nails on her tiny hand.

The day we found the Fort, I was sent home early from school. It wasn't an unusual occurrence by any means, but that day was special. I had been sent home *with a note.*

I was in the third grade and I could hardly read print, never mind my teacher's loopy handwriting, so I gave it to my sister.

"It says you're suspended," she told me, her eyes wide. "Daddy's gonna be pissed."

"I don't care," I replied, tugging my laces tight. We had to move after our last landlord evicted us, and so I was shoved into a new classroom halfway through the school year like a mismatched puzzle piece stuck in the wrong box. I don't remember what I had done to get myself suspended, but I do remember that when my sister read the note, she let out a short, angry laugh and crumpled it in her hand.

She was a few years older than me and had passed from the whimsical days of elementary playgrounds into the slimy grasp of middle school. The new grown-up way she talked was an alien language I didn't understand. The week before she got grounded because she and her friends pierced their belly buttons with an ice cube and a sewing needle out behind the 7-Eleven.

We stood on the edge of the swamp, just a few dozen yards behind our new home. There was a rusted-out pickup in the backyard that the old tenant had left behind. Daddy told us not to climb on it because we might get tetanus, but I had seen my sister perch on the hood like a queen on a throne, a stolen cigarette languishing between her fingers. The swamp was still uncharted land at that point, as intimidating as it was unspeakably exciting.

"Wanna go explore?" she asked. I nodded, simply excited by the prospect that she wanted to do anything at all with me. She took my hand and led me past the tree line. It was cooler in the shade, but not by much. We walked for a long time, sometimes in silence, sometimes while she rattled off the names of classmates and their various relationship melodramas. Middle school already sounded like more trouble than it was worth.

"Look," she whispered, pointing. "A gator." I followed her finger with my eyes and spotted the creature sunning itself on a mossy log jutting out of the green water. It was probably six feet long, but to me looked like an honest-to-God dinosaur.

"Should we run?" I asked breathlessly.

"Nah. An alligator will only bite you if you poke it with a stick." She spoke with enough confidence that I believed her. I always did. Regardless though, I held my breath as we walked past it. Sure enough, the gator didn't do anything. It just gave me a long, slow blink as it observed us creeping away into the brush.

We kept walking, away from the water, and eventually we found the Fort.

"Come on, we can both fit in here!" I exclaimed, immediately crawling inside. My sister held back a bit.

"Are there any bugs?" she asked. She could handle some bugs — like crickets and spiders — but palmetto bugs and centipedes sent her screaming.

"Nope!" I said, even though I hadn't really checked. Brushing her crooked bangs out of her face, she crawled in with me. We sat there, shoulder to shoulder, watching the swamp as the dappled sunlight flitted back and forth across the patchy grass.

It felt safe, at the time. A cool refuge from the oppressive heat, a shelter from the occasional rolling thunderstorm that caught us unaware while we were out exploring.

It still feels that way now. If I close my eyes and rest the cool steel barrel of the shotgun against my cheek, I am invisible. My pursuers will just pass me by, and I will be safe, because I am in the Fort. Nothing can hurt us in the Fort.

Nothing can hurt my sister at all anymore, but I am not so lucky. As much as it pains me, I push myself up and out, not bothering to shake the soft black dirt from my thighs as I continue my trek. The night is long, but not long enough for me to waste time. They'll find me eventually, of that much I'm sure, and I have a long way to go before that happens.

A mosquito lands on my arm, but I swat it away before it can bite. The lemongrass I stuffed in my pockets is wearing off. I reach the edge of the water and yank the bundle of weeds out, tossing them on the ground. If anything, they'll confuse the dogs.

I watch the dark water for movement. If I'd had the foresight to grab a flashlight, I could have scanned the shore for the flashing red eyes of lurking gators. But I ran out the back door as soon as the cops pulled up, shotgun in my hands and my shoes untied. All I can do is pray that they've decided to patrol a different stretch of river tonight.

Crossing the sluggish river that snakes its way through the swamp will throw them off for hours. No sane person would attempt it, especially not in the dead of night.

I am still very sane. Sane enough to know I don't have many options left.

I feel my way along the slippery shore until I locate the old rope swing. When we were children, we had played on the swing almost every day until the summer that June Clarkson got dragged under. After that, the swing was left abandoned.

I reach up and grab what's left of the frayed rope. It's gone green with mold and is dotted with mushrooms, the slow and diligent digesters of the forest. I heard there were mushrooms growing on June Clarkson's body when they finally found it. Mushrooms will consume anything, from fraying rope to wet cardboard to the bloated body of a twelve-year-old girl who had the misfortune of being the next off the rope swing just as a hungry gator swam by.

That was the summer Dad built the chickee, and the summer we started hunting together. I was twelve. The town had an insatiable hunger for dead gators after what happened to June. Every gator head mounted on their wall was one less out in the swamp, hunting their children. We got tags from the state to cull dozens of them, but when the tags ran out, we kept going. The cops turned a blind eye, because they had children of their own to protect. Who could blame us for doing what needed to be done?

Dad and I headed out every morning before dawn on his rusted jon boat. He sat in the back by the motor, and I perched on the bow with a shotgun. We made a good team; by the start of eighth grade I could tag a gator in the eye from thirty yards away.

Seven years later, here I am standing on the same shore with the same shotgun on my shoulder, but this time I'm the one being hunted. Dad was forgiving when I missed a shot, but today I can't afford to make mistakes. A dozen paces past the rope swing I find the shallow part of the river. I hold my breath as I step off the bank, but there isn't time to hesitate.

Dark water fills my shoes, sloshing around my knees as I wade into the middle. The current tugs at my waist as I reach the deepest point, trying to push me further downstream. With every careful step I anticipate the snap of jaws on my leg, or the rush of something huge and scaly swimming between my feet. It's inevitable; the only logical conclusion to this journey is that this place finally takes its revenge on me for all the blood I've spilled and drags me down into the muck.

A little over half-way across my foot catches on a submerged stump, sending me careening off balance. The river is slow but strong, and the second my feet leave the riverbed I'm sucked off the sandbar and out into the current. I thrust the shotgun over my head as I scramble for purchase on the sandy bottom, my legs tangling in old fishing line and garbage as I fight to keep my head above water.

Pain flashes up my leg. It's not the quick snap of primordial jaws, but something sharp and jagged. Probably an old boat propeller, or the edge of a chunk of twisted metal. Either way, I can tell even without seeing it that my blood is spilling hot and fast into the river, and if the gators weren't aware of me before, they certainly are now.

I fight my way to the shore as the briny taste of the swamp fills my mouth and nose. It claws its way under my nails and drips into my ears, swirling through my brain and soaking through straight down to my bone marrow. By the time I haul myself through the sawgrass and onto the shore, there's nearly as much swamp within me as there is around me.

I toss the gun down, mercifully dry, and turn my attention to my leg. In the dark I can't see much, but I can feel a gash about the length of my hand, and probably deep enough to need stitches. I press my palm over it to try and slow the bleeding, but it comes away sticky and wet.

Biting back tears, I wipe my hand on my shirt. This is not the time to cry. I repeat it to myself over and over until the words run together, like a prayer that has long since lost its meaning. *This is not the time to cry, this is not the time to cry, thisisnotthetimeto —*

But the tears find me anyway. There's never time to cry. There wasn't time to cry after Mom left, because Dad was three months behind on paying the rent and the landlord didn't give a shit that he had two little girls at home.

There wasn't time to cry when we hit every Christmas charity event we could find, smiling as we received gifts we knew Dad would turn around and resell unopened. When they figured it out, we caught a lifetime ban from the Salvation Army. They accused Dad of scamming them; they said it was such a shame he was stealing from his little girls.

They painted him as the villain and my sister and I as the innocent victims. But at eight years old I knew that having a roof over my head was better than getting a dollar store Barbie from some lady who got off on my excitement over the second-rate presents that weren't good enough for her own kids.

There wasn't time to cry when the landlord did eventually kick us out, and we had to throw our shit into pillowcases and stuff them in the trunk of the car before he came through with the cleaning crew.

There wasn't time to cry when we lived out of that car for

three months, wiping ourselves down with baby wipes in the dimly lit Wal-mart bathroom before school so our teachers wouldn't call CPS.

There wasn't time to cry when my sister came home in the back of a cop car with a bloody lip, a black eye, and the officer's pointed questions about why she had been out so late in the first place.

There was never time to cry.

But I can't stop it. I sit and sob on the riverbank until I feel like my insides have been scooped out like jack-o-lantern guts and tossed aside. My chest aches and my throat burns from tears and salt and mud as I look down pitifully at the cut on my leg. The dull ache of sadness and exhaustion is replaced by a tightening garrote of anxiety as I realize I can see it more clearly now. The sun has started to rise, and there is no more time to cry.

I stagger to my feet and grab the shotgun from the dirt. My leg throbs when I put weight on it, not enough to stop me, just enough to slow me down. Turning away from the river, I hobble on.

The path only gets thicker and more overgrown as I move away from the shore. It's hardly a path at all anymore. Back in the summers of gator hunting and rope-swinging, the path to the chickee was always clear, maintained by trampling feet and scaly bodies being dragged through the undergrowth.

Now the woods have forgotten those summers, and the brush has grown thick and close over where we used to play. Spanish moss sways above me, catching golden light that leaches through the tree branches. The edges of the boughs are tinged blood-red as the woods rustle to life. The hiding creatures emerge and the hunting creatures find rest, and I am strung somewhere in the middle — both hunting and hiding — as I stagger toward my hidden refuge. The gun drags behind me now. My arms ache too deeply to carry it any further, but I have to.

Steam rises from the ground around me as the climbing sun begins to bake the swamp with its brutal heat. Sweat, blood, and swamp-river-slime dry tacky across my skin as I snake my way around the sweeping oaks, ducking under writhing branches and stepping over the twisting roots.

I pass the rotting corpse of a tree that had been struck by lightning years ago, and I know I'm almost there.

My sister leaned against the tree, watching me with her arms crossed across her chest as I planted my feet. Frowning around the swelling on her lip, she walked over to adjust my stance.

"Put more weight on your back foot, then follow through," she instructed me. I swung at the empty air, and she shook her head. "Put your weight in it, come on." I tried again and stumbled, my momentum pushing me forward. She crouched down in front of me, taking my face in her hands. The bruising on her cheekbone had started to fade, but the welts were still sickly yellow.

"One day, they're going to tell you that trailer park girls are easy and it's all your fault. So you gotta kick and scratch and bite until you make it not worth their while, got it?"

I nodded. I wasn't entirely sure of her meaning at the time, but the dead straight certainty in her tone told me I had better listen. That phrase would follow me through middle and high school, through a maze of wandering hands and sneaky glances.

I didn't ask her what happened to her face. I didn't ask when her boyfriend stopped coming around. I didn't ask when he was replaced by a newer model — a twenty-something guy named Ted who drove a motorcycle and worked at the jiffy store on the corner. I never asked because I didn't know how. I was just a kid; I couldn't save her — but I carried the guilt with me all the same.

Trailer park girls are easy.

It was a dare and a death sentence all rolled into one. All of my actions carried a second meaning because of where we lived. In one quick summer the neckline of my shirt became a marker of my morality, roving eyes became my responsibility, and I finally understood what my sister had been trying to tell me. From then on, I always kept my thumb on the outside of my fist.

The chickee is a little more slumped than it used to be, but still standing. The posts of the platform have been worn white, blanched by the sun from the lumber-yard yellow I remember. Water laps at the legs of the platform where they disappear into the dark water. The bleached gator skull we nailed up over the door has gone green with lichen but it's there, staring out blindly over the scrub brush as I approach.

I smile at it as I pass under it, into my sanctuary. In my child's mind, I had decided that gator was the one that had killed June. It was the biggest we caught all summer, the biggest we would ever catch. Its skull would have earned a decent amount, but Dad let me tack it up on the wall instead. He knew then what I know now — that in order for people to feel safe, someone has to die.

Nearly a hundred gators died by my hand in one summer. I had nearly cleared the swamp of them myself, and every night I slept a little better. I was so focused on gators that I almost missed the real enemy. I hunted gators in the early morning fog, while my sister fought off classmates and cat-callers. I measured hides by the inch, while every inch of my sister's skin was added up and tallied against her.

I stagger through the sun-bleached tarp that serves as the door, and all sorts of creatures skitter away into the shadows. Three walls are still half-enclosed up to my shoulders with warped plywood. Dad had done it after the third time I fell over the edge trying to haul in a gator twice my size. The pallets of bottled water we got from FEMA after Hurricane Irma are still stashed in the corner, covered in dust but unopened. Dropping the shotgun, I rip through the warped plastic with my fingernails and grab a bottle. I gulp down my first one in one go, reaching for another as

I let the empty one fall to the floor. The water is stale and warm as piss, but it's still the most refreshing thing I've ever tasted.

I drain two bottles, then still and listen to the sounds of the woods. A helicopter putters overhead, but it sounds far off. I still have a while before they find me to reign punishment down on me for the crimes they think I've committed.

I don't think they're crimes at all — I see it as simple retribution. A balancing of the scales. When June died, the entire town roiled with an insatiable bloodlust for an entire summer, screaming for the skin of the creature that *might* have hurt her. We'll never know for sure if we got it, no matter what my child's mind believed. But people wanted vengeance, so we gave it to them.

It turns out they're less forgiving when the predator isn't a scaly prehistoric beast, and the victim isn't a blameless sacrificial lamb. In that case, horror and outrage vanish and they say things like *"oh, it's complicated,"* or *"well, we don't really know what happened."*

But I do. I know what happened. What happened was my sister was mean and rough around the edges because she had to be to survive. She came from a place people didn't understand because they could hardly stand to look at it.

People want the swamp to be drained and paved over so they can forget about the untidy ugliness of it. It's messy and sticky and dark, and there are evil things out here. They think that if they can wipe this place out, the evil things will go away.

But they're wrong. The gators have already moved on to the retention ponds behind their manicured little league fields. They're swimming closer than they think: in their backyards, their classrooms, their malls, their grocery stores, their daycares, their family barbecues, their police stations, and their pulpits. I was the only one who had the guts to do what needed to be done and put the beast down, regardless of the incorruptibility of his victim.

When the helicopter fades into the distance, I take the first-aid kit out onto the steps and sit on the stoop to dress my wounds in the cool light of dawn. Wincing, I dump an entire bottle of hydrogen peroxide on my shin and watch my blood boil. When it settles, I pat it dry and wrap my leg in tight gauze. It needs stitches, there's no doubt about that now. It'll probably get infected too, but sepsis is a problem that's too far away to pay any mind to.

The real problem is what to do when they find me — and they will, eventually. Like a rabbit being pursued by a hound, I have bolted for my burrow; but they'll smoke me out at some point. If they have to burn the forest down to find me, they'll do it.

But when that day finally does come, I'll hold my ground until the end. I have more buckshot than they have men and better aim than any of them. Let them come by the dozens; they'll drag me out in a body bag. I'll be the proof, living or dead, that trailer park girls ain't easy.

About Emily Gray

Emily Gray is a writer based in a small North Carolina town. She grew up in north Florida, where she cultivated a deep love of the wildlife and natural landscape of her home state. Though she primarily reads and writes science fiction, she is also passionate about the voices of women and queer people living in the south. When she isn't writing about spaceships, she's probably daydreaming about how many varieties of heirloom tomatoes she can fit in her garden this year.

Budapest to Berlin

Elizabeth Holden

The train was a whim; I paid too much, and I had to run to catch it. But I couldn't sit quietly in my hotel room any longer. I needed to fix what I'd done.

I was panting by the time I found the right track, my arm aching from carrying my suitcase on the dash across Keleti Station. The train hadn't yet left, thank God. It wasn't one of those modern, sleek-nosed machines that sped across Europe at 200 miles an hour. It was boxier, stouter, more old-fashioned, something that would chug along dependably if not especially quickly.

A station employee glanced at my passport, verified I was the same Erin Fischer listed on the ticket, and silently waved me on. Before climbing aboard, I double-checked that the sign on the train said Berlin HBF. The last thing I needed was to get on the wrong train. It was the sort of thing James would have loved teasing me about, if the circumstances had been different.

James. I pictured the last time I'd seen him, his figure striding away and disappearing into a crowd, leaving me alone in Budapest. I could fix this. I could.

I'd been fully prepared to sit up all night, staring at the darkened countryside out of the window, surely unable to sleep. But all that had been available last-minute was a deluxe sleeper cabin. I hadn't hesitated — credit card debt was better than wondering what was happening in Berlin.

So now, instead of heaving my white, hard-shell suitcase over my head onto a narrow rack and tucking myself into a seat, I followed a porter down a gray, skinny hallway lined with gray, skinny doors. He opened the last door, then handed me a plastic card with holes punched through it.

"Your key, miss." He nodded at me. He had a serious face and dark, thick eyebrows that reminded me of James. Everything reminded me of James. "I return at 9 o'clock." He nodded again, then quickly retreated.

I pushed my suitcase into my home for the next 12 hours–the place that would carry me away from Budapest and my bad decisions, and give me the chance to get my future back on track.

The room was small, no bigger than a walk-in closet. There was a navy-blue loveseat on my left, a convex sliding door on my right, a window ahead of me. My suitcase took up the width of the floor. I set it on the couch and opened the door to reveal the most compact shower-sink-toilet combo I'd ever seen.

Where was the bed? The website had shown a narrow twin bed when I'd booked my ticket. Maybe I was just supposed to curl up on the couch? Well, that would be fine. I sat down and rested my head against my suitcase, letting my eyes flutter shut. I hadn't slept more than a handful of hours in the last two days. Now that I was safely onto the train, the roiling ball of tension in my stomach was finally shrinking.

Now I could message James and tell him I was coming. He'd meet me, I knew it. He'd have to. And if he didn't? Well, I had his address in Berlin. I was going to fix this.

An announcement in Hungarian blared over the loudspeaker, distinct but utterly unintelligible, then was repeated in German, of which I could pick out a word or two, then in English. We were departing now. The train would arrive at Berlin at 9:15 tomorrow morning. When the announcement finished, the train slowly rolled into motion. Keleti Station retreated out of view.

I'd only arrived in Budapest three days ago. It was my first trip to Europe, a college graduation gift from James, who had graduated a year before me and was already making what felt like heaps of money with his electrical engineering degree.

When James told me that his engineering firm wanted him in their German office for the summer, I'd been happy for him, but jealous. I had never been to Europe and had long dreamed of visiting. Little did I know that James was already saving up for my trip.

He'd surprised me with news of the trip the week before he left. I'd been deliriously happy — a trip to Europe! "Let's go to Paris!" I'd said. James knew I'd wanted to see Paris ever since I saw the movie *Amelie* as an impressionable twelve-year-old.

But he convinced me otherwise. "Budapest is the Paris of the East! It will be perfect!" he'd said. "Plus, I've already been to Paris. Let's go somewhere new to both of us."

I'd wanted to love Budapest. I'd been ready. And maybe I would have — the rolling hills in Buda, the quirky shops in Pest, the beautiful Danube cutting the city in half. But now it was forever tainted: it would only be the city where James and I broke up. The city where I'd screamed at him in a public square, in front of a crowd of tourists, then lost myself in hysterics when he'd stormed away. I'd stood in front of an enormous Ferris Wheel for nearly an hour, waiting for him to come back, sobbing so hard my gut ached.

I grabbed my phone. *Hey*, I typed, then erased it.

The train was fully out of Budapest and into the countryside by the time I had a draft I didn't hate. Though I'd written paragraphs, most of them had been deleted. In the end I kept it simple.

> We can't leave things like this. I'm sorry for my reaction. I'm coming to Berlin right now, will be at HBF at 9:15am. I need you. I love you. - Erin

Only when I tried to send it did I realize I didn't have wi-fi, and saw no available networks.

I stuck my head into the hallway, looking for that dark-eyed porter or another passenger, but the hallway was empty and all the other gray doors were shut.

Exploring the train, poking my head into different carriages, seemed too hard. It would require me to act normal, friendly, and human when I felt like none of those things. But what choice did I have, if I wanted to reach James? I could wait until the porter returned at 9pm, but I didn't want to wait. I needed internet *now*. I grabbed my odd plastic key card and left the cabin.

There was another bathroom at the end of the train car, a shared one. The toilet flushed from within it, and I wondered if the porter was inside. I considered waiting outside the door. But what if it was another passenger, a Hungarian who spoke no English, perhaps? I didn't want to bother them.

I continued on, pulling open the door at the end of the train car, stepping nervously through the jerky, wobbly space between cars, then emerging in another car that looked identical to my own. Still no people.

What if I'd died on the dash to the train station, and this was the afterlife, just endless gray hallways? The idea spooked me, and I walked faster across the car and into the next one.

Seats. Chatter. People. My relief was disproportionate to the situation.

I still didn't see a conductor, but a man sitting alone had raised his head to look at me when I'd stepped into the car. Since he had a friendly, non-threatening, almost goofy appearance, I decided to approach him.

"Uh . . . szia," I said haltingly, trying to recall the few words of

Hungarian I'd memorized. "Beszélsz angolul?" If he said that no, he didn't speak English, I'd have to keep walking.

"Nem . . . beszélek magyar? Magyarul?" He spoke haltingly, and his cheeks turned bright red.

I bit my lip. "Sorry? I don't understand Hungarian."

The guy started laughing. He had shaggy, curly hair, and it fell into his eyes as his shoulders shook. "I don't either!" He burst out. His English was accented but clear, easy. "That's what I was trying to tell you, I don't speak Hungarian."

My whole upper body sagged with relief. Not just a fellow English-speaker, but someone friendly, someone to briefly distract me from the low hum of panic in my brain. I sat down gingerly in the empty seat next to him. "Do you know how to connect to the train's internet?"

"Oh, there is no wi-fi aboard," he said, pronouncing it 'weefee.'

"There isn't?"

He shook his head, shrugging regretfully.

I stood up quickly, turning my head so he wouldn't see the tears that had welled up in my eyes. Hopefully I could make it back inside my capsule before I broke into full-on sobs. I didn't want to search Berlin for James's apartment! I wanted him waiting for me at the station, proving he still loved me.

"You don't have data? No European SIM?"

I bit my lip, hard, as I shook my head.

"Would you like to use my phone?" The man's arm was outstretched, a dinged-up smartphone held loosely in his hand.

Now the tears fell, but they were tears of relief, and then, of course, of embarrassment that I was falling apart like this. I sank back into the empty seat and covered my face, pressing the palms of my hands against my eyes.

James hated it when I cried. When we fought, and I cried, he accused me of being manipulative. I wished he could have seen me now; crying was absolutely the last thing I wanted to be doing. I wanted to snatch the man's phone, spirit it off to my room, curl myself around it and reach out to James.

The man next to me didn't say anything, but when I finally lifted my head, I saw that his eyes were fixed on me.

"I'm so sorry," I breathed, wiping my eyes once more with my hands. "It's been a rough couple of days."

He reached into the backpack at his feet. I suspected he was pulling out a tissue, which I appreciated, but instead he pulled out a half-full bag of chips. "Crunchip?" He tilted the bright red bag toward me. "They're paprika flavor."

I shook my head. "No thank you."

He shrugged, as if to say 'suit yourself,' ate a few himself, wiped his hand on his faded jeans, then rolled the bag closed and put it back in his backpack. I couldn't help but note the contrasts here: James would never wipe his hands on his jeans, James would never let several days' worth of stubble grow, James would never use an old phone with a dinged screen.

"So, my phone? Would you like to borrow it?"

"Oh —" I should say no. He'd watched a complete stranger break down crying; that was enough to ask of a person, right? My eyes traced the navy fabric pocket on the seatback in front of me. The thing was, I didn't have any other options. I'd use his phone, but I'd do it fast, and then I'd retreat to my room. "Yes. Please."

He passed the phone to me, and I logged into my own email. My heart fluttered. Maybe I'd have a message from James waiting for me. An apology.

In the instant that the screen loaded, it hit me in my gut — James owed me an apology, too. I'd been jet-lagged and over-emotional and had jumped to conclusions; he'd been a jerk. I'd made a huge scene for no reason; he'd left me stranded in a new city. A new country. A new continent. He had at least as much to apologize for as I did.

My first trip to Europe. My graduation gift. My romantic getaway to the Paris of the East. All my friends had predicted a marriage proposal. I'd told them not to be ridiculous. Sure, James and I had been together for years, but we were too young!

Secretly, though, I'd thought the same thing. With both of us now done with school, it was time to start the next phase of our lives. Even as our communication had grown strained in our weeks apart before the trip — James already in Berlin, working in the German branch of the American engineering firm that had hired him a year ago, me finishing my final coursework before graduating — I still thought he was going to ask. It was the perfect time. The perfect place.

Then my email loaded. Nothing from James.

Fine. I copied the message I'd written from my phone onto the stranger's phone, sent it quickly and logged out.

Only now that the message was sent did I really look at the man next to me. He was close to my age — twenty-two — or perhaps a bit older. His skin was freckled, his eyes wide-set and light brown, his jaw covered in a few days' worth of stubble. Unruly curls hung over his ears.

"Thank you so much," I said, hoping he knew how deeply I meant it. It had occurred to me that, if I'd been in his position, I absolutely would not have offered up my potato chips, let alone my cell phone.

He shrugged easily. "Of course."

I was suddenly loath to head back to my tiny room, to be alone with my thoughts. This realization made me scramble to my feet. "Have a good night. Thanks again."

"No worries."

When I glanced quickly back at him on my way out of the train car, I saw he'd pulled out the chips again, and was munching them as he looked out the window.

I locked the door to my cube, pulled down the curtains — not that a random Hungarian farmer looking at the passing train could really see inside–and undressed. My jeans were the same pair I'd been wearing for days, and they felt stiff with grime. I balled them up and shoved them under the loveseat.

The air in the tiny room was stuffy. I found the thermostat, then stood under the vent and let the cool air blow on my bare skin.

If I chose to, I could stand here all night like this. For a moment, the solitude felt okay. This room was my little kingdom, my little habitat. No matter what sort of emotional scene might happen between James and I tomorrow, for the next twelve hours it was just me and the loveseat and the teeny tiny bathroom, alone.

I slid open the curved bathroom door, threw a small, white, square towel on the floor, and ran the shower on hot. My attempt at showering left the whole bathroom sprayed with water. A bruise bloomed on my elbow after I'd accidentally banged it against the wall. I'd knocked my head against the shower nozzle repeatedly while rinsing my hair. Regardless, it was an improvement. When I turned the water off, I used my index finger to carefully write E-R-I-N across the fogged-up mirror, an old habit from childhood that I hadn't indulged in for years.

I paused, looking at my name in the mirror and my foggy image behind it, feeling the low, fast rumble of the wheels on the track under my feet.

A sharp rap at the door startled me.

"Just a second!" I darted out of the bathroom and dug through my suitcase for pajamas. I imagined it was the man whose phone I'd borrowed, then remembered that he had no idea where my room was. As I opened the door, a soft night-shirt and cotton shorts thrown over my still-damp body, the correct answer clicked in my brain: it was 9 p.m.

Indeed, the porter was standing in the hall with his hands clasped behind his back.

"Miss." He nodded at me.

"Hi." I nodded back, waiting for him to explain his visit. He really did look something like James — the brooding dark eyes, the thick eyebrows, the broad shoulders. James was taller, though, and leaner.

The porter took a step towards me. "Your bed."

It wasn't a question. My heart stuttered. I was suddenly aware of how alone I was, how vulnerable I was. "Yes?" I clutched my cell phone in my hand, though what would I do with it? I couldn't even make a call, and I was barreling across the countryside on a train, anyway.

He gestured past me, to the room. "It's time I make up your bed."

"Oh." I stepped into the hallway to let him pass inside, my heart still thumping even as my brain tried to calm down.

With quick, practiced movements, the porter set my suitcase on the floor, flipped the loveseat in on itself, and folded it against the wall. Then he unlatched two metal clasps on the wall I hadn't noticed before, and unfolded a narrow Murphy bed with sheets and a thin blanket already made up on it.

"That's where the bed is!" I exclaimed, unable to stop myself.

He smiled at me, and suddenly his face looked younger, and less like James. "Yes, miss. I return in the morning with breakfast. What time?"

"Eight?"

He noted it down on a tablet, nodded at me once more, and departed.

I collapsed onto the surprisingly comfortable bed. I *did* jump to conclusions. James always said it, and God, he was right. The porter was harmless, here to set up my bed, not assault me.

The fight with James was, ultimately, my fault. I'd been convinced he was cheating on me. Everything he told me about Berlin was sprinkled liberally with mentions of Grace, the other American working at the engineering firm's German office for the summer. Grace this, Grace that, constantly.

"Grace found a great food cart right near our office."

"Grace is taking a German language class our boss recommended. Maybe I should, too."

"Grace double-majored in math and engineering, so I have her check my work."

"Grace says Berlin's club scene isn't as good as everyone says. She says London's is better."

Each little mention, innocuous on its own, added up to something big in my heart. And James and I weren't getting along, anyway. The time difference made phone calls tough, so we mostly texted, which led to miscommunication and bickering. It began to seem suspect that James had insisted we go to Budapest. My reasoning? Paris, my choice, would seem too romantic, and Berlin itself would give me evidence of Grace's presence in his life. One part of my brain was deeply convinced he was going to propose, and another separate part was equally convinced he was in love with his coworker.

I'd asked him about it tentatively as we walked down the Vaci Utca, sightseeing and souvenir shopping. He had carried the bag with gifts for my parents, a big green and red shopping bag with a glass jar of paprika, a white lace tablecloth, and two matching t-shirts.

My parents loved James. We'd been together since our junior year of high school. He was a fixture in my parents' household, letting himself in without knocking, bringing coffees for everyone if he stopped for his own cup, helping them with computer problems, washing the dishes after dinner without being asked. When he surprised me with the idea of the Europe trip, my parents were there, eyes shining, in on the plan with him. They loved him.

I hadn't told my parents we'd broken up, thank God, given that tomorrow I would fix things, we'd get back together. They would have stressed out over it for nothing.

I hadn't told my parents my fears about Grace, either. But by the time I was ready to fly to Hungary, I thought about her nearly as much as I thought about James himself.

"You talk about her a lot," I'd said as we strolled with the rest of the tourist hordes along the Vaci Utca. "And all those pictures on social media of the two of you out drinking together . . ."

He kept walking, not looking at me, not replying. I kept explaining.

"I'm probably being paranoid. It's just hard being six thousand miles away when I'm used to seeing you every day." Yes, I had started out fairly calmly. But by the time we'd reached the end of the street and walked on to Erzsébet Square, with its towering Ferris Wheel, I was shouting. He still hadn't spoken a word, and his silence fueled my panic.

"I'm not sure you actually like me! I'm just something you're used to having around, like an old piece of furniture. Boring little Erin, not a math genius, not a world traveler, not fun or wild or surprising!" It wasn't exactly correct, but I couldn't figure out how to articulate what I was feeling. "I just follow along, doing whatever you say is best. Yes, let's go to Budapest even though I want to see Paris. Yes, let's wait till I'm done with school to move in together. Yes, let's have fucking pizza for dinner when I'm in the mood for curry. I do whatever you want, but I'm not even what you want!"

My thoughts were wild, disorganized, spiraling, but the spiral was orbiting something true.

That's when James had grabbed my arm, stopping me, turning to face me. "Enough." His voice was low and tight. "You know I love you. I would never cheat on you."

Even in the mess of my mind, I could recognize both statements as true. "It doesn't matter!" That was true, too. "You love me, but you don't actually like me! You might not have slept with this girl, but I'm sure you want to! I don't want to be old furniture to you, James, I want to be someone you adore!"

"This is ridiculous. Don't make a scene, Erin."

"Too late!" I barked a laugh, still crying.

"I can't handle you anymore. I can't handle this."

"What the hell does that mean?"

"I just can't. I just . . . I can't do this anymore."

When he walked away, I didn't even understand what was happening at first. I thought he was pacing. He wouldn't just abandon me. He couldn't.

But he had.

I'd gone back to the hotel to look for him. His things were gone. His note was brief.

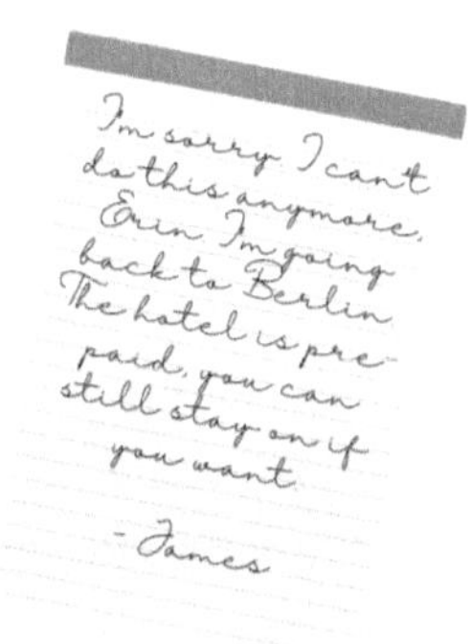

I'd crumpled the note and thrown it against the hotel room wall, then hit my fist against the wall, too, screaming and sobbing, all control lost.

Reviewing the past two days made my stomach ache. There were a thousand different threads woven into that fight, a thousand remarks and conversations and silences, and I couldn't tease them apart to see which were my fault and which were his. James and I had too much history.

I sighed, rubbed my eyes, and rolled onto my side, facing the wall. The train was shuddering to a stop as it pulled into the next station. The announcement blared just as it had before, first in Hungarian, then German, then in English. We'd passed through Slovakia and into Austria.

When the train had fully stopped, I sat up and peeked around my window shade. The station was small, just a little brick building, but the large, rectangular lights on the station wall were fiercely bright. I didn't feel like I was in Austria. I didn't feel like I was anywhere. The train was a liminal space, connecting all these cities but not existing in any of them.

The sky had gradually grown dark. Now, as we pulled away from this first Austrian train station, with the contrast of the bright station lights behind us, it seemed night had fully fallen. I stretched to reach the light switch, not even needing to leave the bed to do so, and flipped off the overhead light. My sleep in Budapest had been brief, shallow, and had provided no rest. Now, alone in my capsule, secure, suspended in space, I could finally rest.

I lay in the dark for hours, feeling the jostling and bumping of the train as it passed into the mountains. I replayed the fight with James. I replayed the first time he'd told me he loved me, in his car on a random winter afternoon. I replayed our first kiss in his parents' backyard, fireflies blinking around us.

Two years ago, when my mom had needed an emergency appendectomy and both my dad and I, coincidentally, had been out of town, James had been the one to drive her to the hospital, the one who stayed there overnight, texting updates to the family, making sure she had everything she needed. He was a good guy. He was woven into the fabric of my life. He couldn't just be ripped out of it because of a stupid fight.

I wondered if he'd written back to me. What if he had told me not to come? What if he hadn't written at all? Once I'd started wondering, I couldn't shake the thought. Damn it, if only I could get online, I could check. I looked at my phone, just in case, its blue screen harsh in the darkness. Still no connection.

It was nearly eleven p.m., but what did time mean, on this train, really? It existed in its own universe. Without allowing myself to think it through, I slipped my shoes back on, grabbed my keys, and made my way into the corridor.

Though the lights in the general compartment had been

dimmed, the curly-haired man was still awake. He looked up at the pneumatic hiss of the door, catching my eye as I stepped inside.

Immediately, he held up his phone, his head cocked in a question. I smiled, relieved, and nodded. He shifted his backpack off the seat next to him, then patted the empty seat. Oh, thank God for this man. I fell into the seat, whispered thanks, and took the phone.

James had written.

Erin, Of course I'll be there. I'll see you in the morning at Berlin HBF. I'll wait by the Bäckerei Heberer. Be safe. Love you, James

There. Okay. I could relax. He would be waiting for me, just like I'd wanted. And he'd signed the email like he'd signed so many others, "Love you, James." I'd been right – this was fixable, reversible. It wasn't a real break-up. Right?

I logged out and handed the man his phone back without sending James a reply. I'd see him in the morning; there was no need to say more now.

"All okay?" the man asked, apparently reading the relief in my body language.

"Yeah. All okay."

He brought out the bag of chips again. "Crunchip?" He was smiling.

With a lighter heart now, I was able to notice my hunger. I hadn't had dinner. I'd picked at my lunch . . . when was the last time I'd actually eaten? "Yes. That would be lovely." I took a chip, sprinkled red with paprika, and tried to eat it with as little crunching as possible, not wanting to wake the other passengers.

"I'm Luuk," the man said.

"Erin. Hi. And thank you again. You're a lifesaver."

"Are you here visiting from England? America?"

"America. Near Chicago. How about you?" It felt good to make casual conversation. The chips, or the email from James maybe — something was giving me energy despite my lack of sleep.

"I'm from Utrecht. You know it?"

I shook my head, took another chip.

"We're in the Netherlands."

Ah, so his slight accent was Dutch. "You speak English so well."

He shrugged, waved the compliment away. "Oh, we all do." Then, with a broad smile that revealed slightly crooked teeth, "How many people in the world speak Dutch? If we want to travel and go about in the world, we need to learn English."

"I guess that makes sense." I stuck my hand back in the chip bag. "You don't mind?"

"No. In fact . . ." He reached into his backpack, and pulled out two thin bars in bright green wrappers, *Sport* written across them in yellow script. "Have a chocolate."

I took one gratefully, too ravenous to turn him down. "What were you doing in Budapest?"

"I was seeing some friends, for a stag night." At my uncomprehending stare, he elaborated. "You know, my friend Sem, he is getting married, so we party together before the wedding."

"Oh, a bachelor party!" My voice had risen, and the person in the seat in front of me, previously sleeping on her companion's shoulder, stirred and glanced back at us. I lowered my voice. "What did you do?"

"You know, go to the famous ruin pubs, drink too much, make asses of ourselves." His eyes crinkled as he grinned at me.

What would James do for a bachelor party, if we got married? His best friends from college would probably plan something. It wouldn't be the stereotypical strip club thing, thank goodness. That wasn't their scene. I tried to imagine what *was* their scene, and found that I couldn't. Life in Illinois suddenly seemed impossibly distant.

"I went to Las Vegas for a friend's bachelorette party last year," I said. "Have you been there?"

"No, but I've seen movies. What happens in Vegas, it stays in Vegas, right?"

I smiled. "Right. I won five hundred dollars gambling, kept playing since I thought I was on a hot streak, and lost it all and more."

Luuk laughed, and I laughed too. James had been frustrated by this story. He thought it was illogical, stupid. I thought it was no big deal, since it wasn't money I'd come with. We'd argued. Why did it seem funny now?

"What were you doing in Budapest?" Luuk asked. "Vacation?"

I nodded. "Yep." I unwrapped the chocolate bar, took a bite, fiddled with the foil wrapper. Should I say the whole thing? Maybe it was a weird thing to unload on a stranger, but why not? It wasn't like I was going to see this guy again. I dove in. "With my boyfriend. Who broke up with me. Who I am heading to Berlin to reconcile with."

"Oh wow." He blinked. "Wow."

"Yep."

"I'm sorry to hear that."

Of course he meant he was sorry to hear I'd had a break-up on vacation, but a little part of my brain imagined he meant he was sorry we'd be reconciling. Maybe he'd been interested in me, found me attractive. It had been so long since I'd considered another man being attracted to me. Now, when I had damp, tangled hair, no make-up, worn-out pajamas, and after he'd met me when I'd started crying? It was unlikely.

"That is who you were messaging on my phone." He said it as a statement, no doubt in his voice.

"I was letting him know I was coming, and then looking for his response."

"And he will be there, in Berlin."

"Yeah. He will." Okay, maybe it wasn't that he was attracted to me. Maybe I'd had that thought because I was the one attracted to him. Oh, it was the sleeplessness, making my brain weirder and weaker, that was all. I'd never once been tempted to cheat on James, never even had the thought pass through my head. Not that finding another man attractive meant I was going to cheat on him, anyway. Why had I even thought that?

Probably he had a girlfriend, some tall, hot Dutch girl.

Not that it mattered.

Obviously.

The train was pulling into another station. It was time for me to go back to my room, get some sleep. Maybe someone boarding even had this seat reserved. I should definitely move.

It seemed difficult. And I hadn't finished the chocolate bar yet. I stayed put as people stirred, grabbed their bags from the overhead shelf, and disembarked. A new group of people boarded and settled in. No one asked for my seat. Luuk and I kept chatting.

"I was going to watch a movie on my phone. Would you like to watch it with me? I'll share my headphones."

"Sure." Why not? It was better than laying in my little capsule, unable to sleep.

He flipped through a few streaming apps, considering options. "How about Ocean's Eleven? Las Vegas, right? You can tell me if it is really like this." His mouth quirked into a smile, and mine echoed it.

"I expect there will be a few more heists in the movie than we did when I was there, but I'll let you know."

We started the movie, each using one of his ear buds, leaning together. My shoulder touched his. His skin was warm, almost hot, even through my t-shirt. I kept my eyes trained on his phone screen, but I didn't take much in.

It was cute, that he'd chosen a movie about Las Vegas since I'd been talking about it. But what else did he know about me, after all? He knew my name, that I was American, fighting with my boyfriend, and that I'd been to Las Vegas. That was it. A trip to Las Vegas was a solid 25% of the information he had about me.

Luuk didn't look at me and see decades of history. He didn't know that I worked in event planning at a hotel, that I'd majored in English literature, that I didn't get along well with my two sisters, that I was allergic to bees. He didn't know I jumped to conclusions, was over-emotional, that I worried too much about my parents' health and happiness, that I got lonely too quickly when I was by myself.

I could be almost anyone. I let the feeling seep into me. On the train, this liminal space that didn't exist in any city or country, Erin Fischer of Oak Park, Illinois didn't exist either.

It felt dazzling inside. I imagined it, felt it. And then I leaned on Luuk's shoulder and promptly fell asleep.

He shifted when the film ended, and I woke up. I'd drooled on his shirt. I hastily wiped my mouth and hoped he hadn't noticed.

"I am so sorry," I whispered.

He waved the apology away as he took out his half of the ear buds. "I fell asleep too." He whispered back. His face was close to mine, close enough that I felt his breath on my neck.

"I should get back to my room."

"Ah." A look of regret passed through his eyes, and I realized, with a twist in my chest, that the attraction hadn't just been one-sided. "I suppose so."

He bent forward, pulling out a scrap of paper and a pen. "Here," he scribbled quickly, "is my phone and email. Look me up if you make your way to the Netherlands one day. You'd like Utrecht."

Still feeling different, like someone else, I laughed quietly. "You don't even know me. How do you know I'd like Utrecht?"

"Oh, everyone likes Utrecht." He laughed too.

I took the piece of paper, tore it in half, and scribbled down my own contact information. "If you're ever near Chicago."

"Thanks." He folded it carefully and stuck it in his wallet.

I started to get to my feet, then he spoke again.

"And hey, Erin?"

"Yeah?"

His eyes were twinkling, his smile holding something dangerous. "Berlin to Utrecht is an enjoyable train ride. In case you change your mind and need something to do."

My heart beat harder. I was glad he couldn't see the red flush on my face in the darkness. "Good to know."

I went back to my room, every nerve buzzing, wide awake. Yet when I crawled into bed, I fell fast asleep. I didn't wake until eight, when the porter knocked on my door to deliver my breakfast.

The breakfast wasn't bad. I sipped my tea, ate a sweet roll and a tiny container of cherry yogurt. We weren't far from Berlin now. James was early for everything, and was probably already heading for HBF.

Would I see Luuk when I got off the train? He'd need to switch trains to head to Utrecht, so we'd probably cross paths disembarking, right? I was glad James would be waiting at Bäckerei Heberer, not waiting at the platform. I didn't want them to meet, though probably it would be fine and I was just being dramatic. I'd watched a movie with him and slept on his shoulder, not had sex with him. It was no big deal.

The train slowed as we entered Berlin. I stood in the hall with my suitcase, in line with a few other bleary-eyed travelers, waiting to disembark. This was it. Arrival in Berlin, no longer suspended from reality on the train. Return of my identity, of my life. I stepped off the train, feet heavy on the ground.

The crowd was huge. Luuk's train car, two away from mine, might as well have been a mile away, for all I could see through the rush of people. Twice I thought I saw his curly head in front of me, but both times I was wrong.

I pulled my suitcase through the station hall. My legs were wobbly, like I was trying to keep my balance on the deck of a ship, a consequence for having been in motion for twelve hours.

What if, despite having emailed me back to confirm it, James didn't show up? What would I do then? I bit my lip, imagining it. I'd panic, right? And then what would I do? Where would I go?

I found a big board with a map of the station, spotted Bäckerei Heberer and headed for it. The crowds hadn't thinned; I was surrounded, people ahead and behind and beside me, crossing in front of me, flowing.

There, just beyond a large group of college kids. His shiny dark hair, his angular jaw. He was far away, head turned towards the bakery's menu board, but I knew the sight of him instantly, innately.

There was my future, laid out in front of me. James and I would mend our relationship, he'd eventually propose, and we'd settle down together. The Budapest breakup would retreat into a meaningless blip in our shared past.

I swallowed.

The crowd was dense, and James hadn't spotted me yet.

I knew him so well. Even at a distance, my view partially blocked, the way he stood with his weight shifted to one side, his head cocked at an angle as he considered the bakery's display case — the sight of him was like coming home.

In my heart, a sense of entering a room, a door closing slowly behind me.

What if that metaphorical door didn't shut? What if, actually, I didn't want it to shut? What if I wanted to keep moving? This whole train trip, I'd had the space to simply exist as myself, not as part of the Erin-and-James unit. As soon as James saw me, that would disappear.

I couldn't articulate it further, couldn't define precisely what I wanted instead. But maybe that was the point. I wanted choice. Agency. Something different.

My nerves were alive, my heart pounding. I kept walking, faster now. I was still surrounded by people, anonymous in the throng.

A few more steps, and then James was behind me. I turned a corner, and James was out of view.

And then I was at the ticket counter.

My God. I exhaled and bent over at the waist, resting my hands on my knees. I had walked past James, past the man I loved, the man I'd spent years with, the man I thought I'd marry. Suddenly I was shaking, tears stinging my eyes. It took me a minute to recognize the overwhelming emotion surging through me: relief.

The people in line ahead of me finished their transaction, and the employee at the counter waved me forward.

"Um, hi." My voice trembled.

"What can I do for you?" The woman's German accent was strong, her eyes kind.

I coughed, cleared my throat. "I'd like your next ticket."

She paused, waiting for the obvious piece of missing information.

"To Paris, please."

She tapped her computer, took my credit card, and handed me the ticket. Her moves were businesslike, calm, blasé. Like there was nothing special about this moment at all. Like I was a random woman who wanted to go to Paris, and so was buying a ticket. Making it happen.

About Elizabeth Holden

Elizabeth Holden owns a travel company specializing in quirky group tours. The extensive time she's spent in more than a dozen European countries, plus her eclectic interests ranging from physics to roller derby, enrich her written work. She believes the ideal conditions in which to write a novel are in the dining car of a train traveling through the Alps, with a pot of tea beside you—though she writes the most at her home in Wisconsin. Her debut young adult novel, Mighty Millie Novak, comes out in August 2024.

Website: elizabeth-holden.com

 instagram.com/ElizabethH_WI

The City of the Silent

C. M. Leyva

I am more dead than alive in a world that fears mortality. What they don't see is the life after death. While the body releases its last breath and the heart takes its final beat, there is still life within them. Muscles relax and contract in response to a symphony of chemical reactions now hitting their crescendo. Humans are not immune to the cyclicity of nature. The cry of a newborn exposed to the light of a world too harsh for their eyes. The final breath of an old man as he reflects on things left undone. Eyes open, pupils now abandoned wells. Dilated orbs accepting the light they've filtered since birth. The body temperature drops like clockwork. A slow decay. One point five degrees every hour, until it matches mine. All the while, I surround them, nurture them as we become one.

While the world below is filled with life, the world above moves at a slower pace. I rest nestled between the sharp terrain of the San Bruno Mountain and the tranquility of the Gulf of the Farallones. The combination of the sea breeze and the mountains allows the rolling green slopes to hide behind a late summer fog. I breed rarity. Fauna that only grows in climates such as mine. I protect the vulnerable as species hide from extinction. On my surface, there is beauty in the miles of green I still possess, untarnished by gray looming buildings piled on top of each other. But this is not my legacy. No. It's the thousands of unwanted souls. Each gravestone reflects the moonlight like silver scars against my skin. I am Colma, city of the dead, and these are the stories of the silent.

The year is 1849. Gold sparkles in the eyes of men seeking fortune in San Francisco, but opportunity always comes with a price. There's a saying that the grass is always greener on the other side. The idea that by giving up what one already has, one can achieve something greater. But what is greater than family? Greater than life? For some, it's a chance at unimaginable wealth.

MURDOCH DOHERTY

"I ain't got that kind of money to lend you."

Murdoch's head drops in exasperation as he rubs the bridge of his nose. He'd worked for Mr. Steele for over five years now, and not once had Murdoch asked him for anything. With one hundred dollars, he could join the next wagon train out of Independence, Missouri for the six-month trip to California. He just needed the money, and Mr. Steele was the only person he knew that would have it to spare.

"I told you I'll pay you back tenfold."

Mr. Steele turns away from the window overlooking the factory workers below. He shakes his head and removes his pocket watch, ringing the bell to indicate it was time to end the day.

"You can't guarantee me shit, Murdoch. Ain't nobody I've known come back yet. It ain't right bringin' your family on that death trail."

Aileen had said the same thing, but Murdoch couldn't imagine leaving without her and their boys. Maybe taking them wasn't right, but leaving them didn't feel any better. He brushes away the thought and stands, placing his hat on Mr. Steele's cherry hardwood desk. The desk alone was worth more than what Murdoch was asking for.

"Sir, I can feel it in my being. This is the journey I'm meant to take. Tell me, what did you risk to get here?"

Mr. Steele's face softens. "I'll give you the money if you're brave enough to do this on your own. We'll bring your family to the house and your wife can work around the farm to pay for her and the boys to stay. That's my offer."

An impossible choice. Walk away from his family for a chance to give them everything they could ever need or want. Or stay and admit he isn't brave enough to take the risk for them. Murdoch stares at the floor, thumbing the shamrock charm around his neck. He hates that he can't answer something he was so sure about just a minute ago.

"The wagon train leaves town in a week. My offer stands 'til then," Mr. Steele says with an empathetic smile. He pats Murdoch on the back and walks towards the metal stairs, each step echoing through the office.

Murdoch couldn't let Mr. Steele walk away. If he didn't take the offer, Aileen would find the words to convince him to stay, and he'd die wondering what their life could have been.

"Mr. Steele," Murdoch shouts, rushing down the steps. "I'll take your offer, sir."

Murdoch puts out his hand and Mr. Steele eyes it with dejection. "May God watch over you."

His rough hand finds Murdoch's, sealing his fate. "Thank you, sir. I won't come back 'til I can pay you what I promised."

A week later, Murdoch kisses Aileen goodbye. He bends down and tells the boys to be good and watch over their mother. Anything to keep from looking into Aileen's eyes. She was strong, stronger than him, but not strong enough to keep the tears from welling. He mounts his horse and kisses his charm for good luck, giving a final wave as he starts towards town. By joining the wagon train, he'd have protection against bandit attacks that often happen to lone travelers. The company he joins is a group of twenty-three wagons made up mostly of families with children around the ages of his boys. Murdoch aches to hear his boy's laughter, but a month into the trip after the second child is run over by a wagon wheel and the third is pulled away by the swift currents of a river, Murdoch is grateful for leaving them behind.

Despite his relief, he still misses his family. He spends the nights looking up at the sky, wondering if Aileen is looking at the same stars. It's only been a little over three months, but he longs to be home again. Murdoch pushes himself up from his sleeping mat to get a sip of water. The wagon train stopped next to a river for the night, and the stillness of the water from the lack of rain reflects the moonlight. He bends, splashing the cold water onto his face before taking a drink.

The next morning, Murdoch is hit with a sharp pain in his stomach, forcing his step to stagger. His horse stands next to him eating leaves from a tree growing next to the river. It hasn't taken a sip of the water yet. The pain returns with more intensity, and the burn of bile slowly works up the back of his throat. Murdoch understands what's coming. Mr. Casper had been unfortunate enough to catch this the first week on the trail. Death could be swift like it was for Mr. Casper, or it could be long and painful. A wave of terror washes over Murdoch as he looks back at the camp. Mr. Casper had wandered off to keep his family safe, but Murdoch fears dying alone. He gives a quick prayer and kisses his shamrock charm, hoping for any luck it can bring. The selfish need for comfort in his last hours pushes him back towards camp, where he knows he brings death to everyone.

Murdoch Doherty and his wagon camp are found by the next wagon train to pass. They're buried as unnamed grave markers guiding travelers along the two-thousand-mile stretch of trail.

SAMUEL KETTERMAN

Those who survived the journey arrived in the lawless world of the gold mining towns. Dirt roads lined with supply stores for work, and saloons and brothels for entertainment. The buoyant tunes of the saloon piano and raucous laughter provided a false sense of security as men sat at gambling tables with shifty eyes. These men — the Forty-Niners — knew what they were willing to risk for wealth. They cheated death once; they could do it again.

Samuel looks down at his cards — first bad hand all night. Sweat drips down his brow and he quickly wipes it away, hoping no one took notice. The California summer heat could be enough of an explanation. But nobody asks, which means he doesn't have to lie. There's no opportunity without risk, which Samuel knows well. Each night he walks in with his earnings from the gold mines and doubles them before stumbling out after one too many glasses.

"Lucky son of a bitch," the bartender says, each time Samuel returns. Earning Samuel the nickname "Lucky."

He lowers his cards with a grin, pushing everything he has into the pot. One bad hand isn't enough for Lucky Ketterman to walk away.

"I've heard of you around town and I ain't lookin' to lose my shirt today," one man says as he folds.

The man next to him follows, but the last remains fixated on the cards in his hand. His hat sits low, casting a shadow over his eyes.

Another bead of sweat rolls down Samuel's hairline. The man in the hat notices.

"Why don't you take off that hat and keep things fair here?" Samuel asks, hoping to create a distraction.

His hand reaches for a shamrock charm around his neck. Something he had picked off a traveler on his way to California.

"You got luck. I got my hat. I think that's fair enough," the man says with a rotten grin.

Samuel's stomach drops at the familiar rough voice of the man next to him. Luck wasn't something he only had at the tables. It had followed him since picking the charm off of a man he had been traveling with. Samuel was the sole survivor of a twenty-three-wagon massacre. Murdoch Doherty had caught cholera, spreading it through the camp like wildfire. Samuel only knew the asshole's name because it was etched into the back of the charm.

Since then, Samuel had walked away from more than one dispute untouched yet surrounded by bodies, had wandered to failed dig sites to find pockets full of gold, but it was a tunnel collapse two months back that almost ended his luck. Thirty men were not so fortunate. One of them being Jacob Tinley, the man now sitting next to him.

"I thought you were dead," Samuel says, as the room shrinks around him.

Jacob pushes his earnings to join Samuel's. "With friends like you, I should be."

They had arrived in Hangtown the same day and decided it was safer to work together than try to survive on their own. However, Jacob seemed to have a black cloud following him wherever he went. This, of course, made him envious of Samuel's inexplicable luck. And understanding the monsters that jealousy can create, Samuel grew cautious of Jacob's intentions. The day the mine collapsed was their last day together. Samuel had asked Jacob to take his spot in the mine. He had filled his cart with dirt and rocks, which he hoped to pan for gold.

"This ain't a good spot," Jacob argued. "I already told you I've dug here twice and come out with nothin'."

Samuel patted him on the back, giving him a confident grin. "I got a good feelin' about this spot today. Just trust me."

Samuel had barely cleared the mine when the tunnel collapsed. Nothing more than a cloud of dirt escaped.

"I should've known better than to trust you," Jacob says, tipping back the brim of his hat and exposing a left eye patch. "You ain't ever looked out for anybody but yourself."

Samuel forces a laugh, leaning back from the poker table. He tucks the charm under his shirt and gives it a pat for good luck.

"Come on now. Looks like some of my good luck finally rubbed off on you."

Jacob nods slowly. "Or maybe you were my bad luck all along."

The click of a gun sounds under the table and the saloon goes quiet.

Samuel "Lucky" Ketterman wasn't lucky enough to appreciate the irony of his tombstone.

Father Bowers

Father Bowers stands at the grave. According to the tombstone, it had been over sixty years since Samuel had met his demise. The world he knew was long gone. The gold picked clean from the earth and replaced by the miners, now tucked away in caskets. Unwanted residents, six feet deep in rich California soil. Father Bowers continues down the row of tombstones no longer maintained. Once the vacant plots ran out, so did the money. And no one would care for the dead for free. Statues vandalized. Gravestones cracked in half. Bronze mausoleum doors removed from their hinges. This was how they honored their fallen. Even in death, their souls had no peace.

When Father Bowers graduated from All Hallows College in Dublin, he was eager to spread the word of God. As a missionary, he found himself traveling to what they knew as the Wild West. He arrived to find a world of sin, with men allowing their darkest desires to take hold. Drunks, thieves, and men committing murder in the name of justice. It was enough to make many of his fellow missionaries question their purpose, but not Father Bowers. He saw a chance at redemption and repentance in each man, regardless of their sins. Desperation created monsters of men. This he understood after seeing what it had done to his father during the Great Famine. Men who knew nothing of the Lord would crawl to him in their last hours. Fear emanated from their eyes as they confessed, begging for forgiveness. Father

Bowers never turned them away, not if they were willing to open their hearts to the Lord.

He had promised the families of those buried in the Catholic cemetery of San Francisco that he would watch over them and keep them safe. It never occurred to him how difficult it would be to keep that promise. Each day, the price of San Francisco's land grew, and so did the lies of the dead. The power the government wielded with nothing more than words was astounding. So much so, they were able to overrule the Catholic Church's argument to allow their cemetery to remain untouched. Greed was somehow greater than God, and now Father Bowers was tasked with watching over the exhumations of each body within his cemetery. So began the solemn procession of one hundred and fifty thousand bodies from San Francisco to Colma.

Father Bowers whispers silent prayers for each soul disrupted from their eternal slumber. Men, paid for the number of bodies moved rather than the care they took, allow caskets to crack and fall, exposing what is left of the remains. Despite the years that had passed since the bodies disappeared into the earth, the smell of death resurfaces with them. The wealthy had been embalmed, preserved in cast-iron coffins, but Samuel Ketterman's remains had become nothing more than dust. Father Bowers places a small redwood box next to his grave, asking the men to transfer the remains from the mangled wooden casket. They don't argue, but their faces say enough for him to discern their thoughts. They toss a shamrock necklace into the box and Father Bowers lifts it to the soft light of the setting sun. Murdoch Doherty's name glints back at him. Another forgotten soul, deserving of his own burial. Father Bowers opens a second box and places the charm inside.

With two small redwood boxes tucked under his arm, Father Bowers stands. The gravediggers throw Samuel's tombstone into a pile they would later dump into the Bay. Peace came at the price of $10 per grave. Those whose families couldn't — or wouldn't — pay found themselves in the company of others abandoned in mass graves. The sun begins its descent into the horizon, which means the gravediggers would be heading home soon to rinse the stench of death from their skin. For Father Bowers, his day is far from over. He continues to the last horse-drawn hearse, as they prepare to travel the ten miles south to deliver the bodies to Colma.

The hour journey is one of silence. Father Bowers sits in the carriage next to a casket. It allows him too much time to think, and he wonders if this is what he was put on this earth to do. A shepherd of unwanted souls. He looks down at the redwood boxes on the seat next to him, wondering if anyone will do the same for him when he's gone. They arrive in Colma just as the city comes alive. The living residents work solely in the business of the dead.

He hears the whistles of the gravediggers as they make their way to the cemeteries to begin their work for the evening. Bodies arrive in the thousands, not just by horse and carriage, but from streetcars and trains with stops at each cemetery. Father Bowers knows the people of this town well. Dirt-covered faces of the living, waiting to welcome the next group of the dead.

Agatha, the local florist, tends to her gardens during the day and delivers each beautiful arrangement at night. Benton, the monument maker, carefully chips away at the granite, unwilling to allow a mistake to pass in his work. Even the barkeep at Molloy's understands his role as he pours the mourners a pint, listening attentively to their stories of the deceased. The tavern isn't a place for sadness, but a chance to honor loved ones. Father Bowers pats the wooden lid of the remains, honored to provide Samuel "Lucky" Ketterman and Murdoch Doherty such a peaceful place for their souls to finally rest.

Harold Poulter

Harold Poulter is a grateful man. One who appreciates the warmth of the sun on his face, the songs of the birds hidden in century-old trees, and the sight of another funeral procession slowly making its way to his cemetery. People who didn't understand Colma would find his world to be morbid and distasteful, but Harold takes pride in his work as the groundskeeper of Holy Cross Catholic Cemetery. It's the same work his father did before him — a family tradition.

"Good afternoon, Harold," Bonnie says, wiping her brow with the back of her gloved hand.

She adjusts her straw hat, looking up at him. Bonnie arrived in Colma just two years ago, and according to the rumors, it was because her fiancé — a nameless man who had died tragically in a motorcycle accident — had been buried here. Harold often wondered if that was true, but he was a firm believer in minding his own damn business. So, the two worked side-by-side day after day, him tending to the grounds while she maintained the grave flowers, ensuring they weren't wilted or missing when the families arrived. He appreciated that despite her being decades younger than him, she put the same amount of effort and care into her work as he did, often arriving before him with her contagious smile and two black coffees in hand.

"The Bowers family will like the new yellow tulips," Harold says, watching Bonnie adjust them in a vase.

He hovers next to her, leaning on his rake to take some of the weight off his bad knee. The sound of children laughing and playing travel from behind him. Sunday Mass had just finished, which meant that Father Bowers, Samuel "Lucky" Ketterman, and Murdoch Doherty's graves resting side-by-side, would be receiving their normal visits from the Bowers family. Bonnie stands, brushing the dirt from her knees.

"Listen, I wanted to see if you had time to join me for lunch today?" she asks, loading her dirt and shovel back into her wagon.

Harold, being a creature of habit, hesitates to respond. The thought of changing his daily lunch routine makes him suddenly anxious. Every day at noon, he eats his ham and cheese sandwich with an apple on a bench outside of the Holy Cross Mausoleum. The town is small — a little over fifteen hundred living — but at

1.5 million dead and counting, Harold found more comfort in the deceased.

"Would it be okay if we saved it for another day?"

Bonnie grabs the handle of her wagon. "Yeah, another day works. Just let me know when."

Harold knows he won't schedule that other day, but he gives her a reassuring nod, nonetheless. Bonnie waves to the children as they approach, and continues to the next set of graves. Harold struggles to bend towards Father Bowers's grave, removing a towel from his back pocket and wiping the dirt from the base. A shamrock is etched into the stone and Harold rubs his thumb across it, not for luck, but just out of habit.

He tips his hat to the Bowers family as they approach and continues up the road towards the mausoleum.

Weeks pass and Bonnie hasn't brought up her request to meet for lunch again. Harold hopes this means he can stop feeling guilty about it, but each time he sees her, her words find their way into his memory. Over and over, haunting him. Each day he sits on his bench and watches her drag the wagon down the road. She disappears out of sight to eat her lunch somewhere alone. The heaviness of guilt ruins his appetite yet again, and he decides to follow her so he can get back some peace. His pace is much slower than hers, but he's able to follow the tracks of the wagon in the dirt. He eventually arrives to find her sitting and talking to two tombstones. His shadow tips her off to his presence and she jumps to her feet.

"Harold, you scared me," she says, clutching her chest.

She isn't scared. She's embarrassed for being caught talking to the graves. Harold's eyes travel down to the tombstones. *Anita Rossi & Daniel Rossi.* Both with the same date of death two years ago.

Bonnie tucks her hands into her pockets, her hat covering whatever expression she's trying to hide.

"My parents," she whispers. She motions to the grave next to them. "And my little sister, Nadine."

The same date of death. Harold always treated these graves the same as the other three hundred and fifty thousand he polished and maintained. They never had flowers or visitors, and he always assumed whatever tragedy occurred had taken them all together to the next life.

"I'm so sorry, Bonnie," Harold says, the guilt burrowing deeper.

Bonnie shakes her head and grabs a small folding chair from her wagon, placing it across from her.

He takes his seat, sinking into the soft grass and placing his paper bag on his lap.

"I should have asked if today was a good day," he says, looking down at the dirt caked under his fingernails.

"Today is a perfect day."

Even without looking up, Harold can hear the smile in her voice.

"I remember the day they arrived," he says.

It wasn't a lie. There was no procession, just three cars with three caskets. The bodies were buried with no words spoken over them except for Harold's silent prayers. He watched the graves for days after they arrived, hoping someone would eventually come looking for them. But each day he passed, they sat alone. A month later, Bonnie arrived as the newest member of the grounds crew. Her face was pale and worn, but many city dwellers looked like that, so he thought nothing of it.

Bonnie took a bite of her sandwich and Harold could hear her sniffle beneath her hat.

"I tried," she chokes out.

Harold had consoled hundreds of families throughout his years maintaining these grounds. He never minded the tears soaking through the shoulders of his shirt as they grieved, watching their loved ones disappear into the earth. Those that were closest to the departed would often stay long after the rest of the party had left. They would laugh with him as they recounted stories of better times. It was those connections that gave him fulfillment in life. Being able to care for people in their darkest times, and bringing comfort to them by watching over their loved ones when they left.

Harold removes his sandwich from the paper bag and allows Bonnie to work through her thoughts as she continues eating her sandwich in silence.

"I tried to come to their funeral that day, but I couldn't." Another sniffle and a quick wipe of a rogue tear tell Harold she's just beginning her story. "There were days I would park my car on Old Mission Road and just sit there for hours trying to convince myself to see them. That if I just saw them, maybe it would make it easier to breathe. Maybe it would lessen the ache that had settled in the center of my chest since they passed. But I couldn't."

Bonnie finishes her sandwich and takes a sip from her bright pink metal water bottle. The dents and chipping paint tell Harold she holds onto things that she should have moved past. She wipes her mouth and sighs.

"You know how the rumor got started about me having a fiancé in a motorcycle accident?" Her curt laugh makes it obvious she doesn't appreciate said rumor.

"No," Harold says, knowing more words aren't needed.

"Have you met Gretchen?"

Harold nods. A money-hungry woman from the city who had bought up several homes in Colma when the housing market crashed in 2008. At no point did she try to make friends in the small town. Harold smiles, remembering the day she was pulled over for speeding around a funeral procession. If there was one thing you didn't mess with in Colma, it was their funerals.

"She saw the newspaper clipping I had left on the front table of the rental and assumed the man on the motorcycle who had cut off my parents was my fiancé. I suppose it was better than assuming it was the family that had died instead."

Harold's cheeks grow hot as his dislike for Gretchen deepens. "She had no right starting rumors like that."

Bonnie finally looks up and Harold sees the red in her now

puffy eyes. "I just wanted you to know the truth. It's stupid, but I worry that if something happened to me, no one else would know about them."

Harold pauses mid-bite, shocked by her words. She's too young to be concerned about her mortality, but Nadine's grave next to him is even younger. He had seen fractures of sadness break through her cheerful demeanor, but he never thought it was because of this.

"Your fears aren't stupid and I promise if anything happens, I'll care for you as I do for them."

Only in Colma were these words of comfort. Bonnie smiles up at him, the same radiant smile she had given a hundred times before; and Harold feels the warmth in his heart, like the sun against his face. There was always hope in the darkness. A light that would never extinguish and they would always preserve that. Colma's legacy is to be a sanctuary for the silent and a place for their stories to be heard.

About C.M. Leyva

C.M. Leyva is a speculative fiction author and registered nurse who enjoys writing character-driven fiction in all genres. Her passion for science and medicine is often seen in her stories while exploring the what-if's around them. You can find her short fiction in anthologies with Outland Entertainment and Flower-Song Press, and her debut novel The Legacies of Traitors will be released in 2024. When she's not working on her next short story or manuscript, you can find her attempting home improvement projects, losing herself in a good book, or playing video games.

Linktree: linktr.ee/cmleyva

The Argus

Amanda Bender

The Argus is six stories of oak and steel with portholes and hatches along its port and starboard sides. A relic people vaguely understand is significant, but no longer know the truth about: It was once a ship that soared through the clouds before it was shot out of the sky.

When it crashed, the Argus's bow drove into the earth like a shovel, burying the bridge so deep in the soil that the rest of the ship stood erect with its rudderless stern reaching for the skies. What was left of the crew patched up the hull and built supports to keep it standing. The crew resigned themselves to never seeing home again, and so they built a new one inside the Argus to live out their days until Time came to take them.

Except Time never did. It just kept ticking.

And ticking.

And ticking.

Months turned to years. Years turned to decades. Decades turned into centuries. But the Argus and its crew remained. Even after explorers found the ship and its eccentric crew in the middle of the forest and settled the land. Even after the settlers turned their outpost into a center for trade. Even after the outpost spread outward. Even after it ate away at the green surrounding it to make space for buildings and streets and people — so many people. And even when the crew learned that one of the roads to the city could take them back to the place they once called home, they remained.

The only thing left of their home is each other and the Argus.

So the Argus and its crew carry on, watching the city stumble and grow, fighting itself and others, doing their best to blend into the world in all its different ages. Some would call the surviving crew members immortal because they've lived for so long without aging. The truth is much sadder though: they're stuck. Caught up in the past, but unable to fully be part of the present.

Ozkar doesn't know what made him walk in. He had passed it dozens of times over sixteen years and on the night he finally went inside it hadn't looked any different. Just an odd, old thing with lights glowing in the portholes and the neon sign humming, letting everyone know it was open. But that night . . . it had reeled him in as if he'd been hooked on an invisible lure.

That night was a year, one month, and thirteen days ago. And he has called the Argus home ever since.

The city outside is ablaze — most of the time figuratively, but sometimes literally. Infrastructure is crumbling. Institutions are stumbling. People are paranoid, hurt, and curt. It used to be a kind place and it's trying to get back on its feet. But it's unsteady and shaken and close to the edge.

Of what?

People like to speculate.

Most are uncertain. Some are pessimistic. Few are hopeful.

The Argus drowns it all out though. Ozkar can't hear anything over the steam gurgling and hissing through the pipes, and the portholes are so scuffed that the scenery beyond it looks like an abstract painting. If visitors didn't come barging into the shop on the first deck, he would be able to believe there was nothing beyond the sheets of steel and wooden planks.

But there are visitors. The Argus is boasting a sale. Ozkar keeps an eye on everyone as they move about the deck. Atticus is talking to an older couple with an easy smile on his face. The wind-weathered helmsman-turned-cashier is the oldest of the crew. He had been sailing across the skies while the others were learning to fly their first balloon. But even though there is gray at the edges of his hairline, Atticus is still trim and sharp.

Ozkar looks down at the book he's balancing on his knees. It's one of the older tomes from the library the captain keeps in her study. Ozkar has a dust jacket pulled over it to disguise its identity. He shouldn't have taken it.

But he doesn't have a choice.

He needs to find a way to stay with the Argus and its crew and he's running out of time.

Someone comes up to the register and places a pile of items on the table. Two books. A deck of playing cards. A gizmo that looks like a watch, but isn't a watch. Ozkar looks at the gizmo.

"Where'd you find this," Ozkar asks.

"Over there," the woman points.

Innocent enough, but Ozkar hears a faint squeak in her voice and then there's also the black smudges on her fingers from where she grabbed the railing to the stairs that lead up to the second deck. There are boxes of gears and gizmos on almost every step.

"Sorry, ma'am, but this isn't for sale."

"But the sign says 'everything must go.'"

"Everything down *here*," Ozcar says and then points to the ceiling. "Not up *there*."

"Name your price."

"It's priceless."

The woman frowns. Ozkar rings up the other items and tells her the total. She gives him a smug smile that makes it clear that she would like to give him a piece of her mind. Before she can,

Atticus comes over and asks what she got. The woman turns and Ozkar uses the opportunity to pocket the gizmo. He grabs his book, slips out from behind the counter, and ducks around the corner.

The ship's first deck has the highest ceiling and its walls are divided by steel ribs originally built to stiffen the ship's hull. Between the ribs are floor-to-ceiling shelves packed with just about every kind of thing imaginable. Tables engulf the floors, displaying records, encyclopedias, and other collectibles. Everything is meticulously labeled. Ozkar shades his way toward the back of the deck. Izzy says he acts like a ghost.

She's not wrong.

The second deck is Izzy's domain. It smells like burnt wires and electricity, and it's packed to the gills with things from all corners of the world. Bronze tools and shields. Hefty tomes and tightly tied scrolls. Busted clocks and bobs and cogs with gears and springs hanging out of them. Parasols and walking sticks. Spears and ink quills. Hand-sewn tapestries and blankets. And then there are the jars filled with neon-colored goo. Claws, crystals, scales, and so much more are suspended in the green gelatin. Each one is covered in symbols that are now only remembered by the Argus's crew. Every piece of hardware on the floor has been harvested for parts for Izzy's latest project.

Her warp gate is fired up and ready to go. The submersible-looking ship that will carry the crew through the time vortex is not.

"Izzy?" Ozkar calls out.

"Over here."

Half her body is inside the ship, her legs dangling out of the side. She's tightening bolts with a socket wrench. Ozkar leans against the ship and hugs the book to his chest.

"You figure out what's wrong?"

"No."

She's the youngest of the crew and the smartest. A mechanic who lied her way onto the Argus before its fatal mission. But Izzy was so smart and sharp that the captain couldn't bring herself to turn her away. Ozkar knows it won't be long until she discovers the crisscrossed wiring and missing heat sinks. When she does, she'll know it was him and he doesn't want to think about how mad she'll be at him.

Izzy hoists herself out of the ship and Ozkar sticks out his arm so she can grab hold of something as she drops down. As usual, she has smudges of grease on her freckled cheeks and has a pair of goggles strapped to the top of her head.

She points at the book.

"Nothing interesting," he lies.

"Were you working the register?" She knows he likes to read during slow shifts.

"I always do from ten to two."

She rolls her eyes. "You know what I mean."

Ozkar doesn't answer.

"You should be packing and planning and . . ." Izzy stops herself. The way she does when she has too many thoughts and not enough words. Finally, she simply asks, "Don't you think it'll be nice to spend time somewhere other than this stuffy place?"

"It's a mess out there."

"Messes can be cleaned up."

"Not all of them."

Izzy huffs and says, "You really lack imagination sometimes."

"Well, we can't all be girl geniuses who are smart enough to build a time machine."

"It doesn't take a genius to clean up a mess."

"Only geniuses say that," Ozkar says and after a moment, he admits, "I want to go with you all."

"You can't though. You didn't —"

"I didn't what?"

"Nothing," she says, a little too quickly.

He doesn't know *exactly* why he can't travel through time, but the short of it, according to Izzy, is that, unlike the Argus's original crew, he doesn't have the cellular stability to handle it. There's something about their ancient DNA that will allow them to go through without any trouble.

Ozkar is about to tell her it sounds like something when he hears shoes tapping against the deck's metal floor. Ozkar and Izzy turn to see a tall woman in knee-high boots and a long overcoat with ducktails and brass buttons engraved with a sigil that is no longer known. Her hair is pinned back in a tight bun. Her demeanor is calm and cool. Her presence is felt, even when she's not seen. If the Argus was a person, Ozkar imagines Captain Ava Penni would be it.

Captain Penni folds her hands behind her back and approaches, her face drawn in a neutral line. She asks, "Any progress?"

Izzy shakes her head.

"Keep working on it. We don't have long."

"Aye, captain."

Captain Penni looks over at Ozkar. "What are we reading today?"

Ozkar holds up the book to show the captain the cover.

"Do you know what's intriguing Mr. Noveck?"

Uh-oh, Ozkar thinks.

"That tome looks to be the exact thickness and height of a book that is presently missing from my study."

Without a word, Captain Penni holds out her hand and Ozkar places the book into it. He hangs his head. "I just want —"

"The less you know about our civilization the better."

"That's not why." Ozkar shakes his head. "I want to —"

"It's out of the question."

"You haven't even —"

Captain Penni raises her hand. "I know *exactly* what you want, Mr. Noveck. It cannot be done."

"You haven't even tried."

Izzy starts to say something, but the captain shoots her a severe look, and she instantly closes her mouth. Ozkar huffs and crosses his arms in front of his chest. He glares up at Captain Penni, imagining all the terrible things he wants to spit at her, but he bites his cheek.

"Promise me, this is the last of these attempts," Captain Penni says, lifting the book in the air.

Ozkar stays quiet and keeps biting his cheek. He won't promise a thing.

Static rustles across the intercom and Atticus's voice rings out. "Shop is closed, captain."

Captain Penni walks over to the intercom and presses the button. "Thank you, Mr. Pelias. Make sure everything is secure for departure."

"Yes, captain." The intercom clicks off.

Theoretically, the warp gate will be able to take the crew *and* the Argus back in time. The submersible is a failsafe. If anything goes wrong, the small craft will guarantee the crew's safe return. But while they don't need to bring the Argus back, Ozkar can tell they want to. It has been with them for so long that it is part of them, one of them, and Captain Penni refuses to leave anyone behind.

Even the watchman.

Ozkar stops. He hadn't thought about the watchman. *Maybe he can help…*

Captain Penni looks down at Ozkar once more and says, "Mr. Noveck, I understand this will be a hard change. But it is the right one. You must pack your things and depart. The world is waiting."

Ozkar looks away. The Argus and its crew should know more than anyone that the world waits for no one. But he doesn't say so. Better to let Captain Penni think he's given up. It'll make it easier to put up a fight.

He isn't out of ideas yet.

Ozkar stuffs his clothes into a sack. Izzy watches him pack. She's leaning against one of the posts on deck four, where the Argus's crew used to sleep. There are dozens of hammocks, pillows, and blankets hanging around. Ozkar has made his home in the far corner of the deck. His hammock is blue and green. His blankets are soft. There are pictures hanging from the walls that he's drawn over the last year. He wants to take everything with him and at the same time wants nothing.

If this plan doesn't work, he doesn't want anything that will remind him of the Argus and its crew and what he let slip through his fingers.

"Where will you go first?" Izzy asks.

Ozkar shrugs. He hasn't given this a single thought. All his time and willpower have been spent on finding a way to avoid having to make such a game plan.

"Will you try to find your family?" Izzy's voice wavers as she asks. She has heard his story and knows she is treading along soft, painful points. But this is Izzy. She is gentle, but direct.

Ozkar's memories come in a flash.

The ground shakes.

A flash.

A bang.

Screaming. The kind that can only be ripped from a person when they are bearing witness to something so horrific and shocking it's beyond description.

He closes his eyes, preparing for what he knows is coming next. He sees his mother's smile and her brown eyes. Bright one moment and then dull the next. Her hand slipping out of his. Her body crumpled on the ground, eyes wide, stare blank. Him being wrenched away in the stampede of people trying to flee.

The memories twist his insides, pulling at his heart until the pain in his chest is so terrible that he buckles over. No matter how hard he tries, he can't push her and the outside world from his mind.

Ozkar falls to his hands and knees. Unable to speak or move or think. The longer he stays there, the more his mind spins. And just when he thinks this is the moment when his heart finally bursts because it just can't beat with such a big hole blown through it anymore, he feels a pair of cool hands tug him upright, a hand on his shoulder, and a pair of arms slide around his neck.

Izzy pulls him into a hug and he just breathes. She stays with him in his painful silence until the wave of grief subsides and he can finally think straight. There are so many things Ozkar wants to scream about, but he knows that none of it will bring his mom back. He knows that even if he finds a way to go with the crew, there will always be a hole inside him that hurts.

He lets go of Izzy and tilts his head back. He stares upward and once again thinks about the Argus's watchman, Mr. Soltesky. The crew calls him Sol. Ozkar's out of good ideas, but he isn't out of bad ones and while this might be the most terrible one of them all, it has the highest chance of yielding a result. He needs to speak with the watchman.

"You think the captain will let me stay a little longer?" Ozkar asks.

Izzy dips her head. "I think she would be insulted if you didn't."

"It didn't seem that way earlier."

"You know how she gets," Izzy said.

Ozkar nods. Captain Penni is a duck on a pond. Calm and cool on the surface, but beneath the water she kicks feverishly. Not for herself but for those around her. He doesn't know exactly how long the crew has been stranded here. But he does know that it's been a *long* time. Years of solitude and service to keep the Argus and its crew afloat. He's heard Izzy and Atticus whispering about the lengths she's gone to protect them.

The thought of crossing the captain and turning to the exiled watchman makes Ozkar's stomach queasy. But he'd still take

Captain Penni's wrath over holes in his heart. Without the Argus and the crew, there will be more holes. More hurt. More moments like this where he can't think or breathe and has no other choice but to put on a brave face and pretend like everyone else beyond the Argus's hull that everything is fine.

At first, Ozkar tore through the books on the first deck, then Izzy's library on the second deck, and, eventually, he dared to search Captain Penni's study. He thought he was out of options, but now, he stares upward. He's on the fifth deck. There is a lift on the far side that creaks and groans when it's used, so pulling the lever to his right is out of the question. He tests the pipes and rungs running along the wall. They are sturdy enough. He grabs hold and climbs.

When he reaches the top, he rolls onto the floor and lays still. He gulps down some air and wipes his palms on his pants. The entire deck is cloaked in darkness. The only source of light is a massive domed window that has a telescope standing in front of it. There are loose sheets of paper scattered everywhere. It smells like ink. Ozkar pads over to where some of the papers are scattered. They're covered in jagged handwriting and sketches. There are notes stacked around hastily drawn graphs and formulas and molecular diagrams. Some have X's through them. Others have been completely blotted out. Every sketch is framed with a circle — the outline of the telescope. They offer snapshots of what the watchman sees from his crow's nest. People walking, sitting, talking. Coffee and food carts. Gargoyles on neighboring rooftops.

Ozkar stands and stares into the darkness, waiting for his eyes to adjust.

"Well, well, if it isn't the little ghoul," Sol's voice echoes across the deck.

Ozkar jumps back.

"Takes one to know one," Ozkar squeaks. The determination

he felt while climbing up here has faded. He looks around, trying to figure out where Sol is standing.

Sol laughs and Ozkar hears a steady *tap, tap, tap* as the watchman walks.

The crew speaks of Sol sparingly. He does not join them for meals. He does not speak to anyone. He is disgraced. Condemned to the sixth floor because Captain Penni couldn't bring herself to banish him from the Argus. The rule regarding Sol has always been simple: Stay away from him.

"What brings you all the way up here?"

"Questions."

"Ah," Sol says. His voice is low and measured. "I see."

"Do you?"

"You want to know the truth."

Ozkar's heart pounds. He forces himself to stay quiet and listen.

"I'll tell you what the others won't . . . for a price."

Ozkar gulps. He knows he should climb back down to the fifth deck. He knows he shouldn't negotiate with Sol, but he can't stay behind. He doesn't belong in the world beyond the Argus's hull. If there's a chance he can go with them, he will take it. Even if it means stooping to Sol's level.

"Name it," Ozkar says.

Sol lets out a whistle. The *tap, tap, tap* of his boots come closer and closer and then . . . In a blink, the watchman is standing in front of him. He's inches away from Ozkar's nose. He's tall and slender and pale. He wears suspenders, a white T-shirt, and a bowler hat. His eyes and hair are the color of ink. He looks like he's been ripped right out of a black-and-white film.

Ozkar jerks back and loses his balance. He's about to fall over, but Sol grabs his shirt. He hoists Ozkar off the ground so that they're eye to eye. Ozkar's heart is beating so fast and loud he thinks it might explode in his chest.

"What do I have to do?" Ozkar barely manages to get out the words.

Sol grins. He says "Bring me my compass and its key."

"You're going to need to be a little more specific. What do they look like?"

"I've watched your world through the window. You know what a compass looks like."

"Alright, well, what about the key?"

"Find the compass and it'll lead you to the key."

"Fine, fine." Ozkar kicks his legs. "Can you put me down now?"

Sol pulls Ozkar closer and whispers, "The helmsman has them. Simply steal them back and that will lead you and me to the ticket we need."

"We?"

"Yes."

"How do I know you're not going to cut me out?"

Sol is quiet for a moment. His stubbled jaw twitches and Ozkar thinks the watchman just might tell him the truth — the irony.

"What will it be, little ghoul?"

"It's a deal, watchman."

Sol drops him. "You'll need to find it before nine chimes."

"Nine?" Ozkar blurts out. "That's not a lot of time."

"No, it isn't and you're already wasting it. Now fly."

Ozkar peeks around the corner. The crew is busy on the second deck. They're helping Izzy find the root of the problem with the transport.

"Huh, that's weird," Izzy says.

"What?" The captain asks.

"The heatsinks are missing," Atticus says.

"How can that be?"

"Mr. Noveck's work, I'm sure," Captain Penni says.

Ozkar winces, but stays quiet.

"We should really bring him with us," Izzy says.

"He belongs here, Miss Valdez," the captain says.

The deck is quiet for a moment and then Atticus asks, "How long will it take you to make new ones?"

"The machining time won't be long," Izzy answers. Ozkar can see she's forcing herself to keep her tone in check. Captain Penni can see it too.

"How much time?"

"Nine . . . ten chimes the latest. We'll be right on time captain, don't worry."

Ozkar slips off his shoes and hurries down the stairs. The first deck is dim, but not dark. The lights give off a dark blue glow. Ozkar moves to the metal trunk where Atticus keeps his collection of lanterns and gizmos. There is a thick padlock hanging on the front latch. Ozkar kneels and rubs the back of his neck. It's usually open. Atticus must have locked it to prepare for the journey through the warp gate.

The helmsman doesn't keep everything on his person like the captain, but he doesn't throw things about like Izzy. He's precise but practical. The key has to be close. Ozkar goes straight to the front desk and sifts through the drawers. There is a box of keys in the middle one. Ozkar pulls it out and tries the keys one by one until, finally, he finds the right one.

The key turns. The lock clicks. Ozkar's heart speeds up. He scans the gizmos and gadgets. Some of the hardware is in boxes, others are not, but all of them are neatly laid out. There are four inserts inside the trunk. Ozkar pulls them out to get to the bottom insert. It's the obvious place to hide something, but Ozkar doubts Atticus ever thought Sol would get this far — or enlist a kid to steal his compass back. Ozkar immediately sees a case in the top right corner with "Soltesky" etched into it.

Ozkar snatches it up. He pops it open. His stomach drops. There is a small gemstone inside. It's been cut and filed into the shape of a cog. But the compass isn't inside. A folded piece of paper has taken its place. Ozkar unfolds it and reads.

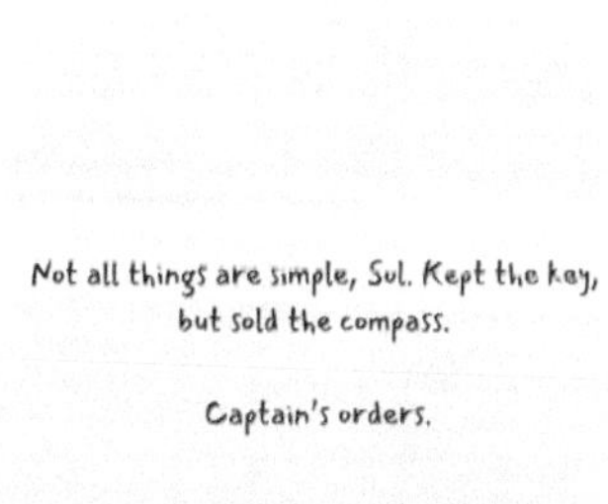

Ozkar slumps against the chest. Heart heavy and mind blank. He tries to tell himself he tried. He tries to convince himself he'll find another way. But he fails. The crew will leave. The Argus will be gone. Then he will be set adrift in a world where he doesn't belong and his family is gone. He doesn't want to move. He wants to keep staring blankly at the wall. But the only thing that will make this situation worse is if he's caught down here. Stealing the book was his first strike. Sabotaging the transport was his second. This would be his third. He hadn't cared before when he thought he was going to succeed, but now that he's not, he doesn't want the crew's last memory of him to be him snooping around like a wicked ghoul.

He keeps the gemstone but puts everything back. Sol deserves to know what happened to his compass. Taking one final look over the deck, Ozkar climbs back up the stairs.

The crew is still on the second floor, consumed with getting the transport ready and making sure the warp gate is properly calibrated. They're also trying to tidy up Izzy's deck for the journey home.

"Ah, Mr. Noveck," Captain Penni says. "Didn't see you come this way."

"I'm light on my feet."

"A handy trait."

"I was just having one final look around."

"You're packed then?" Atticus says.

Ozkar nods.

Captain Penni squeezes his shoulder and gives him a nod. For a moment, he thinks she might smile or there may be a flash of warmth washing over her eyes. But before he can see any emotion, the captain turns away and dives back into Izzy's mess.

Atticus steps forward. "I know you don't want to hear this, but this was never your quest."

"It could've been," Ozkar says. He's not angry. Just tired. The day has been full of so many ups and downs.

"You belong out there" — Atticus juts his head to the Argus's walls — "with the living."

"You guys are breathing."

"It's not the same. We're stuck."

"So am I."

But Atticus shakes his head. "Give it time and you'll come to understand, I think."

Ozkar glances over at Izzy. She has her goggles and ear muffs on. Her face inches away from the heat sink that she's cutting. He should stay and help them. There's only one chime left before they will board the transport and go. He wants to stay down here. He wants to spend the last bit of time he has with them. He can't think about pretending like this is just another thing to fix, a mess to clean, or a problem to solve. His heart hurts too much.

"How much longer?" Ozkar asks.

"Go rest. We won't leave without saying goodbye."

Ozkar lays in his hammock. Every once in a while, he hears snippets of Captain Penni and Atticus strategizing the best way to secure the explosion of stuff on the second deck. Ozkar pulls out the gizmo he pocketed from the lady earlier and pops it open. It reminds him of a pocket watch. Instead of a watch face though, the top opens up to reveal a bunch of silver gears, but the central one that makes them all turn is missing. The case is brass and even though it must be quite old the metal still has a polished look. Ozkar closes it and turns it over in his hands. On the back, there are tiny etchings. Ozkar brings the gizmo closer to his face and his heart starts to skip faster and faster.

The etchings are symbols, like the ones in Captain Penni's books. This is from their time. A switch flips in Ozkar's mind. He sits up and pulls out the gemstone he pocketed. He hops out of his hammock and hurries over to his desk. He pops open the gizmo and sets it on the table. Carefully, he takes off the clear face cover and removes the gears with a pair of tweezers until he gets to the heart of the mechanism. He plucks the purple gemstone gear and places it in the gizmo. Ozkar wipes the sweat from his face on the sleeve of his shirt and then gently replaces the gears. He puts the clear face back on and then twists the nub sticking out of the gizmo's side. He hears a *click* and then the gentle *whir* of gears that start to turn.

The compass. *Atticus didn't sell it. He had lied.*

The gears grind against one another and slowly a small grid projects out of it. Ozkar stares with his mouth ajar. He moves his hand through the grid. The grid becomes distorted, but quickly snaps back into place after his finger passes through. If Ozkar had more time, he would be taking the entire thing apart to try to understand how it works. He knows the projection has to do with the gemstone, but there isn't anything like this that he knows of and it makes him wonder where exactly the crew is from. For the first time, it's not just a question of *when* but *where*.

Sol said the compass and the key would lead them to the ticket they both need. Ozkar turns the knob on the side of the compass and the squares on the grid become larger. Out of curiosity, he touches his finger to the square and as he moves his finger, he finds that it moves with it.

There has to be a way to find my location, Ozkar thinks.

He taps the grid and it snaps to two dots. One is blinking, one is still. Ozkar assumes the blinking dot has to be him. Taking the compass with him, he moves around the deck. As he gets closer to the stairs that lead to the third deck, the grid turns a dark purple, but when he heads for the fifth deck, it turns blue, as if he's playing a game of Hot 'n' Cold.

Ozkar goes down to the third deck and heads for the captain's quarters. The grid stays the same shade of purple. The ticket is inside. Ozkar should have guessed. He closes the compass, kneels in front of the door to Captain Penni's rooms, and waits for the pipes to start hissing. Her door squeaks loudly and the floor-boards have a distinct creak. He'll need to tread quietly. While he waits, he takes off his boots and socks.

When the pipes start to hiss, Ozkar gets to work on the lock. It doesn't take him long. He's done this dozens of times over the last year and even more frequently in the past few weeks. The lock slides open. Ozkar twists the doorknob and slips inside.

The captain's cabin is completely dark. Ozkar stands on his tiptoes, feeling for the lamp that's usually right next to the door. He pats the wall until he feels the lantern's rough metal. He turns on the burner. He keeps twisting it until the flame is large enough to light the room. As always, the cabin is meticulous and sparse. The captain doesn't hoard hardware like Izzy, nor does she share Atticus's fascination with collectibles. But there is a small stack of books and a box of what Ozkar can only assume is filled with keepsakes.

Ozkar pops open the compass. The grid is still purple, but now the dots are gone and the grid is pulsing. Ozkar moves to the right of the cabin. The pulse slows. He moves to the left side and it quickens. He needs to think like the captain. She's ruthlessly pragmatic. He gets down on his hands and knees and feels around under the captain's bed. He searches for a loose floorboard but finds none. He leans over the bed and waves the compass across the shelves. The grid is pulsing but it doesn't speed up.

When he moves to the foot of the bed though, the pulse quickens again. Ozkar frowns. The only thing at the end of the bed is paneling. He gets down on the floor again and when he does the grid blinks even faster. Whatever he's looking for, he's practically on top of it.

The pipes above him hiss and spit and the Argus seems to groan at his inability to find the captain's hiding place. Ozkar pushes on the panels and when he does, he realizes one is on a track. He slides it to the side and inside is a bottle with a greenish, yellow liquid sitting in a glass case. It's locked, of course. But instead of a padlock, it's a tumbler lock. Ozkar spins the tumblers to see what he's working with. Just like many of the captain's books, it has symbols he doesn't recognize. He might as well be trying to spell something in hieroglyphics.

He goes over to the box he suspects holds the captain's keepsakes. But instead, all he finds is a tiny notebook. Ozkar rolls his eyes. It would be just like the captain to have absolutely nothing of sentiment in her quarters. Shaking his head he opens the book. Some of it is written in letters he knows and then there are symbols. The book flips back and forth between the two languages until the very back. In the back, there are names of at least fifty people. Ozkar knows four of them. The rest he does not and yet he immediately understands that these are the people who had been lost when the Argus sailed out of the sky and buried its bow into the ground.

The little book is taped up. The writings on the earlier pages have been traced over. Ozkar looks over at the captain's desk and imagines her retracing the words so that the ink doesn't fade. He imagines her reading the names of the crew she was responsible for and lost every night before she closes her eyes.

This is why she has not given up.

This is why she won't allow herself to crack.

The pipes hiss and bang and they make Ozkar jump. He flips

through the pages, searching for a five-letter word to punch into the tumbler code. The answer has to be in this book. He reads through the names. The captain has translated all of them. His eyebrows rise as he reads the last name on the list.

It's his: Ozkar Noveck.

He doesn't know why, but he goes back to the tumbler and spells his name in the captain's native tongue. He shakes as he turns the tumblers into place. The entire time he thinks that it can't be that simple. And yet, the last letter clicks into place and the lock pops open.

Ozkar doesn't know what to think. He knows Captain Penni isn't heartless, but he never thought she thought so highly of him. He never believed she considered him part of the crew. He swirls the liquid around in the bottle and as it mixes it turns blue.

"What is this?" he whispers.

"Oh good, you found it."

A jolt shoots through Ozkar. He wants to come out of his skin, but he can't bring himself to move. Now that the pipes are no longer clanging and hissing and sputtering, he can hear Sol breathing. The watchman is less than an arm's length away. Ozkar tries to dart and run, but the watchman grabs him and presses a rag to his mouth.

Ozkar's arms are tied above his head. People are yelling. More specifically Captain Penni is yelling. Ozkar opens his eyes and blinks. They're in the crow's nest. It's dark. But the crew has lanterns and Izzy is wearing a headlamp. Sol is standing in front of them. He has the vial in his hand.

"Mr. Soltesky, I won't ask again!"

"You come one step closer and I'll smash it."

"No, you won't," Captain Penni says. She tilts her head high, her jaw set. Her posture says it all: She is captain here.

"Won't I?"

"Not unless all your time up here has dulled your wits."

"Speak plain, *captain.*"

Ozkar looks up. He is hanging from a hook. He straightens his body and even though he's dangling off the floor, his toes touch. He reaches skyward and pushes up onto his tiptoes. And as he reaches, he leans forward. He's dizzy and sweaty, but he doesn't take his eyes off the hook.

"That vial is your ticket home. Smash it and you'll never see it again."

Sol cackles. It's raspy at first but grows steady and screechy. When he stops, he shakes his head. There is a grin splitting his face. "Oh, my dear, dear captain. What makes you think I want to go home?"

Come on, Ozkar thinks. *Come on!*

The rope slides off the hook and Ozkar falls to the ground. He sucks in deep breaths. Thankfully, the crew is so busy yelling at each other no one sees or hears him slip into the shadows. He unties himself and then slinks toward the wall. He circles behind Sol and waits.

"Are you out of your mind?" Izzy asks.

"Completely." Sol's grin grows even wider.

"Mr. Soltesky . . ." Captain Penni starts.

"No!" Sol screams. "No! No! No!"

"Without it, our people are going to die," Atticus says.

"So be it," Sol hisses. "We were leeches. Just like they are out there. We need to let nature take its course."

"Enough!" Captain Penni yells. Her voice cracks as she says, "That's not for you to decide."

"Nor you, *captain,*" Sol mocks.

He tosses the vial in the air and catches it as if it's a ball. The crew instinctively takes a step forward, ready to catch it if it falls. Sol snickers. He has them where he wants them.

"How did you even get it?" Izzy asks.

"I did nothing. Your friend the ghoul took care of it for me."

Atticus scoffs.

"A foolish ghoul, but a clever —"

Sol looks to his right and realizes Ozkar is gone. For a moment the watchman freezes and then Ozkar sprints forward. He leaps into the air and crashes into Sol. They fall forward.

Ozkar and Sol hit the ground hard. The vial rolls out of the watchman's hand. He grabs at Ozkar, but Ozkar keeps rolling. He gets back to his feet and half runs, half stumbles toward the bottle. He snatches it up and pulls the cork.

"No!"

"Don't!"

"Mr. Noveck!"

"Do it!"

"What *is this*?" Ozkar demands.

The crew looks at each other and then Captain Penni steps forward. "An elixir with the power to cure a disease that is plaguing our people. The sickness causes cells to multiply uncontrollably. This stops it."

"We were sent here to find it, but the ship went down," Izzy says.

"No," Atticus says sharply. "We were sabotaged."

The three of them look at Sol.

"You all drank this?" Ozkar asks.

They all nod — even Sol.

"We were all sick when we came here," Izzy says and points to the bottle. "We took it as a test. It cured us. If we go back in time, we can save our people."

"It's all we have left," Captain Penni says. "After Mr. Soltesky . . ."

Ozkar looks at his crew and then at the blue liquid in the bottle. It looks like a lightning bolt in liquid form. The captain stretches out her hand and takes a step forward, but then hesitates. There is a crease across her forehead. He can see through her armor and the list of names comes back to him. This is his bargaining chip.

Just say it, Ozkar tells himself. *Tell her to make you an offer.*

Tell her to find a way to bring you with them and you'll give them the vial. What's another couple of years after waiting so long?

It would be so easy.

They would do it. He knows it.

But he can't bring himself to speak the words.

It feels wrong to rob the crew of the hope they've held onto for so long. Maybe that's what Atticus meant before when he said they are stuck. Ozkar knows what it's like not to have hope. He knows that when they leave, there will be more holes, and hope will leave his heart like it did before he found the Argus. He takes a deep breath, bracing himself for what he knows is coming. He gives Captain Penni the vial.

No conditions.

No questions.

The Argus is six stories of oak and steel with portholes and hatches along its port and starboard sides. It's a landmark people have been taught is important, but no longer know the truth about: The ship was once home to a crew that spent centuries searching for a way back to their home so they could save it.

The Argus was the crew's parting gift to Ozkar. They had wanted to bring it back. But, to Captain Penni, it didn't seem right to rip the Argus away from him. So although the crew was gone, the airship remained. At first, Ozkar had cried because he could stay within the comfort of the Argus. But now his eyes well up every time he thinks too much about how empty the ship is after he closes the shop for the evening. Everything is still just as the crew left it. He can't bring himself to change anything. He's a ghoul on a ghost ship, stranded in the middle of a bustling city.

Ozkar rings up the last customer and follows them to the door.

"You're a bit young for a clerk," the customer says.

"Not really," Ozkar says, waving off the comment.

The customer shrugs and wishes him a good night. Ozkar does the same. As soon as the door closes, he flips the sign on the door over to let everyone know the Argus is closed. He goes over to the register and counts the money. He enters the earnings into the ledger and starts to add up totals for the week. He needs to bring down more items from the second deck. He also needs to add to the troves.

The idea of having to go to an auction house or dig around an estate sale to bring in more items makes Ozkar's skin crawl. Izzy and Atticus always loved going because it was one of the few times they were able to leave the ship. Ozkar and Captain Penni never had a desire to go.

I made a promise, Ozkar tells himself. He had sworn to take care of the Argus and that's what he was going to do. No matter what.

The bell chimes as the door swings open.

"We're closed," Ozkar calls, without looking up.

"I can read."

Ozkar peeks up at the stranger standing in the doorway and his heart beats a bit faster. It's a boy about his age with dark hair and bright eyes. His shirt is tucked in and he wears a fitted jacket. His hair is short and combed. Everything about him is precise.

He makes Ozkar feel like a mess. Of course, he *is* a mess and plenty of people have come into the Argus put together, but this boy . . . Ozkar's cheeks burn a little as he tried to comb his curls and straighten his shirt.

"We open at 9 o'clock tomorrow," Ozkar says, getting up from the stool.

"Yes, I know." The boy doesn't take his eyes off Ozkar. "But I haven't come to shop. My business is with you, Mr. Noveck."

Ozkar stops and takes a step back.

The stranger with the dark hair and bright eyes reaches into his jacket and pulls out a wad of papers. He holds out the paper and juts his chin at it.

Ozkar doesn't move.

"These are my qualifications," the boy says. He then pulls out an envelope with "Mr. Noveck" scrolled across it and says, "And this is an explanation for why I'm here."

Ozkar tilts his head to the side. There is something familiar about this stranger. He knows that he should be cautious, but something inside him says, *Hear him out.*

"Who are you?"

"My name is Albert Penni Langman. My great, great, great, great-grandmother was Ava Penni. You called her captain once."

Ozkar leans against the counter for support. He is doing the math in his head and trying to work out how . . . And then he understands.

"The cure worked," Ozkar whispered.

Albert smiles and nods. "They were heroes."

Ozkar lets out a laugh and puts his hand on his forehead. For a moment he thinks he might melt from the feeling bubbling up from his stomach and into his chest. The cure worked. The crew was . . .

Gone.

The warm feeling turns to a wave of sickness as he realizes what this means.

"I didn't know any of them," Albert says. "But from the stories my family and my people have passed down, they were larger than life. Is it true?"

Ozkar nods and gives a sad smile.

"They lived well?" Ozkar asks.

"They did." Albert lifts the letter.

"I don't think I bring myself to read that. Have you read it?"

"No, but I can take a guess. It's a promise passed from one generation to the next until it came time to find you. Turns out that it's my responsibility. All of ours, actually."

"Ours?" Ozkar squeaks.

Albert puts the envelope and his papers in his pocket and goes to the door. He leans out and waves for the others to come in. Another boy enters and he's followed by two girls — twins. Ozkar can't help but stare. The boy is tall and broad and the girls have black hair and dark blue eyes. The boy looks like a young version of Atticus and the twins could be Izzy's sisters.

"You seem to be taking this well," one twin says.

"Are you joking? He's so pale I can see the vein in his forehead," says her sister.

"That's from a lack of sunlight, not shock," says the boy with broad shoulders. He crosses his arms.

"Good point, Bat" says the twin.

"When's the last time you got out of here?"

"Belle," her sister hisses.

"Gwen," her sister hisses back.

"It's a fair question," Belle insists.

"If we're going out, I vote the soup place three blocks over."

"We can't go out for soup, Bat! We just got here," Gwen says, giving Bat a look. It's the same look Izzy used to give him when he was getting on her nerves.

Bat keeps his arms crossed and shrugs.

Ozkar is waiting for Albert to silence them, the way Captain Penni would. But he doesn't. Instead, he has his hands drawn behind his back, taking it all in. He's smiling wide and there's a lightness to him. Ozkar tries to think of a time when Captain Penni smiled like that.

Finally, Ozkar clears his throat and to his surprise, they all immediately fall silent. Everyone turns and gives him their undivided attention. Ozkar gulps.

"Why are you all here, exactly?"

Gwen snaps her head over to Albert. "What were you two talking about in here? The weather? You were supposed to be explaining things."

"I was. I thought it would be easier if we were all here," Albert says.

"He mentioned responsibilities that are falling on you all," Ozkar says. "Whatever that means."

"Responsibilities, Al? For goodness sake." Belle shakes her

head. She has Izzy's directness, he can feel it. Ozkar winces, preparing for what's to come. "We're here to join your crew."

"What?"

"I didn't stutter."

"But, I'm, I'm a . . ." Ozkar pauses for a moment to collect himself. "I'm a ghoul. That's what Izzy used to call me. Jokingly. But it's true. I'm . . . I'm not a captain."

"Ava Penni left the Argus in your charge, correct?" Bat asks.

Ozkar nods.

"And you've kept it running," Gwen says. "Although it desperately needs work. Why didn't anyone mention *that* to us?"

"It crashed! What did you expect?"

While the others debate the Argus's structural integrity, Albert pulls out the envelope again. Before Ozkar can blink, Albert is across the room and standing in front of him. They're the exact same height so he has no choice but to look him directly in the eye. Ozkar hesitates to take the envelope, but finally forces himself to do so.

Keep it together, Ozkar tells himself.

The letter inside has turned yellow, but the ink is still bold and clear. He recognizes Captain Penni, Atticus, and Izzy's handwriting. They all take turns narrating and explaining and joking and reminiscing. Pride and joy leap from the page and fill Ozkar up. It makes him read the letter over and over and over, and each time he does, the truth sinks in deeper and deeper and deeper.

He shakes his head in disbelief.

The truth is that this new crew is not bound to the Argus the way their ancestors were. It is a part of their history, but the city that surrounds it is just as important.

They are not stuck.

"Well captain?" his crew asks. "What now?"

Ozkar isn't quite sure. All he knows is he is no longer alone.

About Amanda Bender

Amanda Bender is a marketer by day and a writer by night. But through it all, she is a storyteller at heart. She holds an MFA in Creative Writing from George Mason University. She was a contributing writer at *LitReactor* until they closed their digital doors in 2023, and you can read more of her creative works in *Rune Bear Magazine* and *The Book Smuggler's Den.* If you're looking for a reading rec, a book reviewer, or just curious about the lessons in craft Amanda is learning and applying as she writes her next project, visit her blog Live by the Shelf, or follow her on social.

Website: livebytheshelf33.com

Soiled Tears in the Mangrove

Sara Kapadia

***Trigger Warnings for child brides*

For eighty years, my roots have burrowed deep into the soil of Bengal's Sundarban region. I have been home to many creatures. My branches have risen up into the stagnant humid air, reaching for brighter skies, while my tendrils hang like a mermaid's tresses providing the monkeys ample climbing material.

It is not only water that my roots have soaked up, but the tears of countless young girls.

Girls. Not maidens. Girls as young as eight years of age. They come adorned in red, their heads hung low, ushered in with hushed adult voices. The stench of child marriage has always been one of bitterness, a loss of innocence and tears, so many tears.

Not so long ago another group came through the forest: the same smiling elders, the same older man, dressed in shimmering silk, the same forlorn mother. Let's not forget the girl, trembling, her chubby arms barely ready for the burden of womanhood she would now have to bear. A crow squawked in my branches making the wedding party look up. I shook my branches in frustration. The mother held her child closer. A breeze made my leaves rustle loudly and fall like confetti all over the Humans.

I couldn't stand the sight. Another child being forced into a marriage with a grown man.

Didn't these humans have any sense? A child that age was supposed to be climbing trees, not huddling under it being wed. Now she was closer, leaning on my trunk, my tendrils caressed her back, I wrapped them close around her, but slowly so no one realized I was moving. Her tears fell to the ground, seeping into the soil, salty and sweet. My roots tasted the promise of a future she would never have.

"Beti, come closer," the village elder said, holding the little girl's chin in her hands.

The mother put her arm around her daughter, maybe sorely aware that the villagers are not real friends but agents of barter, haggling a child's innocence for a fair price. How much is a child's life worth? If my leaves were made of money, I would have gladly shed them to save this blameless girl.

The mynah bird that nests in my branches called out. Heads turned. All except for the little girl looking at the ground. Her head covered in a red saree she wears, heavy gold bangles on her wrists, smelling of incense and jasmine. She has been prodded, primed, and dressed for the occasion.

The groom, a grown man of about thirty, stepped towards the child bride; she cowered. No more than ten years old, the little girl bit her lower lip and clung to her mother. Torn between duty, poverty, and shame, I see a moment of distress in the mother's eyes. But then she pushed her desperate daughter forward into the groom's arms.

"Amma, please take me home," the girl cried, falling at her feet, voice breaking over gulps of air.

The mother said nothing as she turned toward my trunk, hiding her face from the elders. The groom lifted his quivering child bride up with his grimy adult hands. She looked like a small doll, unable to talk back, rigid with fear as if she were made of porcelain, an object to be played with. I groaned under the weight of the horrific event that was about to take place.

I thought back to the baby monkeys playing on my branches only yesterday, carefree, and well cared for by their parents. Even monkeys had more freedom than the little girls in this village. If only there was something I could do. Looking down, I saw they had the groom and child bride sitting at the base of my trunk. The villagers encircled the couple. I cringed as I heard that word.

Couple. Made up of a thirty-year-old and a ten-year-old.

The eldest woman took two garlands of jasmine and roses and placed them on the little girl and the groom. A tingle of dread traveled from the tips of my branches to the ends of my roots. The ground shifted slightly, and one elder almost fell.

That's when I realized: I could save this girl.

I began to shake my roots, bit by bit. The soil loosened around the trunk.

"Earthquake," the mother yelled.

I let the full force of my roots convulse through the ground. The Humans stumbled. Then while the groom was on his knees, and the others were looking away, I whisked up the girl with my tendrils and into the safety of my branches.

Her mother called for her, "Mina, where are you?"

The little girl held onto my branches and peered down at her mother. If she wanted to return all she had to do was answer her worried mother; but she stayed silent.

The groom rose to his feet, dusted off the soil from his clothes and then ran to the elders. Soon they separated into smaller groups and called out her name. As they dispersed into the forest, the calls faded away.

She was safe, finally free. I curved my branches around her to create a nook for her to curl into. I covered her with my leaves. Soon she was fast asleep.

When the sunlight broke through the clouds the next morning, it was a brand-new day. Mina shuffled about, opened her eyes, and stretched her arms out. It was long known that there was magic in the forests. The creatures knew about it, as did the nymphs that lived within the trees. Humans had never seen this kind of magic before. I wondered if I should reveal myself to this innocent child.

I was just a mangrove tree in the magical forest, my powers were not as great as the mighty banyan trees, and yet I had been able to rescue little Mina from that awful wedding. She sat up and leaned on my trunk. Slowly I rearranged my leaves to shield her from the bright sun. Could I reveal my abilities to Mina? Surely she realized the way she got into my branches was not normal.

Mina swung her legs over my biggest branch and looked down at the ground. She couldn't jump down. Did she want to leave? I had to speak to her.

"Do not be afraid." I whispered.

"Who's there?" Mina said, turning her head.

"I am the tree on which you sit," I replied slowly making sure to sound as gentle as possible.

Mina touched my bark in awe. "But how can a tree talk?"

I purposefully moved my branches around her to show her my capability of motion.

"Wow, you can move . . . Wait, are you the one who pulled me up? Away from that man?" Mina stroked my bark in a way that was almost grateful.

"Yes, you are too young to get married," I answered as she licked her lips. "You must be thirsty. Here, have some rainwater that I have stored away." I lowered one of my largest leaves with some drops of water from the last rains just two days ago.

Mina sipped from the leaf and let out a deep sigh as a mynah bird hopped down. "Who is this?" the bird chirped.

"You talk too?" Mina gaped.

"Well, of course! All the creatures speak," the mynah bird retorted. "Who are you?"

"I'm Mina."

"She will be staying here too." I told the mynah as it pecked at her sari. "Well, if she wants to."

"I can't go back to the village; they will marry me to that old man." Tears welled up in Mina's eyes. "I miss my mother, but I don't want to go back."

"I will look after you," I whispered, embracing her with my smaller branches.

Every night after that Mina slept in my branches. The years came and went. Upon my instructions, Mina weaved herself clothes from my thinner tendrils. She learned to collect rainwater. She made a sturdy structure in my upper branches. She befriended the forest creatures. The monkeys taught her to collect fruits and nuts. The mynah bird moved into my branches as well. Even the antisocial cobra warmed up to Mina, showing her where she could climb to see the best sunset.

Mina was happy, cheerful, and above all, free. I am sure she missed the village, but she had friends in the forest, she had access to the delicious produce of the Sundarbans, and every night Mina and I would weave stories about princesses who were warriors. From time to time, Mina would even share the stories with the trio of forest nymphs who had become her best friends. Yes, life was good in the forest, and Mina was free. There had been less and less girls being taken to the forest, and the ones that were married off were older than Mina had been when they tried to wed her.

When Mina turned nineteen, strange humans appeared in the forest. They came with tools and cameras. They surveyed the whole area. They spoke in deep voices. Some wore suits and ties. They spoke of building a resort.

"We'll flatten this part near the water, ideal views from here," said the tallest man.

A man in khaki pants wrote on a clipboard and instructed a young boy to take measurements of me. Me, an ancient mangrove.

"Yes, this one will have to go," snorted the man in khaki pants.

"Definitely," the tallest man agreed as he swatted away a crimson rose butterfly.

"Oh my gosh," Mina whispered. "They want to cut the forest down."

My insides shuddered, and I was sure some of my sap seeped out.

Over the next few months more human men came with more clipboards and more discussions of the fancy resort they wanted to build right here.

One day while Mina was collecting moss, a different man came into view. This one was alone. He had no clipboard. He was simply looking around. Tall and well built, he was younger than the other men. A crimson rose butterfly landed right on his palm. He was unique.

We didn't see him again for a couple of weeks. But when we did, he was running and bleeding.

He limped over to a great banyan near me, trying to hide.

"He's injured," Mina gasped from her perch in my branches. "I could help."

"No, Mina, it's not safe," I warned, but before I could say more, she was already climbing down. The man looked startled when Mina appeared, seemingly out of nowhere.

"It's okay, I can help you." Mina's voice was altered, and she had an expression on her face I had never seen before.

"It's not safe; someone's chasing me," the man whispered as Mina helped him up. "They shot at me."

"Why are you being chased?" Mina said.

Very slowly I lowered my tendrils closer to hear better.

"I'm a forest ranger looking for the elusive glowing Kankra plant. If I can find it, I can make sure this area is protected." The man bent down to assess his bleeding leg. "If I find it, they won't be able to build a resort here."

"Oh, I know that plant . . . the nym —" Mina paused and cut herself off. "My friends showed me how it glows."

The man's face brightened. "Yes! That is the plant. You know it?"

"I know it and I can show you the plant, but you need help right now." Mina put his arm around her shoulders and started to step towards me. "My name is Mina. I will help you."

"I am Raju," the man said, smiling, although the pain was obviously making him grimace.

"Bring us up," Mina said softly, standing at the base of my trunk.

"Who are you talking to?" the man said.

"There are things humans don't know, but I was raised here in this tree, and she is special. She understands me." Mina explained.

My leaves shook in pride. "Minaaaa . . ." I said softly.

"Who is there?" Raju flinched.

"Just trust me. It will be okay." Mina wrapped her free hand around my tendrils.

I was scared that Raju would be too shocked, but I knew he needed to heal, so I lowered my tendrils, wrapped them around Mina and Raju, and lifted them both up.

"What is happening!" Raju huffed.

Mina beamed. "This is my home. It's okay, you'll see."

I gradually unraveled my tendrils as I placed Mina and Raju at the platform Mina had built in my upper branches.

Raju looked about. "This is where you live?"

"This is my home. The tree looks after me." Mina stood with her arms open.

Suddenly the foliage below shuffled. Men with guns came rushing through.

"Shhh . . ." Raju gestured with his finger over his mouth.

Mina peered down at the men, who were thrashing about in the shrubbery.

I moved some of my smaller branches to make sure Mina and her guest were fully hidden. Moments later the men and their guns were gone.

Just to be sure, Mina and Raju stayed quiet for longer. When Mina was sure the men were truly gone, she turned to Raju and tended to his leg. Taking some of my soft leaves and some thin tendril fibers she wrapped his bleeding leg.

"Thank you, Mina," Raju said, putting his hand on her arm.

"I know it seems strange, me living in a tree, but this tree rescued me." Mina sat back against the thick branch that formed the main support for her little tree hut.

"Saved you? From what?" Raju asked, looking more comfortable now the bleeding had stopped.

"Ten years ago, they tried to make me marry an old man. My mother was extremely poor, and the elders told her she had to marry me off." Mina had a glazed look in her eyes. "I was only eight."

"Oh, that's illegal! But I heard that they hide in the forest so that the authorities aren't aware of the ceremonies. I am sorry, Mina. That is awful." Raju shook his head.

"I live here in this tree. The forest provides for me. And I know I mentioned nymphs, humans don't believe in them, but they do exist." Mina sat close to Raju, her fingers moving closer to his. There was just something about him, it pulled her to him. Her gaze settled on his perfect lips. I wondered if questions rustled her insides. Were his lips as soft as the flowers of the delicate beli plant? Would he teach her about the city? Would he think she was wild and dirty? Would he . . . like . . . her? Why was I tormenting myself thinking about what she might ask him. I couldn't know, but yet a mother, even a tree mother always knows.

Raju's eyes widened. "Wow, nymphs."

Mina's glazed eyes refocused on him. "Oh, yeah, nymphs . . . We have so much in this forest."

Mina tossed her hair over one shoulder and ran her fingers through her tresses. The forest life suited her; she had grown into quite a beautiful young girl. Every week she would put special oil in her hair from the Guribantu nuts. The sun had tanned her skin, and now that she had become so skilled at weaving, she made intricately patterned clothes from fibers she found from trees and foliage. Her face had lost her childish fat, and her features were sharp, with huge oval brown eyes. I could tell that Raju found her quite delightful from the stolen glances.

"Here, have this, I picked it yesterday." Mina handed him a half coconut shell with water and flesh inside. Mina ate from the other half, scooping the succulent whiteness out of it. Raju slurped the coconut water and then ate the flesh too.

"Now you should rest." Mina pulled out a blanket made from overlapping leaves and placed it over Raju's legs.

She laid down on the opposite side with her own blanket and I tightened my branches around her hut. The sun was setting, and the air began to cool.

For three days and three nights, Mina cared for Raju, giving him berries, nuts, and the delicious Nipa Palm fruits. She prepared the Nipa seeds that were soft and juicy, and then showed him how to eat the sugary sap from the flower stem.

Raju became stronger and soon could put weight on his leg. He stood in the tree hut looking down on the forest. Mina had asked the mynah bird to send a message to the nymphs who arrived later that day.

Their translucent wings beat in the air, and they landed on the platform. Raju's mouth remained open, and released a gasp. Finally, he reached out his hand to one of the nymphs as if to make sure she was real.

"This is Dipal; she is the one who knows where the glowing Kankra plant is," Mina told Raju.

"I need proof that it is real. Can we go to see it?" Raju asked Dipal.

"You are injured," Dipal whirred her wings. "I can bring it to you."

"The plant? The glowing Kankra plant, you would bring me one?" Raju's face broke into a smile.

"Yes, I can bring it to you," Dipal sat closer to Raju, and then Mina shuffled between them.

It was obvious that Mina was already very fond of Raju. I worried for her. What would happen when Raju went back to the village. Would she go with him? Would my Mina leave me? A tiny bit of sap left my bark as I thought of the future.

The mynah bird arrived at the platform and brought me back to the moment.

"So, you have met the nymphs," the mynah bird said to Raju.

"I have never met a speaking mynah." Raju laughed.

The nymphs and Mina giggled, and soon everyone was chuckling, including myself.

A day later, Dipal brought the mysterious gleaming Kankra plant to Raju. She gave it to Mina who then placed it in Raju's open hands. The luminous leaves made his fingers glimmer.

"This is incredible!" Raju exclaimed.

Mina's eyes twinkled and reflected the bright fluorescent color of the plant.

"I must take this back to the authorities. I must get this area protected. The resort must not be built," Raju announced.

I was mistrusting of humans, especially men. After all, they were the ones who married the innocent girls. Yet if this one wanted to safeguard the forest, I might not be cut down after all.

The night came quickly, and I had become accustomed to seeing Mina happy with her new mate. Somehow life felt more complete with both of them sleeping amongst my treetop, but it couldn't last. Raju had to return to the village.

Mina climbed down to my lower branch and held her arms up to Raju who struggled to place his injured leg on the branches. Seeing him straining, I swathed him with my tendrils and dropped him to the ground softly.

Clutching the plant specimen, Raju leaned over and kissed Mina on the cheek. "You saved me."

"And you will now save all of us," Mina said, her voice breaking.

"I will come back. I will come back soon." Raju embraced her; his voice muffled in her thick hair.

Weeks went by, and even though the nymphs came by to keep Mina company, and even though we still told stories at night, she was dejected, lonely in a way she had never been before. I was no longer enough for her. There was nothing I could say or do.

Mina missed Raju.

Then one day, as Mina was scrounging for mushrooms, Raju came casually strolling in, as if it were the most normal thing in the world. Mina dropped the mushrooms and ran to him, flinging her arms around him.

"I told you I would be back," Raju tittered.

"Raju, I missed you." Mina sobbed.

"Don't cry, look what I have." Raju pulled out a piece of paper from his pocket. "See, the forest is protected. No one will tear it down. It is safe and protected. It says so right here, now it is a conservation site, and no one can build here."

"Oh Raju, you did it. You saved us all," Mina said exuberantly.

I watched Mina and Raju in a spinning embrace, and I knew then that the future would be different. My little girl had grown up.

About Sara Kapadia

Sara is an artist, educator, yoga teacher, academic, and writer who uses a transdisciplinary approach in her projects. All of Sara's degrees specialized in education. Sara has a bachelor's from the University of Cambridge, a master's from the University of London and a PhD from Claremont Graduate University. As the founder of an academic, peer reviewed, open access publication called The STEAM Journal Sara created a hub that focused on art and science.

Sara's fiction writing is based on folk stories from South Asia and uses fantasy to transport the reader to other worlds. Her artwork draws from the textures and hues found in nature.

Sara lives in a colorful home with her husband, two foster kids, two rescue cats and rescue dog, and lots of imaginary creatures in Los Angeles.

More can be found about Sara at **www.sara.kapadia.com**

If Walls Could Talk

Nico Vazquez

If you watched me, you would see me come to life. The pictures dancing across my ink-stained wallpaper like magic, like something out of storybooks.

Wendy Ainsley was something out of a storybook, she just hadn't figured that out yet.

The pirate ship that sat high on the wall moved slowly across the painted moon, the shadow of a man standing with sword high on the edge of it. Mermaids by the empty fish tank jumped, and if you looked close enough, you would notice the water droplets on the floor beneath them and the spray on the curtains from their games.

Wendy told her walls stories about running away, dreams about being someone else. And as she spoke, she drew dragons and lions and beasts with sharp claws and gentle souls lost in the trees. She drew pirates and mermaids and their squabbles over the sea. And she drew a boy, with eyes like the weeds and a crooked smile, older than his face.

She told them the stories she dreamed of living. The life she longed to have.

I was a garden once. A long time ago. Somedays I think I still am. What is a garden if not shelter for those smaller than its roses? And now I am simply a shelter for one smaller than my walls.

With a violet crayon, Wendy gifted me eyes. She took care with the lashes, curving each one just such. Her brother John thought she was odd, but she didn't mind that much. She simply stuck her tongue out and continued her work. If walls could see, as she truly believed, then they deserved eyes.

Wendy spent the bulk of her life leaning against me for comfort. When her parents would fight and when the other kids at school would poke their fun. When she'd been forced to move out of the room she shared with her brothers and her father had taken her storytelling journal. Wendy didn't have many people to talk to. She couldn't talk to her brothers because she was the older sister; she had to be strong, if only for them. But the walls of her room, they didn't expect anything of her.

As Wendy got older, despite her father's constant push for her to grow up, when she was all alone, she still held her dreams tightly. When she was sixteen, she once sat by the wall, drawing those eyes and ears, and trees and leaves and flowers, rebuilding a garden she had never seen. She'd never stopped telling her walls stories. Even as she took on more and more responsibilities in her real life. She had long since ceased her drawing in class and telling her brothers of fairies. But her bedroom was covered with her tales.

Wendy, now nineteen, sits beside the wall, running her fingers over the faded adventures while lost in her thoughts. She is quiet. Saying goodbye. Looking much older than her face. She thinks herself all grown up now, looking over the dreams she will have to put away in the morning. Her new life sits in boxes, far too little of them for her to have hope that things will be interesting. Her expression is troubled as she clutches one of her art pens tightly in her hand. She'd already given the others away to her friend. It had been a rash decision. And maybe a little dramatic, but Wendy had decided it would be much too upsetting to have them if she couldn't use them the way she'd always wanted to. Now she regrets it.

She stares at a blank space between her finding Peter Pan's shadow and the two of them going to save John and Michael from Hook at the cove. When she'd sat down, she'd wanted to draw an ending. But none would come.

"Maybe it's better if I don't end it," she says finally, turning to face the violet eyes on the wall. "You never got an ending. An old tree, cut down to build a new home." She smiles fondly at the familiar idea that there is still magic here from the old garden. "Oh, what the fairies must have left behind to give you eyes like that, as though you know when stars are to be born." It was something her mother always said about them, when her father wasn't around to chide her encouragements of Wendy's wild imagination. "Do you know how my future is going to go?"

The violet eyes stare back at her. Unmoving.

Wendy nods. "Probably for the best that I don't know, isn't it?" She lets the pen roll out of her hand as she stands, looking around the room. Her eyes are glassy and her smile tight. The weight of her future is a constant stress. "All good dreams have to come to an end, don't they?" she says.

Outside of her window, a shadow droops at the shoulders.

Everyone besides Wendy knows that there was once a time when her dreams were not just dreams.

Moonlight trickles into the darkened bedroom long after Wendy has gone to bed, casting shadows and illuminating her fitful sleep.

Wendy tosses and turns, as she does most nights, her mind running away from her.

The light stretches, inching itself further into the room as a gust of wind billows the curtains. If you stop and pay attention, at night you can still hear the sounds of the garden the room used to be. Still smell its soil. Still sense the presence of fairy magic. As the light stretches its tired fingers, it brushes the drawings on the walls.

Wendy calms her fretting, stilling with a deep breath as her dreams of worry and adult life cave into memories of happier times. Before she worried about the mundane responsibilities of ordinary people.

A faint blue light catches the leaf of a rose Wendy had sketched earlier that day, the pencil still nestled in a space between the carpet and the wall. It sparks, like fire on a wick, the little bit of moonlight weaving its way over every line until the rose glows with life, the smell of it perfuming the air and slowing Wendy's frantic breaths. From that rose the little light hops to the next flower, and the next, and then the next one, and the grass she'd drawn, and the sun — a beam of warmth catching the cat's attention — the light carries up the wall to every drawing it touches. The flowers sway, filling the room with the familiar scent of the garden that once stood where Wendy's home does now. The scene of mermaids at a cove comes to life, one of them shaking out her hair as another splashes water at her. The mermaid frowns as water drips from her curls and Wendy's curtains.

The moonlight sparks, the light from the window stretches, and soon the whole room sparks to life, pictures chattering and vibrant like living things. The spark dances, sparkling and springing through the room like it's proud of its work. As it rolls, it realizes that something is missing.

Moving through the room and the pirates and the lost boys on their swings and Wendy's little brothers dressed in leaves talking to fairies, the spark searches for the most important memory.

Tucked away behind her dresser, is a drawing Wendy never looks at, nearly as forgotten as the memory itself and faded with age. It's a drawing of a little girl, only twelve and still so full of unabashed wonder. Her blonde hair is tied away from her face as a little boy with eyes as old as the garden hands her a stolen pirate's sword with a mischievous smile.

A jealous fairy crosses her arms, sitting in a nearby tree and looking away from the two. The spark bounces into the image, slowly waking the drawings as they shake their heads and rub their stiff arms, looking about the dark corner. Little Wendy blinks, holding her new-old sword to her chest and taking careful steps to the side of the dresser where she can almost see the light from the sun peeking through.

The little spark rolls on the carpet, catching her eye. It bounces up and down, trying to tell her something. The boy from the drawing pokes his head out from behind the dresser, his chin on little Wendy's head. She moves away, making him stumble, and turns to face Little Peter. He frowns at her before getting distracted by the glowing ball of moonlight hopping about and the sound of the drawings in the room bickering and splashing and laughing in their scenes. He blinks.

The little spark curls again, then turns and zips away toward the bed. "Well come on," Little Wendy says, turning to Little Peter. "I think it wants us to follow it."

Little Wendy wastes no time sheathing her sword and jumping up, trying to catch the blanket. She jumps and jumps, finally catching onto it before falling back down with a frustrated huff. Behind her she hears a laugh, and her cheeks heat in embarrassment. Crossing her arms, she looks up at Little Peter floating above her head and sparkling with fairy dust.

"Cheater," Little Wendy grumbles.

He laughs again and Little Wendy shushes him, waving her hand at the boy tumbling around in the air, already adjusted and as lively as the real thing. "Shh shush shush, you'll wake her." Little Peter claps a hand over his mouth, looking up to where the actual Wendy lays sleeping. He lowers himself a bit to float beside Little Wendy. "Ya need a hand?" he offers.

Little Wendy pouts but takes his hand reluctantly. Little Peter whistles, signaling the drawing of Tinkerbell to come help. Very reluctantly the fairy pokes her head out from around the corner, looking uninterested. Peter waves her over, gesturing to Little

Wendy and waving his arms in a mock flight motion. Tinkerbell flies out from behind the dresser and crosses her arms, giving them a scolding look.

Little Peter frowns. "Aww come on, Tinkerbell. Don't be like that."

Little Wendy crosses her arms again, throwing back an equally scolding glare.

Little Peter wipes his hand exaggeratedly across his face. Tinkerbell blinks back at him, not budging. The two eyed each other for a while before Tinkerbell finally rolled her eyes. Her voice is a jumble of bells as she tosses fairy dust at Little Wendy, hitting her in the face and making the girl cough. Little Peter gives her a disapproving look, to which the fairy simply laughs.

Little Wendy concentrates on flying though she's annoyed with the fairy, Tink never seemed to like her much. The two of them fly up to the top of the bed, Tinkerbell trailing behind curiously. Little Wendy drops beside her older self and stares in befuddlement. As she watches the real Wendy sleep, she looks around the room. She sees the boxes packed away for college, the trash can with drawings and stuffed toys hanging out of it, the journal where she knows the real Wendy would have written to herself, attempting to convince herself that this is all for the best. That she's too old for fairytales. It's heartbreaking to Little Wendy. With all her wide imagination, she'd never imagined that she'd give up.

She wrings her hands in the front of her dress, face drawn in sadness.

Little Peter frowns, scrunching up his nose. "Well . . ." He pouts. "Maybe it's for the best anyways." He kicks a bit of dust as it floats by, his hands behind his back as he looks everywhere but at the two Wendys, afraid he'd give himself away. Peter likes games, but he isn't very good at keeping secrets. There had never been any need to with the Lost Boys. They were his family, but now that included Wendy, it was hard not to treat her the same way. He feels guilt heat his face as Little Wendy turns around, baffled and clearly upset.

"For the best?" she questions a bit too loudly, putting a hand over her own mouth with a startled jump. They both eye the sleeping Wendy, but she doesn't budge. "For the best?" Little Wendy whispers. "How could this be for the best? What have I done?" Her eyes drift around the room, from the boxes to the walls. "How could I give all this up when I've seen so much? Why would I stop believing in magic?"

Little Peter's expression is uncharacteristically grim. "But you don't remember magic anymore, Wend." He crosses his arms. Though he knows full well it's unfair to judge her for it, he can't hide being a bit cross that she could forget about them so easily. That she never did remember him.

Little Wendy shakes her head, her blonde hair bouncing aggressively with the movement. "No, but she does remember. Look around." Little Wendy smooths the front of her dress, looking down at the details, from the shade of blue to the little tears from fighting off pirates and falling from trees. "She drew us . . ."

Little Peter's shoulders droop as he takes in the room around them. On the wall beside the bed he notices a familiar scene, a young Wendy with her needle and thread, carefully sewing his shadow back into place. Little Peter looks at his little shadow which frowns as it takes in the memory. Knowing that he was out there missing his Wendy. As much as he wants to wake her, he knows this is what she needs.

"Her memories . . ." starts the creaky voice of an older woman, "are all but dreams for her now. Merely drawings on an old wall."

Little Peter, Little Wendy, and — despite all her feigned disinterest — Little Tink all look curiously over the side of the bed toward the voice. There was a sound like the walls settling. They watched the face Wendy had drawn on her walls stretch forward, the eyes blinked and the ears wiggled, the mouth twitched and stretched and it scrunched up its nose. It has been some time since Little Peter, Little Wendy, and Little Tink have been awakened by the moonlight, and this is a drawing that none of them have met yet, though she looks much older than the lot of them. Little Tink's face lights up with recognition and without a word to the others she flashes forward, startling Little Peter.

"I know her, I know her!" calls Tink.

Little Peter and Little Wendy follow her down, floating at eye level to the woman. "Tink says she knows her," he whispers to Little Wendy. Peter listens as Tinkerbell explains. As the fairy speaks, he translates her chimes for Little Wendy. "The house used to be a magic garden. A fairy garden. Tinkerbell says she used to live here before they cut everything down." Little Peter looks appalled at the story, unable to believe anyone would cut down a fairy garden to simply build a house.

Little Wendy gapes at the woman. "Goodness . . . Was there nowhere else they could build their house?"

"She says that they used one of the trees to make this room. Oh, you're one of the magic trees. That's why the moonlight makes the drawings move isn't it?"

"Whether it is I, the moon, or Wendy's own magic, or all of us together, I cannot tell you. Only that magic does live here." The old tree's eyes shift up to Wendy's bed. "But slowly, she is losing her faith in it."

"Where is she going?" asks Little Peter, looking at all the boxes. "Why are all her things put away?"

"Wendy thinks herself a grownup now," explains the tree sadly. "She is going away to school."

"To learn to write storybooks?" asks Little Wendy in a smaller voice. The tree blinks slowly, her mouth turned down. Little Wendy scrunches up her face. "Well, we have to stop this and change her mind. Magic is real. If she knows that, then she will know that she doesn't have to be a boring grown up. She's me."

"She doesn't remember being you," snaps Little Peter, sitting in the air with his legs crossed and his chin propped up on his hand.

Tink nods, though she casts concerned glances at Peter, not liking seeing him upset.

"Her memories are not as lost as you think," says the wall, giving Peter a pointed look. "Her memories may only be pictures and stories to her now. But she still keeps a part of Neverland close." Her eyes shift to a shelf where a small music box sits open, a ballerina guarding it.

Little Wendy flies up to the shelf, eager for any proof that this is not all she will have, cautiously peering into the music box. Nestled into the side is a small acorn that Little Wendy recognizes immediately, now attached to a small silver chain tarnished with wear.

"She still has it." Little Wendy bounces in excitement, grinning and hopeful again. "She still has your kiss, Peter! She still remembers something! She must!"

"It is faint," says the voice of the old tree, her eyes droopy as she looks toward the sleeping Wendy. "But if you never lose one thing, it will be your stubbornness."

Little Wendy flied back to stand beside where Peter is still floating, holding her own kiss close, the little acorn digging into her palm.

Little Peter stiffens as he often does when he's troubled. He touches the kiss in his own pocket — a thimble. He had thought Wendy too grown up to keep his, and he questioned if, maybe, she did remember him, if only a little.

The old tree blinks slowly, looking him in the eye. "There is nothing that can be done for it. Whether she remembers or not is neither here nor there. No matter what you decide, she will know you again."

Little Peter's brows furrows. "What's that supposed to mean?" he asks, frowning again.

Little Wendy waves her hand at him, dismissing the question. "We should wake her and stop this nonsense." She pulls at Little

Peter's arm. He pulls away, surprising her by seeming cross. Tink looks rather pleased at the gesture, nodding her head and voicing her thoughts that they should definitely, one hundred percent, not wake Real Wendy.

Though he isn't pleased about it, Peter nods. "Tink doesn't think we should. And I think she's right. We should just leave Wendy alone. She could freak out or something bad could happen."

Little Wendy stares at the boy with a confusion that soon gives way to a hard glare. "Something bad has already happened! I can't grow up like this, I'm miserable. I-I've forgotten you . . ." She holds the kiss tighter, trying to ground herself. Peter goes quiet, looking away from her.

Little Wendy turns toward the wall. "Won't you convince him? I'm right, aren't I? We should wake her. We should tell her that it's real. That she can't stop believing in magic, she can't grow up." Little Wendy's voice reaches more and more hysterical of a pitch the more she goes on, her eyes damp. "It's too important. The Lost Boys and Hook and the mermaids. She could be tricked or-or she could —"

"She could just grow up. She already has, Wendy," Peter says bitterly.

"Why would you want that?" Little Wendy asks accusingly. "You never grow up! Why should I be forced too?"

"She won't remember," says the wall. "It is Neverland's Magic. Eventually all children forget."

Little Peter still does not look up, kicking the ground and glaring down at the carpet. "Yeah. All children."

"Except for one," says the wall, her voice full of pity that only seems to annoy Little Peter more.

"I don't understand." Little Wendy looks between the two of them. "You can't do that; I won't be kept out of the loop." Tinkerbell mocked the girl's tone, zipping up to sit on the windowsill and watch.

"You couldn't remember your parents," starts Little Peter. He crosses his arms, still refusing to look at Little Wendy. "You and your brothers were . . . forgetting things. About here." He starts pacing, floating down till his feet touch the ground. "You were talking about wanting to see your mum, and about school and writing picture books for a job. You-You wanted to grow up." Peter's face scrunches up at the thought. "You wanted to go home."

Little Wendy only looks more upset. She shakes her head. "Only for temporary. I wouldn't forget about Neverland. I couldn't." She lets the sentence hang in the air between the four of them, tense and sad. Tentatively she looks between Peter and the wall. "I could never . . . could I?"

"You are not the first child to leave Neverland," says the wall softly.

Little Wendy blinks, a tear rolling down her cheek. She wipes at it furiously with the back of her hand, sniffling. "I'm waking her," she says sharply.

Little Peter's eyes go wide. "Wait!" He zips after her, following her to the side of the bed.

"Wendy!" she calls. "Wendy, wake up!" She lands on the sheets, stumbling. "Wendy! You have to wake up, look at us! Look at your drawings! Talk to your walls, you were right!" Little Peter lands beside her and reaches to grab hold of her wrist and pull her back.

Little Wendy yanks away. "Please wake up!"

"Shh," Little Peter hisses. Tinkerbell is frantic, zipping around and yelling, though all Little Wendy hears are faint angry bells as the fairy tries to put her little hands over Little Wendy's mouth. Little Wendy shoves Tink away, only making her angrier. Peter gets between the two of them, holding up a hand and giving his fairy friend a look as he reminds her of her promises to him and the boys. Tink glares, stomping her foot, but decides against shoving Little Wendy off the bed.

Little Wendy ignores the both of them, sitting on her knees

beside the grown-up Wendy. Little Peter looks sad, walking forward to crouch beside the crying girl.

"I can't wake her myself, can I?"

Little Peter looks at the sleeping girl, who's barely stirred despite the noise. "I don't know. Maybe not."

"You knew I would forget, didn't you?" she prods. Ashamed, Little Peter refuses to meet her eyes. "Didn't you?" He nods slowly. "Why then? Why bring me back?"

He looks up at her then, surprised. "Because you wanted to go home. And . . . and the old tree was right. We aren't the same. You didn't belong to Neverland."

She frowns. "But . . . But I *did* belong. I must have. You told me I was the Queen of Neverland." She touches her hand to her sword. Her little eyes teary as she says, "I earned that title."

"Would you have chosen any different if you knew for sure you'd forget? Could you forget your mother? Your father?" he asks.

Little Wendy looks down. Then shakes her head. She looks up toward the curtains. It will be morning soon. She stands. They are almost out of time. She looks back to those violet eyes. "Are you sure? That I will know Peter Pan again? The grown-up me?"

The wall blinks slowly at her, sleepily. Little Wendy nods back. "I think I understand."

Little Peter tilts his head. "Understand what?"

"Look," Little Wendy says, pointing to a drawing of the moon, a pirate ship having trailed across it finally, breaking the clouds. "That's Hook's ship."

Little Peter lifted his head to the ship, watching. It had barely moved, unlike the other drawings that had kept going and going through the night. "Why is it moving that slowly? Has it always been there?" he asks, looking to the face in the wall.

"That drawing represents that which hasn't happened yet," says the voice of the old wall. "There isn't much time now. As I've said, it matters not what you decide. Wendy will remember you."

"What does it mean?" Little Peter asks, looking to Little Wendy for answers as he often did.

Little Wendy looks back to the ship. On the head of the deck, she sees Hook, but he isn't looking straight ahead. Instead, his gaze is turned down, looking directly toward the sleeping Wendy as his ship sails toward the brightest star, the second star to the right. "He's trying to leave Neverland," she replies. "He's almost to the star."

"But why?" Little Peter asks. "Wendy's been gone from Neverland for years, why would Hook want to come here?"

"I cannot tell you the motivations of others," says the wall. "Only what I see."

Little Wendy can't hide her relief, the excitement moving through her apparent as she claps her hands together and places them in front of her face. Her eyes are wet. "Then I will remember again. I will know Peter Pan. Soon."

Little Peter stares at the drawing of Hook. He is not nearly as excited as Little Wendy despite his longing for her to remember him. Hook had not left Neverland in a long time, whatever he wanted with Wendy, it worried him. "Yeah . . . soon."

With that, the moonlight fades entirely from the room, retreating back through the window. The drawings cease their moving and return to their original places as though nothing had ever happened. As though the walls are simply wood and plaster and paint.

Little Peter reaches into his pocket, pulls out a tiny thimble and runs his thumb across it. Little Wendy sees him and tilts her head; smiling, she pulls out the small acorn from the pocket of her dress. She holds it up and Little Peter mimics her movement. They pocket them and she reaches out to take his hand. The grown-up Wendy begins to stir, rubbing the sleep from her eyes just as Little Wendy and Little Peter are carried away by the shimmering lights to their space behind the dresser.

Wendy opens her eyes and looks about her room. She swore that she heard a familiar voice, but all she sees are shadows chased away by the sun peeking up through her curtain. Too tired to commit herself to waking this early, she throws off the covers and trudges to the window. A curiosity pulls at her, nonsense left over from her dreaming. Despite the thought, she pokes her head out the window, looking about in an attempt to catch something before it can hide from her view. Unknown to her, Pan's shadow is just a bit faster, ducking around the corner to the outer wall of her home. Wendy frowns, shaking her head. "It's time to grow up," she mutters to herself before closing the curtain.

She walks back to her bed, rubbing her eyes, wanting only to push the day away a little longer. Soon she dresses and takes her boxes downstairs. She refuses to stop and take another look around, but she spots her pencil against the wall. She grabs it, puts it in her pocket before leaving. She grips it tight as she closes the doorknob to her childhood room.

But if she had listened to the voice in her head, the little nagging that sounded like a bell and turned around, maybe, just maybe, she would have felt the spray of the water on the floor by the windowsill. Or heard the laughter from the mermaids splashing. Or caught the little spark of moonlight still trying to glow a little longer. Maybe she would have seen the violet eyes she had drawn for her walls all those years ago, blink just one more time.

Maybe she would have heard them talk.

About Nico Vazquez

Nico Vazquez is a poet, multimedia artist, and author. They received training in writing and performance art through mentoring with local group P.O.M.E beginning at age fourteen and have been finding new ways to create and share since. His work often includes educating others on topics centering gender, sexuality, and race, through discussing his own experiences as a biracial trans person. When he's not creating or educating, Nico can be found wandering graveyards with friends or dancing with a hyper chihuahua and a tsundere cat.

Published works include poetry books 'I Am Arrogant and Cruel' and 'Lovely Thoughts At 3AM'.

As well as a short stories in the anthologies 'Places We Build In The Universe' and upcoming 'As We Convene: An Anthology of Time and Place' both edited by Lauren T. Davilla. You can find more information on his website ignicovazquez.weebly.com and social media.

The Great Indoors

Jennifer Kaul

My running slows to a stop when I see the For Sale sign piercing my front lawn. My jaw clenches as my eyes trail toward my house, noting the PureOx car in the driveway, the lockbox on the door.

Shit.

I try to ignore the hazy sky, the tickle at the back of my throat as I storm up the porch steps, through the front door, and into my two-story house. I find my parents in the kitchen, sitting at our table with a woman I don't know. At a glance, they look as unfamiliar as she does: older, wearier, their weekend wear pale beside her bright blue suit.

"Perseus." My dad stands. My mom fiddles with the bracelet on her wrist. "We were just speaking with our community liaison."

I look from my parents to the woman who smiles eagerly at me. "Our what?"

"Community liaison," the woman repeats. "For your new pure-oxygen home. I think you're going to like what I have to show you." She gestures to the empty chair at the other end of the table, but I don't move.

I've heard of these places before. Greenhouses in the middle of nowhere, supposedly the up-and-coming housing trend. A girl from school, Vanessa, left for one a few months ago, and no one's seen her since.

My eyes move to plead with my parents. "Could we at least wait until after senior year?"

My dad sighs and my mom shakes her head. "We already put down a deposit." Her voice is apologetic yet doesn't waver.

The woman continues, seemingly unfazed by my reaction. "Your parents have reserved a unit in our newest community, OxComm. It's a state-of-the-art, all-inclusive development with everything you could ever need — on-campus restaurants, parks and gardens of course, daily activities, leisure excursions, and more." She makes a few selections on her tablet and turns it toward me. A slideshow begins, displaying pictures of a plant-filled paradise.

"The plant-to-person ratio is among the best available," she tells me like I care. As the images change, I glimpse people eating, hanging out, sleeping, always smiling, always surrounded by plants. "Your unit will include a premium plant package of your family's choice. Most importantly, it will provide you with clean air so you can enjoy a long and healthy life."

The presentation ends with the same PureOx air bubble logo that brands the woman's blazer and car. Beneath it are the words, *OxComm. Join us in the great indoors!*

The woman makes a few selections on her tablet and turns it toward me. "Now, all I need *you* to do is sign here." She holds out a stylus and points to a blank line on the tablet's glowing screen.

I reach for the tablet, leaving the stylus untouched. I scroll up and start reading the new tenant agreement, its terms bouncing around my head like air molecules.

Weekly oximeter checks.

Activity limits.

Food allowances.

Scheduled shower days.

The list goes on, but my mind is too fuzzy to read it right now.

I turn to my parents. "When?" is all I can manage.

My dad looks away. "Three weeks."

Suddenly, I feel like I'm suffocating. I need to get out of this room, away from this woman and the strange lifestyle she sells.

My mom's voice follows me as I rush out of the house. "With how quickly the air is degrading . . . We're just trying to keep you safe."

Soon I'm running — across the front lawn, past the menacing sign, and down my street. *The air is fine,* I tell myself. *They can't make me go.* I run harder, faster, until my lungs burn.

I blink, and our moving day arrives. I sit on a plane with my parents. It's different from the ones I've been on before — the ride feels smoother, the air smells fresher, the cabin's small without feeling cramped. Still, I feel claustrophobic.

The last few weeks were a downward spiral of garage sales, donations, and packed up cardboard boxes. Our house? Gone. My car? Gone. Senior year at North High? Gone. I said goodbye to my friends, not knowing when I'd see them again. *If* I'd see them again.

My eyes pass over the people sitting across the aisle from us. There's a family with two young kids, an older couple, a pair of young men. *Our new neighbors.*

"Are you sure I can't stay with Tyler?" I ask for the hundredth time. "His parents said it would be okay."

"Percy." My dad gives me a warning glance. "We've talked about this."

Before he can continue, a voice comes over the speaker. "Here we are, folks. Home sweet home."

My mom looks out her window and gasps, a smile spreading across her face. I follow her gaze to the ground below but refuse to give her the reaction she's hoping for.

The complex is like a cluster of air bubbles spilling over from an adjacent river. It gleams in the sun, its crystalline shell tinted emerald green by the plants inside it.

As we begin our descent, most passengers oohing and ahhing, my parents try to reassure me.

"We love you, Percy," my mom says for what feels like the fortieth time that day. "This will be great."

"A family adventure," my dad agrees. "You'll see."

Or I won't.

I tuck my earbuds firmly in place, flip my hood over my head, and keep my eyes on my phone until it's time to deplane.

Soon after landing, we arrive in a small vestibule, all twenty or so of us. Our liaison is there to greet us.

"We are now in OxComm's filtered entrance," she explains. "In seconds, the air we dragged in will be stripped of pollutants through our advanced filtration system."

I feel a light change in pressure — a push and pull, as if the air has a pulse. Once it stills, I inhale deeply. Doesn't seem any different to me.

Our liaison removes her shoes and instructs us to do the same. "You will find more suitable footwear in your welcome bag," she explains, handing a large fabric bag to each of us. "We protect our plants so they can protect us."

I dig through my bag, past pieces of fruit and sample size toiletries, until I find a thin pair of plastic socks. A sticker informs me they're eco-friendly and derived from plants. Of course they are.

Seeing no alternative, I step out of my sandals and store them in the cubbies provided. Then I slip on the plant-based socks. Once everyone's ready, the inner door slides open. The woman beams. "Welcome to OxComm."

My breath catches. It's the most beautiful place I've ever seen.

Broad-leafed trees reach up to the ceiling. Bushes boast every possible shade of green, and flowers sprinkle the room with color.

I step inside and onto something surprisingly soft. Looking down, I find a carpet of emerald moss. The footwear is so thin and malleable, it feels as if my feet are bare.

The air is fragrant without being overpowering. Bird songs and the hum of insects surround us.

I glance over at my parents, at their wide eyes, their mouths gaping in awe. The fact that it's so perfect here only makes me hate it more.

We wander down the path, in and out of parks, restaurants, health services, and shops. It's like a cross between a greenhouse, a fancy hotel, and a futuristic mall. People mill about, "recent recruits," the woman tells us with a wink. We're the third group to arrive.

Everyone I see looks as happy as the people in the PureOx presentation. Everywhere I look, there are plants.

Soon, we're back where we started. As the woman gives some final instructions and asks for questions, a dragonfly zips by. Its buzzing wings sound familiar enough, but there's something strange about it, something I can't quite place.

"Here at OxComm," our liaison says, "we understand the human connection with the outside world. To incorporate a touch of wildlife while maintaining an environment as clean as our air, we created our own community of critters."

She holds out her hand and the insect lands on her palm. I step closer to study it. Its iridescent wings quiver as its head flicks this way and that, but it isn't an insect. It's a tiny piece of tech.

"Cool," a young boy murmurs beside me.

The liaison addresses the adults in the group. "Our creatures perform all necessary functions from aerating the soil to pollinating our plants. No more mosquito bites. No more bee stings. No more pest control of any kind."

"So there aren't any bugs at all?" a small voice asks. I glance over to see a younger girl standing next to the boy. Her mouth is curved into a fish-like pout, and I can tell she's trying not to cry.

The woman smiles knowingly. "We offer nature-viewing stations that I bet you'd like, as well as nature sound recordings. And our creatures aren't so bad once you get used to them."

As if on cue, the insect lifts off from her hand. It stops briefly, gently, on the girl's shoulder, flipping her frown before it flits off and disappears into the foliage.

Minutes later, we're standing in front of our unit. Tall grasses flank the modern wooden door on either side, and three large stones act as a walkway among the moss.

"We should be able to just stand here," my dad says, positioning his face in front of a retinal scanner. There's a beep, and the door clicks open. "Voila!"

I roll my eyes and push past him through the open door. "Whoa," I breathe. Our unit is a meticulously-pruned jungle. Ferns blanket large sections of the floor. Vines climb the walls in tangled patterns. The colorful plant life creates a stunning contrast with the modern white furniture and walls.

"Do we have to do anything for these?" I ask, tugging at a leaf on the nearest tree. The sunlight streaming in gives the room a light and airy appearance, but I still feel heavy inside.

"Plant care is included," my dad replies, rummaging through his welcome bag. "Honey, have you seen a list of food options?"

My mom holds up the binder that was sitting on the table. Not our table. The one we'd sat at for as long as my memory can reach has been sold, along with the rest of our lives.

"Let's see." She flips through the pages. "Dining. Here it is." She turns the binder toward me. "You choose tonight."

I take her bait and join her at the table. It feels like we're on vacation instead of getting settled in a new home, a never-ending cruise on a static ship. "Let's just order in."

While we wait for our food, we unpack the few things we brought with us: my track medals and trophies, my dad's favorite books, my mom's sheet music and guitar. My parents gush about how pristine this place is and how wonderful our lives here will be. I look through the boxes, realizing again and again that what I'm searching for isn't there, isn't even mine anymore.

By that evening, I need some time away. "I'm going out for a bit," I tell my parents, and I head for the door before they can protest.

"Have fun exploring!" my mom calls after me.

"Yeah right," I mutter as I exit our unit. I wander down the hall and into the community's shared space, ignoring the people that occasionally pass by. When I spot a bench near the park, I sit down and take out my phone, desperate for a glimpse of life outside of this strange new place. But scrolling through my socials only makes me feel worse.

Soon, the sun sets. Artificial lights cast an eerie glow on the plant life surrounding me. I glance around and realize I'm out here alone. Everyone else must be unpacking or getting ready for bed.

A rustling sound startles me, and I follow it with my eyes. A metallic black and white bird soars out of the bushes and into view. Its big eyes and fiery red crest remind me of a woodpecker. The bird perches on the branch of a nearby tree and starts hammering the trunk with its beak. It's almost like it knows I'm at my wit's end.

The noise pecks at me until I can't take it anymore. I pick up a nearby stone and throw it. Not at the bird, but near it, just to see what happens.

It stops and stares straight at me.

I hold its artificial gaze for a beat, then two, then *click*. The bird blinks.

"Aren't they beautiful?"

I jump up, startled, and turn to face a girl about my age, standing a few feet behind me.

"The tech or the trees?" I ask, but when I look back for the bird, it's gone.

"These plants," she continues. Her auburn waves fall just

below her shoulders, and her eyes are as green as the trees. "Living off nothing more than sun, soil, and water. Creating life yet no waste. Providing food, shelter, shade. We wouldn't exist without them."

I shrug. "I never really thought about it that way."

"My mom helps take care of the plants here, and it's amazing all they can do. Did you know that some plants communicate with each other? And they harvest light through photosynthesis. They —" She stops, likely registering my indifference. "Never mind."

She checks her phone. "It's getting close to curfew, anyway, so I guess I'll see you around."

This catches my attention. "Curfew?" I ask, hoping I somehow misheard her.

"10 PM on weekdays, 11 PM on weekends?" Her voice goes up with her eyebrows, like she's waiting for me to nod in recognition, but my face must betray how stunned I feel. "Don't you have the app?"

I blink at her. "The app?"

"PureLife?"

I shake my head.

"You should get it," she tells me. Then she waves and walks away.

I take out my phone and download the app. Once she's out of view, I work up the courage to open it. My pulse accelerates as it loads.

Welcome to PureLife! it greets me. *Please create an account.*

I enter the needed information and soon I'm in. I already have a list of tasks that are past due, as well as a series of reminders.

I can't take all of this. I'm so mad, at my parents for dragging me here, at whoever created this prison, at all these stupid plants. I take a step to leave and step on a rock. "Agh!" I shout. I kick the nearest flower and a few petals drift down to the ground. It feels good to watch them fall. I'm about to behead another when all of the lights go out.

Damnit. I tap my phone and find an alert. I missed curfew.

I turn on my phone's flashlight and try to find my way back. Blinking fireflies (*not real ones*, I remind myself) flit away as I follow the beam of light.

When I finally make it back to our family unit, my parents are in their room for the night. I change and crawl into bed, suddenly hyper-aware of the tiny tech ants churning up soil in the landscaped corners of my room. I wonder how many there are, what they're doing. I envision a trail of them burrowing deep into my ear as I sleep. The plants cast hungry shadows on the walls.

I count the months on my fingers. Seven more months until I'm a legal adult. Seven more months, and then I'm getting the hell out of here.

When my eyes open the next morning, all I see is green. I groan. Not a dream.

I drag myself out of bed and throw on a t-shirt and shorts for my morning run, even though my time on the track team is over. I think about the goals I had less than a month ago. Captain of North's varsity track team. Winning the district championship. An athletic scholarship to a college of my choice. I want to scream.

Instead, I slip out of our unit so as not to wake my parents and follow the path to the gym. On my way, I do a quick internet search for pure oxygen homes. They're everywhere, it seems — China, India, the US, the UAE. But what's the end game? People living and working in bubbles for the rest of their lives?

I arrive and try the door, but it's locked. Seeing a retinal scanner, I position myself in front of it and hope I remember how it works. It beeps and a message appears on the screen below. *The gym is at full capacity. Please try again later or reserve a time.*

I glance through the glass windows and count the people inside. There are only eight.

After another failed attempt to open the door, I open the PureLife app and check the next available time. There's a spot in a half hour, but it won't let me take it. An error message informs me that today is one of my designated rest days.

Whatever. If I can't run in here, I'll run outside.

I return to where we entered the complex the day before and try the door. Again, nothing. I ram my body against it, then try to pry it open with my fingers.

"What are you doing?" I look up to see the girl from the night before.

"Trying to go for a run."

She watches me, her eyes a mix of pity, amusement, and concern. "It doesn't open," she tells me. "We're supposed to stay inside except for pre-approved excursions. Haven't your parents told you anything?"

"So we're trapped here." I kick the door, and the pain that shoots through my toes reminds me I'm no longer wearing normal shoes.

"Trapped?" she exclaims. "It's the people out there who are trapped! Do you know how many people would kill to live like this? How many are dying because they can't?"

I scoff at the urgency in her voice. "I'm going to die of boredom soon if I can't find something to do."

She shakes her head. "You don't deserve to be here. You have no idea how bad things are, how much worse they're going to get. My dad died of lung cancer, and he didn't smoke a day in his life. Haven't you felt the effects of being outside in the past few years? The added congestion, the tightness in your chest? Between the pollution and smoke from forest fires, the air out there is more harmful than people realize."

"I'm sorry to hear about your dad," I tell her. "But that has nothing to do with me. When I'm outside, I feel fine. Better than in here, at least." I turn and head back toward my family's unit, cursing as a small black and white bird zips past.

When I get back to our unit, my parents are finishing up their morning coffee.

"I tried going for a run." I don't bother smoothing out my voice. I feel so raw, so ragged, that I don't care if they hear how angry I am. "The gym was maxed out at eight people, and the building wouldn't let me leave. Oh, and there's apparently a nightly curfew, too. It might have been nice to know about some of this stuff."

My dad sighs. "We were hoping to tell you a little at a time so you wouldn't get overwhelmed."

I stare at them in disbelief. "You moved me to this weird place right before my senior year without any of my friends or anything to do. Consider me overwhelmed."

That's when a notice flashes across our TV. There's been an air leak.

We watch as a map appears on the screen. It shows the entire complex with a flashing red light indicating the location of the leak. I lean closer. It's at the entrance.

I picture myself kicking and clawing at the door, and my skin prickles. I try to keep a blank face as we're told the issue has been resolved.

"It's probably just a minor issue with the infrastructure," my dad reassures us. "It's a new building, so a few growing pains are to be expected. Better for them to happen sooner rather than later. And look," he adds as the screen changes, "it says that the air quality control system adjusted to counter the leak. Even if the quality levels were to dip a little, whatever we're breathing now is still a hundred times better than what we were inhaling a few days ago."

There's no way the air outside can be as bad as they think. Even if it is, someone will find a way to fix it. Meanwhile, I'm stuck in this bubble feeling as if I might burst.

I text Tyler. I tell him about the restrictions and how I wish I was still at home. Because, despite everything my parents said, I still do.

Tyler: *Sounds like something out of a sci-fi movie, and those experiments never end well.*

I send an eye roll emoticon. *Hopefully I can escape before the complex self-destructs.*

Tyler: *My parents asked about you today. They're still cool with you staying here if your parents ever agree.*

Thanks.

He sends a thumbs up. *Good luck. I need to get ready to meet up with the guys.*

Normally, I'd be joining them, too.

See ya, I say, wondering if it's true.

Later.

I click off my phone, trying not to think of the photos they'll post, photos that are missing me. I spend the rest of the day like I have the past couple: watching movies, watching the walls, and watching the world go on without me.

A single ant crawls across my desk and a chill skitters up my spine. Before I fully think through what I'm doing, I smash it with one of my books. There are hundreds of them creeping around my room. One won't be missed.

I swipe the tiny broken creature onto the floor, feeling a little bit better, a little more in control. *Screw the scheduled rest time,* I think, and I go for a run in the park.

That night, we go out to dinner at one of the community restaurants. I move the food around my plate but can't get myself to eat it. The food here tastes different, and when I mention this to my parents, my dad offers me a grim smile. "It's vegan."

"OxComm is Earth conscious in their operations onsite and off," my mom says as if reading off a script.

I start to respond but stop myself when I overhear someone at another table.

" . . . wouldn't be surprised if someone was stealing the air and selling it for profit."

"Did you hear that?" my dad whispers to me and my mom.

"Hear what?" I ask, my voice innocent.

"Someone talking about the air leak. That it might have been intentional."

"Nonsense." My mom waves a hand as if trying to clear the air of such unsavory ideas. "People and their conspiracy theories. I'm sure there's a logical explanation."

Like some kid trying to yank open the door.

My dad sighs. "There are always those who find ways to take something good and use it to their advantage. It's all about supply and demand. And air is our most precious resource."

I roll my eyes.

"I'm serious," he says. "Think about it. You can survive without food for a few weeks. Water, a few days. Without oxygen, you'd be dead in seconds."

"So what you're saying,"— I lower my voice and lean in — "is that we should buy stock in OxComm or find a way to start smuggling out the clean air."

"Shhh," my mom hushes us, glancing around. "Enough of that talk. Now eat your dinner."

"I liked it better when I knew what my dinner was made of," I grumble.

After dinner, my parents stick around for a neighborhood social. I pass. Instead of being miserable surrounded by strangers, I decide to be miserable sitting alone, seeing what I would be doing if I wasn't here.

I scroll through my feed to see my friends at Tyler's house, checking in at a movie theater, hanging out at the beach. I study the picture of my friends by the water and try to ignore the smoky sky and the fact that a couple of people are wearing the same masks they sported during the pandemic.

Even though I'm breathing cleaner air, I can't help but feel jealous. I don't care how bad things are going to get on the outside. At least my friends are getting to live their lives now. Meanwhile, I'm trapped like a bug in a glass jar. There isn't much for me to do besides miss my life outside of it.

It's getting darker and, as much as I hate to admit it, this place creeps me out. I try to shake my feelings loose and, not wanting to miss curfew again, head back to my family's unit.

As I approach, I see something that makes me freeze. That damn bird is hovering in front of our unit.

In front of our retinal scan.

To my horror, the system beeps and our door slides open. The bird flies inside.

I rush after it, into the unit, and into my room.

When I find the bird, it's hopping around the floor near the edge of my desk. It's almost as if it's looking for something.

I picture myself crushing the robotic ant, then scold myself for being paranoid. There's no way anyone could know about that.

I grab one of my track trophies and approach the bird slowly from behind.

Before I can formulate a plan, it turns and zips past me. After a moment's hesitation, I chase after it.

We race through the hall, into the community's shared space, and down the main path. I hear laughter from the neighborhood social, but it becomes muffled as I follow the bird into the park. I lose sight of it as it disappears into the trees, but I'm not giving up that easily.

I step off the path and into the plants. Tall grasses bend beneath my feet and branches break as I force my way deeper into the brush. I watch for a flash of red, but all I see is green. I listen for any hint of movement but hear nothing but the stupid nature recording.

Finally, I spot it, high up in a tree, looking as if it belongs there. Its strange, wide stare, then *click*, it blinks. It leaves its roost to fly around me. *Click. Click. Click.* Then, it clings to a branch near the wall and taps its beak against the glass. I watch it for a moment, confused, but as a crack in the glass begins to form, I realize what it's doing. It's creating an air leak.

What if someone *is* stealing the clean air? And what if that person's framing me?

Just in case, I take out my phone and start filming. At least that way, if someone asks, I can prove it wasn't me. I'm a few seconds in when something small and fast dives at me. One, then two, then three dragonflies swoop around my head. I try batting them away while keeping my phone on the rogue bird intent on breaking the glass.

As one of the dragonflies zooms past, I catch a glimpse of my reflection in one of its oversized eyes. Of course. Cameras. The bird must have them, too.

After another minute, I think I've gotten enough evidence of my own. I take one last look at the eerie scene unfolding before me, and I run. I stumble out of the brush and back onto the path, swatting at the dragonflies that follow.

"Perseus? Is that you?" I look up to find my mom staring at me, my dad and a few other adults walking up behind her.

My dad looks from me to the plants. "What in the —"

An alarm buzzes, and a voice comes through a speaker. "Alert. Air leak detected in Park 3." A nearby screen lights up with a map that displays the space behind me.

"Percy?" My mom repeats. This time, her voice holds a hint of fear.

Several people sprint past us into the mass of plants, carrying cases and tools. A man approaches. He addresses me as my parents look on, my dad shaking his head in disbelief, my mom's eyes wide with terror. "I'm afraid you'll have to come with me."

The man leads us back to our unit. "I can explain," I begin as we sit down at the table. But before I can pull out my phone, he pulls up images and video footage on his tablet. Me kicking the flower. Walking around in the dark after curfew. Trying to pry the door open. Smashing the ant in my room. The final image is of me standing near tonight's oxygen leak.

My dad's voice shakes as his eyes bore through me. "Do you have any idea what you've done?"

"This is grounds for exclusion," the man says. He turns to me as my mom inhales sharply. "Was there something you wanted to tell me?"

I glance down at my phone, then back up at the man's tablet. I tuck my phone back in my pocket. "When do I leave?"

"Perseus!" my dad shouts.

"We're so sorry," my mom murmurs, tears welling up in her eyes. "He won't do it again. We'll pay for the repairs. Isn't there anything we can do?"

"Tyler's parents said I can live with him," I reassure her a little too quickly. "At least until I'm eighteen."

My dad gets up and starts pacing. "Is that what this is about?"

"I never wanted to come here," I tell him. "*That's* what this is about."

The following day, I pack up my few possessions. I hug and kiss my parents goodbye. My mom is beside herself and my dad is still pissed, but they promise to visit, and I promise to call and text.

And just like that, I'm boarding the plane to return home. Well, not home exactly, but something closer than this. I watch my parents waving through the window.

Then someone steps up behind them, waving her hand right along. It's that annoying, self-righteous, tree-obsessed girl. I wonder why she's here to see me off, if she's delusional enough to have thought we were friends. But then a metallic bird lands on her shoulder and a satisfied grin passes over her face.

I wonder which of us is happier that I'm flying free.

About Jennifer Kaul

Jennifer Kaul is an author of children's and young adult literature, a freelance education writer, a former teacher, and a cautious optimist. Her YA short story, "The Price of Words" was published in *Lunch Ticket*, and she has written nonfiction children's books for Capstone, DK, and more. In addition, Jennifer's middle grade science fiction adventure, *Uploaded*, was chosen for mentorship through Author Mentor Match. Many of Jennifer's pieces stem from the happenings in our world and the what-ifs that swirl around her head as a result. Her hope is, through her writing, to encourage thought, spark conversation, and make the world a better place.

Website: jenniferkaul.com

Misread Signs

Christian H. Morales

I was standing at the corner of W 37th St, waiting for the traffic light to give me the go on my way to the subway station, thinking about how things went wrong on my date that night with this girl I met at a friend's party. At first, things had been promising, but it all fell apart when I decided to tell a joke that had worked every single time I told it.

"A few years ago," I began to say, and she paid attention with a beautiful smile drawn on her perfectly-structured face. "I dated a girl allergic to pineapple. One day — I think when we were dating for six months or so — I really wanted to eat pineapple. The desire possessed me for at least a week, until I could no longer hold myself. One morning, I got up early to go for a run and then went straight to the supermarket and bought a bowl of the most delicious pineapple I had eaten in a long time. Once I'd finished, I forgot about the whole thing and carried on with my day. That afternoon my girlfriend arrived at the apartment and we had sex. I almost killed her."

At that moment everyone who heard the joke laughed, but my date made a grin of discomfort and said, "I am allergic to peanuts and one day my ex-boyfriend had to take me to the hospital because he ate a bag of peanuts and forgot to tell me about it. That same afternoon we were making love and the reaction was very violent." That killed the mood for the evening. The worst thing is that I've never dated a girl allergic to anything in my life. The joke was only a joke.

I was thinking about her expression — about the discomfort displayed on her face — when I heard someone calling my name with a hint of doubt — as one does when seeing an acquaintance, but is not entirely sure is the right person. The light finally turned red. Instead of crossing the street, I turned to face the person who called me. Standing in front of me was a beautiful woman with long black hair that fell straight to her shoulders, framing a face worthy of a Renaissance painting. Her black eyes smiled at me along with her lips. The first thing to cross my mind was *God, how can you make them so beautiful!* The second thing was that I knew her, but couldn't place her in my head.

She saw the bewilderment on my face and laughed with an unbridled laughter. "How come I recognized you at first glance, and you can't recognize me?" She stood in the middle of the sidewalk, arms crossed. Her pose stirred something to the surface of my mind. "It seems to me that the eternal love you once professed had an expiration date after all." The sound of her voice made everything flood back to me in a violent wave of flashbacks.

"Luna," I managed to say.

"Wow," she said, without losing her smile. "You were about to hurt my feelings."

As we stood on the busy street facing each other, I thought back to my past life. In the twelve years I'd been living in the United States, I had never seen anyone from my past. By the time I crossed the border down in Texas, I had cut every bond in Honduras and decided to restart my life as a new person in a new world. It had been going well until I bumped into Luna — or I should say, until she bumped into me.

The traffic light turned green again — my cue to stay there and talk to her.

While we waited for the red light to stop the traffic again, we talked about how long it had been since we last saw each other — we were fifteen or sixteen. We both disagreed on the last time we met; I was sure it was a week before her departure, and she was completely sure it was the night before she left Honduras. We laughed like fools, only paying attention to each other, yelling details of things that proved each of us right — things I hadn't thought about in over a decade — while people passed around us.

"Look," I said. "I know you may have plans, but would you like to go for a coffee or something to catch up properly?"

"I have a couple of hours to kill," she said, shrugging. "I know the perfect place, close to here." She turned to tell the girls she was with — whose presence I hadn't noticed because I was way too focused on her — that she would see them at the party they were going to.

I felt great for a second; not every day a beautiful woman like her left her immediate plans to catch up with a man who used to be her boyfriend when they were kids. Back then, to see her or talk to her, I'd get on my bike every afternoon, pedaling for thirty minutes to her neighborhood. Back then, cell phones were something that only upper middle-class people could afford in a third world country.

Her friends agreed and continued on their way after giving me some curious looks. They were pretty in their own way, but they couldn't match the beauty Luna inherited from her Honduran roots. There are no women in the whole world like Honduran women.

We crossed the street illuminated by the headlights of cars impatient to get on their way and the building lights along the street. She walked gracefully, with a confident ease. "It's amazing how little you've changed," she said.

"You are more beautiful," I said.

"I know," she said and laughed. "I'm sorry. Thank you very

much. People don't usually tell me that I'm more beautiful. I think they take for granted that I've always looked good, but you know what you're talking about."

Luna and I had met in the days of our transition from childhood to adolescence, when I stopped being interested in toy cars and she in Barbie dolls. When I was — without realizing it — focusing my attention on the long legs of girls at school and she stole her older sister's makeup to look prettier. I was thirteen; she was twelve. It was the year 2000, and in Honduras, we were recovering from the aftermath left by Hurricane Mitch, the economy was supported by the American and Korean textile industry, and the presence of the maras was a simple rumor, nothing people worried about in the short term.

I met Luna during an afternoon party organized by the seniors at her school to raise funds for their prom. That afternoon, when I had arrived in my neighborhood, bag full of books and my uniform dirty from playing football at recess, the first person I ran into was my pal, Chino. He told me about the party so I ran home to drop my bag and change my clothes. I told my mother that I had to meet with my study group to do homework, taking my BMX to the meeting point where Chino, Omoa, Galle, and Zurdo were waiting for me. They were all boys older than me, Omoa the oldest at eighteen. We pedaled, feeling the gusts of wind created by the cars that passed us at forty miles per hour.

We left the bicycles in a grocery store near the school; the owner would take care of them for the modest price of five lempiras each. We walked towards the school with our heads up, watching the girls fluttering from here to there like butterflies in a garden. Chino got us into the gymnasium without paying the required tickets; the girl selling them was one of his many preys.

Once inside, we stood at the end near the speakers where the newest reggaeton was loud and clear. The music was good, and while many of the kids danced, we were too preoccupied with playing the role of guys too cool to get caught up in the atmosphere. However, I had a crazy desire to approach two of the girls I liked to invite them to dance. I didn't though because of my own inexperience; I was the youngest of the group and the only one who hadn't kissed a girl in his life.

I saw Luna for the first time when my friends decided they wanted to buy some sodas. I won't say a lightning bolt struck me when I saw her because the one I liked was her friend. I'm not going to lie, the skinny girl was pretty, she had a sweetness that still glowed in her even on that Saturday night in the streets of New York so many years later, but her friend was already playing in another league. Obviously, I had no chance with her, although I guess Galle thought he did, because the next thing I knew, he was standing next to me, asking me to be his wing-man, which meant I had to distract the other girl, Luna, on his behalf. He took the pretty girl aside and left me there, speechless, nervous, and sweating cold with Luna — who seemed to be having a lot of fun with the situation.

"Do you remember how nervous you were the first time we met?" she asked me as we sat down at the table. The cafe was semi-busy for a Saturday night. We sat away from the noise to talk without interruptions.

"Do you still remember that?" I laughed.

"I remember everything about my childhood, about home," she said.

"From time to time, I think about those years in Honduras," she said with a glow in her black eyes. At that moment, I found her the most charming woman I've ever met. "Those were good years, full of special memories for me, especially the last three."

The waiter arrived to save me from my own thoughts. Luna ordered a hot chocolate while I ordered an espresso. "It was surprising to run into you like that, in the middle of nowhere. I had no idea you lived in the States."

I told her I had eight years living in the country, five of which I had lived in different neighborhoods in New York. I told her — with some embarrassment — that the reason I came to the country was because of a girl I loved. We were together for two years in Honduras and only needed one year living together in Houston to see everything go to hell.

"People change once they get here," Luna said. "I've seen it a lot. It doesn't surprise me anymore."

"I haven't changed," I said. "I'm still basically the same person."

"Maybe you have changed, and you don't know. That's something that also happens with people."

"Come on, you know me. You know it would be really difficult to change who I am. I'm pretty much the same person I was back when I was fifteen . . . maybe a little funnier."

"I don't know," she said, wrinkling her nose and looking adorable. "For me, for example, it would be impossible to conceive the idea of you leaving Honduras to follow a girl. No one does that, yet you did." She laughed and shook her head. "I can't say that I know you because we were still children when we had our relationship, however many years it was."

The seed that bore the fruit of our relationship was planted that first time we met, but the thing germinated a couple of weeks later in one of the cliché places in a love story: the bus. I don't consider myself the romantic type, but I'm a man who knows how to tell when a moment in his life is important. From time to time, I give mental reviews to the chronicle that is my life, especially everything related to women because, whether I like it or not, they all left a mark on me, something indelible that makes them special regardless of the way things ended with each of them. Luna had a special place in my heart because she was the first woman I loved and everything about our relationship happened in the most natural way.

I met her for the second time on a bus, on my way to meet my best friend at the movies. I remember waiting for the bus with some impatience. I remember it stopping and the door opening and the three steps I took to get in. I remember the driver with his hand on the handle that opens and closes the door. I remember the door closing behind me as I paid my fare and turning my body to find a free seat on the back of the bus. And then, all I remember were her black eyes on mine. An explosion expanded within me, starting below my belly button, diluted once it hit my chest; my legs lost their strength, my hands began to sweat, and I'm pretty sure my face gained some color. Luna was alone in her row, sitting by the window as though she was waiting for me the whole time. The sun hitting the bus bathed her, making her matte cinnamon skin glow with a dreamlike light. Her black hair fell in waves to her shoulders, framing a face where her smile didn't seem that of a simple human being but that of an angelic one.

I still don't know when my feet took me to her. I stood next to her seat, rapt by her presence, and asked her the stupid question of the day, "Is this seat taken?" She smiled and shook her head. If at that point I was not in love with her, I certainly was when I saw the dimples on her cheeks when she smiled.

Even today I don't understand how I managed to have a normal conversation with her. I've never been so nervous in my life before or after that moment.

The first thing I ever did for a woman was ditch my best friend that afternoon to be with Luna in the public library. The library was not remotely close to being one of my favorite places to spend my free time, but there are moments in life when you have to be willing to do something if the reward in the end is invaluable.

Luna and I were together the whole afternoon. We only spent one hour in the library because she couldn't focus on her homework. The rest of the time we spent walking directionless, going into stores where we tried clothes on for each other's amusement. It was an exceptional afternoon, crowned with a couple of ice cream cones I bought at a stand outside the city park entrance. In the park, we sat on a bench to talk until it was too late to prolong our escapade. On our way back to the bus station – walking slowly — I took a deep breath to give myself the courage I needed, then I took her hand. It was the first hand I held in my life.

The return trip should have lasted about thirty minutes or so, but I was so lost in my happiness that the journey seemed to last only five minutes. I wanted to continue on the road with her, pass by my neighborhood, and accompany her to the door of her house; I didn't give a damn if that meant that I would have to walk five miles to get home. She saw the struggle on my face and told me she wanted to see me again; she gave me her phone number, kissed me on the lips, and said we were dating. That night I went to bed with a smile I couldn't remove from my face for more than a week.

"Can you believe that happened almost twenty years ago?" I said.

"Time has passed so quickly, we're old people now," she said as though she was some ancient creature when she was actually at the peak of her beauty. The tall and squalid teenager I met was long gone; in her place was now an elegant, sophisticated woman that had kept the same smile and dimples of the teenager I loved.

"What's up?" she said.

"Nothing," I said. "I just don't know how I didn't recognize you at first glance when you really haven't changed at all. You're still the same girl I met on the bus back then — only prettier."

"And you're still the same flatterer," she said, laughing softly.

"We've talked a lot about the past. Tell me what's happened since we broke up," I asked. She shrugged, disregarding her possible answer, but the truth is that her life had been interesting. When her father decided to expatriate the whole family from Honduras, Luna was just fifteen. The last time I saw her was during her birthday party, which was a farewell to all her friends. Then, she boarded an airplane that took her away from me.

"When we first moved to the country, we lived in San Antonio," she said, "in the middle of a community of Mexicans. Those were difficult months because adapting to a new culture is never easy, as you may know, especially if you're a teenager and have no friends to share your feelings with. At the beginning it was mainly hard for my dad. He had to work a lot and went out of the state a lot too."

"Yeah, I know the drill."

"Luckily, he found a steady job in a construction company in Dayton, Ohio. So, we moved again. I liked Ohio a lot more than Texas, and it was there where I learned to speak English."

"What about the boys?"

She smiled that smile that had so many hearts. "What about the boys?"

"Did you forget about me easily?"

"Not really. I had short-lived crushes on some boys at school, but never had the chemistry to get into an actual relationship with any of them. That was the reason I never gave away my virginity to any of them. I guess in some part of my brain I was reserving that part of myself for you."

"Really?"

"Yeah. But one day I realized I was one of the few virgins in the entire school, and that was kinda lame. I mean, I was giving sex more importance than it really deserved. I ended up having it for the first time with the most random guy I could find a week before leaving town for college. It was good, but not the life-changing experience everyone made me believe."

Her greatest dream since she'd moved to American was to live in New York City — it was unimportant if it was the Bronx, Brooklyn, or Queens; although, her final aspiration was to live in Manhattan. With that goal in mind, she had sent her college application to study business at Columbia and NYU. The rejection letter from Columbia hurt, but the smile at her acceptance from NYU for the next fall was enough. There, she met the man she considered her second boyfriend — a guy from Seattle, who was fascinated by Luna's beauty.

"But he was too damn jealous and possessive," she told me. "I'm a woman with a high sense of independence. I'm willing to fight tooth and nail for it if needed. And he couldn't deal with that. The next time I started dated someone, I put all my cards on the table. I'm a woman who knows what I want. But none of them ever knew how to deal with the freedom I gave them and expected in return."

"Did you only date Americans?"

"No. I dated Latinos too, but they're the worst," she said.

"Come on, we can't all be so bad. Surely you never dated a Honduran."

"My husband is Honduran," she said quite naturally. I could hear inside me how my rising expectations were crushed. "He's the only one who knows how to deal with me."

"You're married?" I said in my best casual voice, trying to recover from the news.

"Yeah, for two years now," she said. The husband was a Sampedran, a man ten years older than her. She met him when the law firm she works for hired his company to do the remodeling of the new floor they had rented due to a planned extension. At first, she didn't pay him the slightest attention, but one day the guy had the nerves to approach her office with no other excuse than to ask her out. She accepted because he made her laugh after he introduced himself – his name was Andrés. They were both from the same state in Honduras and Luna always felt an almost child-like nostalgia when she met people from her country.

On that first date, he showed her how relaxed and funny he was. Most importantly, he made the conversation about her, by asking her many questions about her life, which worked perfectly because Luna always found pleasure in being the center of attention. They went out a few more times and he never pressed her in any way. From the first date, she expected him to invite her to his place so she could refuse the idea to see how committed he was to win her over, but the invitation never came and eventually it was Luna who ended up inviting Andrés to her apartment.

Things happened so naturally that one day Luna found herself thinking she hadn't even put her cards on the table. A short time later, Andrés got on one knee and asked the million-dollar question. She did not respond immediately; she needed to meditate on the whole situation and its outcome. She didn't love him — she knew perfectly well what love was — but she did like him enough to learn how to love him in time. He made her feel good and safe. He made her laugh — which was more than many of her friends had in their marriages—and the sex was good. He had made it clear with actions that he was a good man, and she knew that it was more than unlikely that she would find a good man in a city like New York.

"The relationship is good," she said, "the life together is good, and we both want the same things, for now."

Outside, the city kept breathing as it always did and inside the cafe people began to leave. "We never have big fights," she said and smiled. "However, if I'm honest with you, Andy lets me get away with things all the time. I'm master and commander in our marriage." She laughed with the musical laughter I remembered from so long ago. "But enough about me, tell me about you, what happened to you and —" The ringtone of her cell phone interrupted her question. She answers the call and I wince a bit at the high-pitch of her friends' voices. The conversation lasted less than a minute.

"Time flies," Luna said as she put the cellphone back into her purse. "I'm sorry I have to go, but I don't want to end our conversation this way. Can you give me your phone number?"

I gave it to her without thinking twice.

We stood up to hug and say goodbye; she kissed me on the cheek before leaving the cafe. I watched her walk away and disappear from my sight while I stood in front of the cashier, waiting for the girl on the other side of the counter to charge my bill. As I watched her struggling with the computer software — and blushing with embarrassment in the process — my mind reviewed the events that developed in the last hours.

I still couldn't believe that the woman I had had my date with before Luna found me hadn't laughed at the pineapple joke. The date with her had been exceptional until the moment I told the joke. Hell, if I hadn't told the stupid joke, maybe the date with her would still have been going on and I wouldn't have seen Luna. If I was reading the signs correctly, then the joke put something better in front of me, something that could promise better things. If the signs were correct — and I thought they were — Luna and I were destined to meet that night. She was married, yes, but in all the time we talked she never mentioned her husband in depth nor did she let me know how much she loved him. No, all the time we talked it was about us and our relationship when we were teens. I was her first boyfriend and that had to count for something.

I paid for the drinks and left the cafe. Standing alone in front of the window, I couldn't help but think how pathetic it was for me to have shared the night with two beautiful women and not ended it with either of them in my apartment. I started walking towards the corner where Luna and I met, when we almost collided with each other.

"Good," she said, almost breathless. "I thought you were gone."

I don't exaggerate when I say that an irresistible desire to kneel and shout thanks to God for the new opportunity almost overcame me.

"Look," she continued, "I'm going to a friend's birthday party, and I know perfectly well that I'm going to die of boredom in that place with the pretentious idiots who are her friends. I know you may have plans and stuff for the rest of the night, but would you like to come with me?"

"So I can die of boredom by your side?" I said. She laughed.

"I didn't want it to be so obvious, but yes," she said, giving me one of those heartwarming smiles. I gave her my arm and she held onto it, amused.

There's this thing that happens in movies all the time when two lovers find each other: they would walk aimlessly, spellbound with each other, perhaps only aware of the city and its fascinating energy as their senses rebuild that physical trust they once knew. As we walked to her friend's party I felt as if trapped in déjà vu, fighting this unbearable urge to hold her hand in mine the entire time, unable to keep my cool because I couldn't believe my eyes.

She was actually there with me, the sound of her voice was coming to my ears, the overwhelming quality of her beauty was filling my retinas, the smell of her perfume was getting me high, altering my brain chemistry.

I needed to record everything about this night: the people walking and talking around us, minding their business as we minded our own, the noise of the traffic going up and down the street, the horns of countless cars honking into the void of the night, the brownstones' windows lit in yellows and whites, matching with the lights illuminating our path filled with shadows created by the trees decorating in green the colorless sidewalks of good old New York. I needed to save everything in my memory: the yellow cabs and their angry drivers, the guy jogging with his head covered by huge headphones completely lost within himself, the girl walking in front of us holding her phone before her to take a selfie she would later post on Instagram, the group of friends gathered in front of the bar on the other side of the street engaged in conversation and chain-smoking, and the fact that these four specific details of the night took place when her hand brushed mine during our walk.

We arrived at a brownstone building looking exactly like the rest of the buildings on the street. Luna directed me through the stairs up to the third floor and to the door where the laughter and the noise of conversations came from. We entered the apartment with my mind working as fast as it could, trying to crack the meaning of my presence in that place. Why did Luna come back for me when the easiest thing to do would've been to meet again another day when we had more time to catch up? Even as a teenager with wild hormones running through my body, I had tried not to create false expectations related to women. I kept doing the same as an adult, but all the signs were there, and they told me that Luna was as hooked on me as I was with her. I didn't want to overthink her motives; I didn't need to know them, as to be there with her was more than enough. I was her first love, and she could never forget me despite all the time that had elapsed.

Sure, she was married. She might even be happily married, but a woman's heart is filled with contradictions. I decided to stop thinking about it and let go of questions that would only ruin the fun.

Luckily, the party's atmosphere was relaxed and everyone seemed to be having a good time. The music was good and the drinks were strong. Luna's friends cornered us and began shooting so many questions. They were morbidly curious about my history with Luna. They smiled the whole time we told them and laughed like hyenas when I told them about my failed date and the joke that caused the reunion with Luna.

"It's the work of destiny," one of them said seriously.

Luna laughed at the remark, but inside I hoped it was true. They managed to get from me — in a clever way — personal information that I would only have liked to share with Luna in the privacy of my bed. I told them my reasons for moving to the United States, and how those reasons ceased to be important when my girlfriend and I broke up. I'd then decided to keep it simple and hopped from bed to bed- women in Houston, to New Orleans then Jacksonville, and finally Brooklyn.

"And you've been single all this time?" another one asked, looking at me with calculating eyes. I said no. To lie was pointless, especially because I didn't care much about that part of my life. "In Jacksonville, I married a Cuban woman who found it extremely exciting to sleep with other men even while married. I mean, the marriage itself was a mere joke. We were very good friends and she just wanted an excuse to avoid getting serious with the different men she dated and who ended up falling in love with her. Every time one of them wanted to take things to the next level, she told them that she loved me, that I gave meaning to her life, and she would never break my heart." Luna and her friends were fascinated with the story and didn't blink as they listened to me. "We were more roommates than husband and wife. We both were dating different people at the same time; sometimes we even sat at the kitchen table to have breakfast together with our lovers.

Sometimes we had seasons in which neither of us were in the mood for other people, and we put our marriage vows into practice."

"So you guys did have sex?!" said Luna.

"Yeah, but at the end of the day it was only sex. Everything happened naturally and usually the initiative was hers."

"I don't know if I'd be capable of doing something like that," Luna said.

"If you can detach yourself from the sense of possession — which is what leads to jealousy and the given suffering — and you decide that what you want is to have fun, then everything is possible," I said. "Eventually, she met a man she fell in love with, and we got divorced. She stayed in Jacksonville, and I came to try my luck here in New York. We're still good friends — just from a distance."

Luna received a new phone call and walked away from us. I saw her leave the room through an open door onto the balcony. When I finally satisfied her friends' curiosity, they left me alone. I went after her and found her contemplating the beauty of the city at night. I stood by her side.

"I still can't believe you're here," she said, smiling.

It's now or never, I thought. I circled her waist with my left arm and brought her to me to kiss her. When my mouth searched for hers, it found her open palm. I froze.

"What are you doing?" she asked in a tone that left no room for doubt. "What the fuck! Did you forget that I'm married?"

I was stunned, frozen like a statue, disoriented by my own stupidity. "I'm sorry," I babbled. "I got confused with the signs you were sending me."

"Signs? What are you, still fifteen?" she said. She turned away from me with her face red and went back into the apartment, furious.

Did I stand there — with the city as background — thinking on how I made a big fool of myself? Hell no. Of course not. The human being will never be exempt from committing errors in judgment — men above all; we are very fucking stupid, especially when it comes to things of the heart.

The next time we met was exactly four months later on the 1 Line. I got on it at Dyckman Street that Thursday afternoon on my way to the Bronx. I saw her at the end of the car. It was impossible to overlook her, to ignore her shiny black hair tied in a ponytail, her perfect features exposed to the admiration of anyone who had eyes. I waited for her reaction as she saw me. God, she looked as gorgeous as she did that last Thursday night lost in time. The effect she had on me remained the same.

I was still standing in the car when the train began its crawl; she took her briefcase from the seat and put it on her lap, leaving the space next to her free. It took me ten steps to reach her. I sat next to her without saying a single word, with nothing but a smile on my face; she smiled weakly as well. Mine said, "I knew we would meet again" and hers said, "I can't believe this is happening." I enjoyed just being in her presence, wondering if I should touch her hand. It was right there within my grasp. So I did. She just laughed and shook her head.

"Don't tell me I'm misreading this," I said.

She shrugged and squeezed my hand before letting it go. Maybe the only choice she had was to let go.

About Christian H. Morales

Christian H. Morales is a Honduran living in La Vergne, Tennessee, since 2019. He moved to the United States to pursue a career as a published author. When he's not working in construction he's in his apartment trying to keep up with his writing goals and reading challenge. His stories have been published in Maudlin House, Latine Lit and Malarkey Books.

Must Be Some Witches in the Atmosphere

Shelli Cornelison

From my vantage point at the intersection, I can see past the parking barricades along Seaside Boulevard and out across the whitecaps. Water's been choppy ever since the hurricane. People haven't calmed yet either. The sun clings to the horizon in all its gilded tangerine splendor, but another night's about to fall. There is no escaping it. Power has been restored to most of the island, thank Goddess. And people are finding their senses of humor again, as evidenced by the new graffiti painted on the boarded-up windows of a restaurant facing the Gulf: *Free Buffet On The Roof! Oysters On The Half Shingle!* Laughter is a balm in times like this.

But the nights are still tenuous. Nerves are shot. Some memories have become distorted, either exaggerated or minimized, but others don't falter, playing on a loop in technicolor terror. Grief is chaotic, everybody processing their own shit in their own way. All of us are grieving something.

The light turns green, but my knuckles are white on the steering wheel, my foot like a brick on the brake. My eyes fixate on the dancing vortex of water rising up from the surface. This one's miles out. I should move my foot to the accelerator, but there's no one behind me, anyway, so I sit and watch the waterspout expand. They spin up every day now. Usually small, they form quickly, linger over the water long enough to spike anxieties, and then dissipate. Not-so-gentle reminders, proof that anything can happen, and even the experts are really just making educated guesses. Mother Nature does what she wants.

As if a witch should need reminding of that.

I am in no shape to make important decisions right now, but I ease my foot off the brake and head for the west end, toward the two-hundred-year-old abandoned pirate stronghold that later served as a military fort. Now, it's nothing more than Blade Island's crumbling figurehead — unless you're a local witch. To us, Fort Meachum is the covenstead.

The funnel continues to churn the waves in my side mirror. If I didn't know better, I'd swear it was chasing me.

The majority of our sisters are already inside when I pull through the heavy, rust-clad iron gates. No traffic out here, not only because the hurricane destroyed most of the vacation McMansions on stilts, but because the elders will have warded the area, ensuring no non-witches can venture into our domain while we gather. When we are in the fort, our sacred temple in the ruins, Blade Coven is free to be. Blessed be for that.

A lone howl undulates on the humid evening currents, greeting me as I step out of my car. The wolves are exiting their rampart cave to stand sentry for us. *If only one had been present for Maelynne at the herb shop, we wouldn't be mourning our most beloved high priestess. Even witches aren't invincible.*

In a fair and just world, we'd be able to take the wolves into town, instill them at doorways in Shipyard Square to protect all the brave merchants — witches and non-witches alike — who are trying to bring back the tourists as soon as possible. The island depends on tourism, and the media's exaggerated coverage of our "post-storm violent crime sprees" isn't helping. But even with desperation driving some people to inhumane acts, we must harbor the wolves here, keep them a secret.

A pack of wolves would be perceived as a grave threat to tourism. They'd be relocated, forced to live in some fenced-off reserve, or separated and sent to zoos.

Or worse.

I lay my hand on the hood of my best friend's car as I walk past it. It's cool, letting me know Georgie's been here a while, probably came out early to help prepare, like I should have done. One deep inhale and a slow, measured exhale. That's all I allow myself before I step inside. Anything more and I may shatter where I stand. Better to keep moving, one foot in front of the other.

The only person I've seen in the week since Maelynne's death is Georgie, but my eyes find Odelle the moment I enter. Even in the uplifting glow of so much flickering candlelight, sorrow weighs on her strong features like an anchor. Her silk headwrap is mermaid print, the one that had been Maelynne's favorite. They are not the fair curvaceous sirens that beckon to tourists from coffee mugs and wine glasses in every gift shop on the island. These are fierce mermaids with sinewy biceps, sharp fangs, forked tongues, tresses of sea serpents, and eyes of emerald flames. More beautiful still.

It guts me to see our elders suffering as they draw strength from deeper realms to staunch the pain scraping at their marrow. Odelle most of all. Her regal warmth and sage generosity all encased in raw granite just to get through this night. Her wife, Yvonne, is by her side, but she is faring no better. They are both imposing women, in body and personality, but they seem smaller than before.

Yvonne's loose dark curls that once framed her face now obscure it. Odelle's square shoulders appear rounded, their commanding sharpness weathered away. I tell myself it's good that they have each other, but even as I think it, I know all they can do is share the pain, not erase it.

We take our seats, face the head table where the Elder Quad sits, an empty chair in the middle that should be occupied by our fallen high priestess. Staring at that stark empty space, there is no room left for fantasy, no more hoping that maybe there had been some terrible mistake.

Maelynne is gone. But the coven must go on, and for that, we need a new high priestess.

Yvonne and Odelle light each other's candles, as is their tradition. At the other end of the table, Wren and Alecia light their own. The opening wind blows through the roofless chamber, whistling through cracks in these vine-covered stone walls, signifying Goddess has blessed our gathering.

Then the wick on Maelynne's candle lights of its own accord, and my dam bursts. It is so unexpected: the sharp, blackened hardness of her absence now suddenly aflame. I am not alone. Tears begin to fall from every witch in the fort.

Maelynne's soft strength was unique—her wide blue eyes and brilliant smile gave the illusion of a small, sweet southern belle, but she was a force to be reckoned with. There wasn't an herb she didn't know every use for, not a hurting heart she couldn't comfort, but also not a bad intention she couldn't recognize from a mile away.

And she was a powerful witch, who could and would protect those she loved, or even a perfect stranger if they were in need. But with all that strength and knowledge, she was still no match for a bullet fired so quickly, so unexpectedly.

Georgie squeezes my hand, and I am genuinely thankful to have her here. I am grateful for all of us who are still here, no matter how difficult the choices that lie ahead. To say we've been through worse as a coven would be an overstatement, but we have survived horrific things in the past. Together is how we get through this.

When the worst comes, we go it as one. We are sisters forever, come what may. The teachings of my initiation come back unbidden, or maybe my agony has called forth these mantras. I need to trust in them now more than ever. I am trying.

My faith is fortified when the decision is unanimous. Of course, Odelle should step into the role. She could have been high priestess ten years ago, but she deferred to Maelynne, said her gentle spirit was what we most needed after the betrayal of our former high priestess, Adeena, a reckless, deceitful witch, who put herself before the coven. Her selfishness was not behavior befitting a member of Blade Coven, but taking a man's life was an unforgivable offense. We may exact revenge from time to time, but we don't play Goddess. Adeena's demise was sanctioned, a necessary sacrifice to protect our ways, to save our sisterhood.

Odelle graciously accepts the appointment, and so it begins. Like the island around us, the coven will recover. All in good time.

As we leave, we toss fresh meat to the wolves in thanks for their protection and as consolation for having kept them from roaming free to hunt tonight. "Feast well," I say in reverence. The guardians in the coven will make it up to the pack with extra time outside the fort in the coming week. Even a hurricane couldn't decimate the feral hog population. Not to mention the nutria are multiplying like mad with so few people around to kill them. The wolves will feast well for some time to come. And the sooner they're back to the natural order of obtaining their own food, the better for us all.

It is easier to protect the pack outside the fort right now with the west end laid bare, looking more like a war zone than a vacation haven, but the rebuilding will begin soon down here, now that the main parts of the island are starting to reopen. Locals get taken care of first. The part-time residents who own the vacation homes like to think they're locals, but they will always be tourists to us. And neither the locals nor the part-timers can be trusted not to hurt our wolves, so their hunts will go back into stealth mode soon, courtesy of the powerful coven who loves them.

Georgie and I catch up to Brielle and Mia outside. Every

witch has flown home for this. They tell us flights are still cheap, three months after the storm. The rest of the country probably thinks we're all still eating cold canned goods in the dark. Media doesn't stick around to chronicle the recovery, just get in and film the initial devastation, and get out, move on to the next disaster.

All the PR to bring back the tourists' dollars will be up to the island. "Hey," I say. "How about we skip all the rejoicing around a bonfire tonight and go grab a glass of wine somewhere? The Highlander is open."

"Sounds good to me," Georgie says as Brielle nods.

"Make mine tequila," Mia says.

My shoulders melt a little. I need this. I may need tequila, too.

No one orders wine. We are all in for tapas and tequila flights.

"Can I swap the mezcal for another reposado on my flight?" I ask.

"The bartender really hates making subs on flights," the waitress says, balking slightly at me.

My jaw locks and my eye twitches. "Maybe the bartender should be glad he has customers right now and do what-the-hell-ever I ask him to."

Georgie intervenes. "Let it go, Charlotte. I'll take your mezcal. You can have my reposado. It's fine."

She knows I hate when she uses my full name, and I know she only does it when I need to be reined in. I know this, but I still want to stand my ground. "It's not like I asked for another añejo!"

"Char, it's all good," Brielle says.

"Mezcal doesn't even belong on a tequila flight." I'm not letting this one go. I'm right, dammit.

Mia laughs. "Girl, you're just looking for a fight tonight. We're all pissed off at the world right now. It's not the waitress's fault. Not the bartender's either."

We toast when our flights arrive. Blancos up, cheers to bad

bitches and good witches, and down the hatch. I can already tell I'm going to need a second flight. And I'm going to argue about the mezcal all over again. "So, I saw the biggest damn waterspout I've ever seen in my life today," I say. "Off Magellan Park."

"You know they act up after a big storm," Brielle says. "There was a hell of a lightning show over the canals as we were driving in."

"Yeah," Georgie says. "Lightning started another marsh fire last night. The Sabo Mansion took a strike, too. Liam got called out."

"Out of your bed?" Mia teases.

"Unfortunately for me." Georgie makes the swap in our flights before I can complain again.

"People are spooked, saying it's never been like this before," I say. "What if these elementals don't settle on their own? This hasn't happened in our lifetime."

"They will," Brielle says. "It takes time."

"But if they don't? The old stories aren't good."

Mia flags the waitress and nods her head toward me. "She's going to need another round." Then she turns to me and demands my keys. I hand them over and shout after the waitress. "No mezcal!"

Brielle drags a tortilla chip through the guac. "The Blade's been spared for years. This island was due for a big hurricane, but they upset everything. You know that. We are not going to have to wage war with any rogue elements. This is all normal."

"It sure doesn't feel normal." My second flight hits the table, and I realize there is no mezcal. I look to the bartender and he winks. It may be the first time I've smiled in a week. There's a glimmer in his narrowed dark eyes, and a hunger evident in his smirk. His demeanor is cocky, the attitude of a hot guy whose kindness has an ulterior motive. And I should hate that more than I do, which is not at all. A stranger could be good for me right about now, possibly better than the familiar. Less complicated, anyway.

Georgie's cousin Reed comes in, all badge and swagger. He pulls a chair over, sits down next to me, and shoots the añejo from my fresh flight. *He'll pay for that later.* "I hope you're off duty, officer."

"Trust me, I'm functioning on sheer adrenaline at this point. It would take more than one shot to affect me." His hand brushes my knee under the table.

Reed hangs out with us for a while, basically until he's eaten all our ceviche and calamari. None of the ugly stories about what he's seeing on the job gets shared with us, just the funny ones. Reed's always good for a laugh, and he drops enough money on the table to cover more than half our total bill before he leaves. "Y'all be safe," he says. "There's a lot of weird shit happening out there. Head home soon, okay?"

We promise. And then we order more food.

The rising sun breaks through my bedroom blinds like a machete to my skull. My mouth tastes like I ate a bowl of used cat litter and fermented seaweed for a midnight snack. Stumbling to the shower, I trip over one of my shoes. Won't even hazard a guess where the other one might be. Being pummeled by hot water is the only thing that could possibly make me feel human again. Followed by a barrel of coffee. And a boatload of greasy carbs.

Oh, sweet Mother, since when does my shampoo smell like cotton candy? I am not going to be sick. I am not going to be sick. I am not going to be sick.

After fifteen minutes of lying spread eagle in my towel on my bed with the ceiling fan on high, I am delusional enough to believe I can walk down the hall without holding onto the wall for support. My compromised equilibrium disabuses me of that fantasy right quick. If only we were the type of witches Hollywood shows the world, I'd probably have some magic to cure myself. Each of our magic is individual and distinct, and mine doesn't include healing.

Communicating with ghosts isn't much help with a hangover, unless one with a depth of herbal knowledge chooses to show up and guide me.

Sitting on the edge of my bed, I let my eyes scan the room, wondering if now that I've thought of her and expressed my need, Maelynne might appear to me. But no, it's too soon. I hope she'll come to me if I ever really need her, but until it happens, I have no reason to believe I'll ever see her again. Hope is a powerful thing though.

I spot my keys that Mia used as a paperweight for the note she left on top of my coffee pot:

Hydrate, babe. Water first. Coffee later. This too shall pass.

My flight leaves at noon. I'm sure you'll still be passed out, but keep me posted on the atmospheric activity. Not convinced Brielle is right about it being normal.

Summon me if need be.

Rifling through my tea chest, Maelynne's labels look like sacred texts now. If she were here, she'd mix up a combination of fennel and chamomile, extolling the virtues of each for an upset stomach, and then she'd scold me for being out of dandelion. I can hear her now . . .

"Well, at least you've got ginger. Sugar, the liver is resilient, but yours is gonna need a little help today. Sip on this until it's gone. Here, wear this citrine pendant. And the matching earrings. Better

put some in your pockets, too. Rub a little of this rosemary oil on your wrists."

By the time she was done, I'd smell like an herb garden and be so weighed down in crystals no waterspout could take me. Shit, it hurts to smile.

My worn couch cushions sink just enough to cradle my hips and keep me from falling over sideways, which is appreciated since my core muscles are too weak from heaving to do the job, and I really need to drink this tea. The first sip burns my tongue as I point the remote at the TV.

A local weatherman materializes on the screen. His head cocks to the right as he stares at the sky. "Lots of boiling and convection up there today, folks. We may be verging on a rare phenomenon." The sky roils. Puffy white cartoon-like clouds succumb to the dark gray blanket rolling over them. Whipping like a tablecloth yanked by a magician, the dark gray rapidly recedes to reveal an unfurling lighter gray underneath. The sequence repeats. It's as if the sky is mimicking the tide, but in triple time. A waterspout forms to the left of the screen. No one on the scene sees it yet. They are all focused on the magic show above.

The anchor in the studio interrupts to say, "Well, Dan, I guess even the best meteorology school in the nation couldn't prepare you for encountering skies like this in real life."

"Actually, Meaghan, I am quite prepared," Dan says, launching into a babbling diatribe about whatever rare weather occurrence he is trying to convince himself he's looking at. I change the channel before Meaghan accidentally steps on his balls again.

My phone lights up with a text. It's Georgie:

Brunch. Hash Hut. Meet me there at 10.

All I want to do is drink this tea and go back to bed. Instead, I take a gulp and respond:

10:30. Best I can do. See you soon.

The skies are still menacing when I park at Shipyard Square. I keep my eyes on them as I walk down the pier to Hash Hut. Georgie waves from a table on the deck. Second level, of course. *I know she asked to sit upstairs just to torture me. I'd kill her if I had the strength.*

"I ordered you coffee," she says. "Figured you'd need it. You look better than I expected."

"Thanks to Maelynne's teas. I still feel like shit, just not as bad as before."

"Yeah, you still look like shit, too, just not as bad as I expected."

Best friends are fun. I should get three more. When the coffee comes, I ask for a basket of biscuits. The waitress is young, maybe sixteen. She says she's only running drinks, not taking orders. I slide a ten across the table. "Can I get those biscuits now?"

"Yes, ma'am." She pockets the money and scurries off.

"When did I become a ma'am?" The coffee scalds my already burnt tongue.

Georgie stirs sugar into her cup, clockwise, as she speaks. "I'm pretty sure you were born one."

She is not a kitchen witch, but we've all picked up habits from Yvonne over the years. If Yvonne catches us stirring counter-clockwise, she will ask what exactly we are trying to banish. I can think of a few things we should be trying to reject right now, but stirring widdershins wouldn't get the job done. The sky clears, lets the sun beat down on us, but I know it won't last. Agitated elementals have never drifted away politely. "Did you invite me to brunch so you could be mean to me?"

"No. That's just a bonus. I needed to get out of the house. Go somewhere I could make some noise. Liam's sleeping. He got called out again last night."

"When are you going to tell people you're living together?"

"We are not living together. It's temporary. My condo is

almost ready for me to move back in. I ordered wallpaper yesterday. Painters come on Wednesday."

"Yeah, we'll see." The biscuits arrive and I snag one before the basket meets the tabletop. "How many fires is Liam investigating now?"

"A lot. The cops think we've got an arsonist. They can't believe this many fires have occurred naturally."

"What does Liam think?"

"He doesn't give up much about his work."

"Aw, secrets aren't good for a relationship."

"Well, I'm keeping a pretty damn big one from him."

"You have no choice in that. It's the burden of being a witch in a relationship with a non-magical man." I shove the basket toward her. "Have a biscuit while they're still warm. And before I eat them all."

"He's plenty magical, thank you very much. Just in very non-witchy ways." She winks, and lightning cracks from the clear blue sky. The flash looks more like a wall than a bolt. It's blinding.

Someone yells from the back of the deck. "That hit a building on campus!"

They might be right. The bridge to Blade Junior College is visible from here, and that strike definitely hit something. Classes were all canceled after the hurricane. Too many buildings damaged. And now this. At least there isn't anyone in the dorms. But there are people working out there to get the buildings repaired and ready for fall.

I lay my hand over the moonstone in the silver cuff on my left wrist, pray for anyone harmed and all who are called to render aid. Sirens fill the air. Here we go again. This one in broad daylight. The strikes that ignited the marshes and the historic mansion all happened overnight.

"You up for going to see Yvonne and Odelle after we eat?" I ask.

"Yeah. It's time."

"The House of Love is looking good," Georgie says as we pull up to Yvonne and Odelle's Victorian. There is no sign on the house proclaiming its name, but we know it as a place of unconditional love for true witches with true hearts.

"Between Odelle's influence and Yvonne's baked goods, I don't think we have to wonder how they got so many contractors on the job," I say.

The first floor flooded, had to be gutted to the drywall, but the interior has all been restored and most of the exterior is done, too. You'd never know the island had even suffered a hurricane if not for the unnatural shifting of the skies happening as we walk to the front door.

Yvonne opens the door to greet us before we have a chance to knock. "Well, if it isn't the most glamorous witches in town." She takes a step back, surveys me separately. "Oh, honey. Rough night last night?"

"Thanks for noticing." I step into her outstretched arms and let her hug me.

"Oh, it's just a little tell-tale puffiness around the eyes. You're still gorgeous." She releases me to embrace Georgie. "Odelle is in a reading right now, but she should be done soon. Y'all come in, keep me company in the kitchen."

Odelle's readings are done in a separate building around back. There is no sign on it either, but word of mouth is all the advertising she has ever needed. She's a gifted medium, even called in to help law enforcement sometimes. I'm afraid of what she might share with us today, but we can't keep tiptoeing around the facts.

Yvonne passes us savory scones made with fresh herbs from her garden and smoked cheddar. I'm beyond full from brunch, but I would never say no to her offerings. Thunder rolls in the distance. Through the window over the kitchen sink, I watch a spontaneous, swirling gust strip wild rosebuds from vines that have only just begun to recover. Odelle flings open the door to her office, a commanding presence with her caftan whipping around her legs. She lifts her eyes to the skies and shakes her head. As she lowers her gaze, she spots us through the kitchen window. She retreats and closes the door, returns to her customer, but she will come into the house soon enough.

And then there will be no more hiding, no rationalizing or wishing away what we've known all along: the storm is not over. It has left behind the equivalent of an emotional echo, like a specter with no ability to communicate, just a visual replay of horror, except agitated elementals left unchecked can grow stronger and wreak new devastation. We have to stop them, deplete their energy before they go too far.

I squint at the blue door to Odelle's reading cottage, expecting to see my brother Mason, to beckon him, call upon him to quell my fears the way I've been able to do for years now. He always reassures me that I can do hard things. But it isn't the ghost of Mason who comes forth. It is Adeena, our false priestess felled by Maelynne ten years ago.

She has never appeared to me before, and of all the places she should not be, outside Odelle's door is at the top of the list. Her mouth is open as if she is screaming, but whether in pain or anger, I cannot tell. The echo of Adeena is not welcome. Not here, not anywhere on Blade Island. But if this image of her is merely an emotional echo, why would she appear here instead of at the fort where her life force was extinguished? Perhaps what I'm seeing is more.

What if it's Adeena's spirit keeping the elementals restless, giving them strength, empowering them to become more than the echo of a storm? If they are feeding off Adeena's vengeance, we may be in for a bigger battle than I imagined. Shit. I picked the wrong day to be this hungover.

The sweep of Odelle's cottage door reopening explodes Adeena's specter into thousands of pixels, and then merely a suspended spiral of dust until the wind takes her completely, clearing the way for Odelle's customer to step onto the pavers that lead around the side of the house.

Odelle lingers in front of her blue door, raises her arms and tilts her head back, licks at the air as if to taste what bitterness remains. And then her deep throaty laughter fills the yard. Her head hinges forward, comes back to center. She purses her lips and blows dismissively, as if she is dispelling nothing more than a nuisance, a fly or a cluster of gnats. There was no love lost between her and Adeena by the end, and Odelle is indeed powerful enough to send such a taunting reminder. I only hope we are strong enough to back her up when the moment of truth comes.

Adeena was nothing if not calculating while alive, and her spirit is obviously intelligent enough not to have shown itself until our numbers were diminished. I am convinced we are definitely dealing with more than an echo of her wickedness.

All our far-flung witches will return to The Blade anytime we need them, and some can return quickly if summoned. Those like Mia possess the power of transmutation, or teleportation, but most still rely on traditional modes of transportation and wouldn't be able to appear so suddenly. Adeena knows this, and she surely knows Maelynne is gone now as well.

Odelle steps into the kitchen, her eyes wide and wild. "What do we do first?" Georgie asks.

"Head west, young witches, head west."

Fort Meachum. We are strongest on our sacred ground. "Should we summon Mia and the others who could get here quickly?"

Odelle waves my question away with the scone in her hand. "Already taken care of, baby girl." She takes a bite with a smile on her face, chews deliberately. The resolve in Yvonne's expression as she calmly sips from her teacup bolsters my courage. The two of them have squared off with evil before. Our elders will guide us. We will go it as one. And we will prevail. We have to.

The sky rages angrier the closer we get to the fort. Blue lightning flashes over an untamed stretch of marshland to the right and over the Gulf to our left. These waves are unprecedented for the Texas coast, hurricane high. But no surfers' paradise — the surface is all erratic chop, not to mention the ball lightning illuminating a cluster of water spouts like strobing bulbs, like a giant hand is hurling fistfuls of electricity at us. It only makes sense that Adeena would punctuate her unwelcome return with bursts of flames. She did some of her worst work with pyrokinesis.

Weatherman Dan is probably on location somewhere on the island sharing irrelevant facts about barometric pressure and jet streams with viewers at home. Knowledge can feel like a level of control sometimes, but being able to define something and being able to control it are two totally different things.

Georgie is quiet in my passenger seat. I know she's preparing, focusing her energy. My nerves are raw and sizzling, my focus fragmented. I need to get it together, but that would be a whole lot easier if I knew exactly what we were heading into.

Lightning flashes across my windshield, a cloud-to-ground strike that I'm positive hit the road between my car and Odelle's in front of me. Was it meant as a warning, or intended to hit one of us and it missed? Odelle accelerates and I follow suit. Headlights close in behind me, more sisters of the coven answering the call. Blade witches on a mission.

Mia greets us when we enter the fort. "What took y'all so long?" Two other sisters have also teleported back to the covenstead from out of state. The three of them have released the wolves, and they are already in their usual guard positions, but this is no usual gathering. The pack senses it in the air. Their hackles are up, bristling with a heightened wariness, low growls emanating as they look to the volatile sky.

I squint and find Mason standing atop the crumbling walls, my brother looking down lovingly on us, another type of protector. But I can feel others. Okay, so it isn't only the living enemies of Adeena who will face her here tonight.

More spirits take form along the walls. I don't know these

faces but I know they are on our side, perhaps people Adeena wronged long before I joined the coven, before I knew I was a real witch, and long before I realized that not all who practice are good. It is comforting to have these extra forces joining us, regardless of their motives.

Odelle walks to the center of our temple, raises her hands to the sky and begins to pray to Goddess.

We all begin our own prayer rituals. The air heats up around us. As our voices rise and our energies coalesce, a gentle breeze begins to move between us. Goddess acknowledging and blessing our gathering, cooling the sweat on our skin.

A feeling of familiarity washes over me as if I have fought this entity before. I haven't in this lifetime, but I'm ready.

The clouds part to reveal a bright blue sky and, though we can't see the Gulf from here, the sounds of the crashing waves have ceased. Brilliant peace, the deceptive behavior of a charlatan from every angle. We all turn to face outward, our backs to the center, surrounding Odelle and watching for the first maneuver.

Lightning bolts ignite the marsh around the fort as if they've been flung to the earth by ten splayed fingers.

Georgie, Mia, Wren, and Alecia all concentrate their telekinesis to conjure waves, pulling them across the beach. They flood the marsh, so at least the fires don't have a chance to spread.

Odelle's deep laughter is carried on the strengthening breeze trapped inside the stone walls, circling us and filling the space with a hypnotic rhythm. We join hands and sway as one with the winds.

The ghosts atop the walls rise up, and then they, too, move along the perimeter of the enclosure, hovering overhead as they patrol, vigilant for signs of the witch who harmed them and eager to return the pain threefold.

Our chants and prayers mingle with Odelle's laughter and grow louder as our voices claim their echoes, become a multi-layered battle hymn. The wind whips, and overhead the gray blanket begins to spread, but all our hands go up, palms flat, denouncing it from every direction, and it dissipates.

Lightning bursts in the sky, feeding Odelle's anger. "Enough with the aerial theatrics! Show yourself!" She spins as she laughs again, her arms still raised high. Not a hint of fear about her. We continue to raise our voices in prayer around her.

Ghostly laughter mixes with Yvonne's lively guffaw, scoffing as it resounds. If there was one thing Adeena hated most in this world, it was for someone not to take her seriously, to blow her off, disrespect her. This will provoke her like nothing else, and if she shows herself as a result, it will be in a fury. I snicker, continue to sway. Soon, we are all daring her with our giggles.

Adeena's spirit shrieks as she descends. She hovers just inside the walls, outside our circle. "Let her in," Odelle commands. We release our hands, disperse enough to allow her to walk into the center, the echoes of our laughter still rimming the fort. The wolves move closer and tighten the circumference of their posts while the ghosts stare down at our current high priestess, facing the malevolent spirit of the one who deceived us all.

Another form takes shape next to Odelle: Maelynne, glowing as beautiful as ever, her blue eyes undaunted by death. "We meet again," she says to Adeena. She leaves unspoken the results of their last meeting in this very spot, the encounter that took Adeena out for good. Or so we thought.

Adeena backs away, quickly realizes she is retreating and freezes. She postures anew, but her weakness in the face of two such great witches reeks like a sack of rotten potatoes. The stench of her fear hangs in the air.

Had she not shown herself, not let her pride get the better of her and keep her from ignoring Odelle's challenge, we might never had known her true current state. But here she is in all her rotten glory, still powerful, but vulnerable.

My eyes search for Mason. *Please don't get involved. Please stay up there.* He smiles down at me. This is not his fight. He knows.

Odelle shakes her head. "I can smell your fear. We all can. Nasty, like your soul."

Sunlight glints off the bullet Maelynne rolls between her fingers. "Your natural abilities never were very strong, were they? Always needed to rely on something practical to get the job done."

"I'm stronger than ever," Adeena says. "You've seen the results. The water obeys me. Lightning is raw electricity at my command. I'll burn this whole fucking island when I'm ready."

Our palms all remain raised to the sky, our powers concerted in effort to prevent Adeena from controlling the elements.

"No," Maelynne says. "You have trespassed against Gaia this time, and she will not be fooled like the average witch. Besides, you just spoke your intention to destroy what she has created. I'm disappointed, Adeena. I truly am. You were so cunningly vindictive when you were alive. Death has made you stupid in your arrogance." Maelynne flicks the bullet and it travels at the velocity of one launched by a trigger. Adeena ducks it and we all laugh because Maelynne has stopped it mid-air several inches before it would've reached her.

Odelle tilts her head from side to side, cracks her neck. "You forget I've been to the other side. Seen your wretched fate. I don't know how you escaped, but I guarantee you're going back."

Adeena's voice cracks as she shouts a command. Nothing happens. At Odelle's nod, we all lower our hands. Adeena tries again. Still nothing.

Maelynne releases the bullet. It exits through Adeena's back. It's not particularly devastating to the physical manifestation of her, but her pride and ego were always larger than life, and it is the degradation that wrecks her. Another round of our laughter compounds it.

Odelle, on the other hand, stands imposing and formidable as she contemplates her next move. She appreciates the deliciousness of seeing Adeena humbled so mercilessly as much as any of us, but she has not come here to play cat and mouse games. She is our high priestess and it is her responsibility to protect the coven, to eradicate any legitimate threats. Adeena is currently cowering in shame, but if she is not fully dealt with, she could regain strength and try again, come back at another time when we are unsuspecting and exposed.

With a flick of her wrist, Odelle sends Adeena crashing into the wall. Her crouched body lifts up as if it's being pulled by a cable. I watch as Odelle's hand controls Adeena, lifting her above the walls. Odelle flings her out into the marsh. Lightning follows immediately, but Odelle's hands are at her sides now. She isn't the one controlling the elements. Goddess has intervened.

The last time I heard Adeena's screams, I was outside and she was standing below on this consecrated ground. The smell of her fear was nauseating earlier, but as she burns, it becomes even more intense.

Another wave crests above the fort, lingers majestically for a moment before it crashes and washes Adeena's ashes from the marsh, sweeps her out in a rush of saltwater, back to the deep. And whatever lies beyond or beneath. Wherever Odelle has visited and returned from to tell such awful tales. Exactly where Adeena belongs.

I greet the new day with no hangover, no malicious skies above, just newborn birds chirping incessantly outside my window. And the hum of water rushing through my pipes before the shower shuts off. I roll over and watch Reed walk out of my bathroom and saunter over to his duffle bag, his perfectly toned muscles all still flushed from the hot water.

"Hey babe," he says as he pulls up a t-shirt. "I forgot my razor so I used yours. You know you're supposed to change the blade in that thing, right?"

My phone buzzes. "It's your cousin," I say. "She wants to get brunch."

"Who can afford to go to brunch as often as she does? You tell her about us yet?"

"No. We've all been through a lot lately. I should let the dust settle before I spring this on her."

"The storm was almost four months ago, Char. People are getting back to normal."

I laugh. "Some of us were never normal."

"That's what I love about you. Tell Georgie I said hi."

"Not happening." He fastens his holster and kisses me quickly. I watch him walk away, the gun on his hip his only means of propelling a bullet. Fat raindrops hit the window and for the first time in months, I don't recoil at the thought of a little rain.

About Shelli Cornelison

Shelli Cornelison writes for young adults and those not so young. You can find her short stories in Hunger Mountain, Castle of Horror Anthology – Femme Fatales, Smokelong Quarterly, Ghost Parachute, and other publications. She occasionally remembers she has a Facebook account and even less often remembers to update her website at **shellicornelison.net**

Most Distracting Place on Earth

Alexandra Z. Lazar

Fifteen words.

Only fifteen little words.

Elle stared at the letters on her laptop screen, her fingers poised above the keyboard as she re-read the opening line of her college admission essay. Months of brainstorming and researching, countless failed attempts, and who knows how many sleepless nights led to this. She had even spent the whole flight working on it instead of looking out the window and watching clouds drift below her like the fluffy remnants of freshly-shorn sky-sheep.

And all she had were fifteen stinking words.

Elle shook her head, trying to clear away the fog of exhaustion *and* the whimsical image of giant, naked sheep grazing on tree-tops. She had more important things to think about now. The right first line would grab the attention of the admissions committee and make them want to read more. The wrong one would bore them so much that they'd throw the essay right in the trash, her future along with it.

Elle leaned closer to the laptop balanced on her knees as if the words would write themselves if she just looked closely enough. How could she convince any college that she was worthy of their creative writing program if she couldn't even write a decent sentence? Of course, being stuck in the cramped backseat of a rental car wasn't exactly conducive to creativity. But it was unfair to blame the setting when she hadn't made any progress at home either. No, the problem was *her*. She had assumed that long hours of distraction-free travel time would be the perfect opportunity to make a dent in her essay — to accomplish enough that she could actually enjoy herself once they reached the theme park. But no. The white page mocked her. Just as empty as her useless, empty brain.

The cursor blinked. Its rhythm mirrored the throbbing twitch of her eye.

Blink. Twitch.

Blink. Twitch.

Blink. Twitch.

The car hit a bump on the Florida road and her laptop jerked backward, smacking her in the forehead. Elle moaned.

Her mom glanced back from the driver's seat. "Problem, honey?"

With a growl of frustration, Elle slammed her finger down on the backspace key, deleting her opening line — her only line — for the seventeenth time that day.

Farewell carefully-researched quote from a famous author. Intended to make Elle sound smart, it just seemed cliche instead.

"It's garbage. All of it."

Annie peered over at the page. "All of *what?*" she quipped.

Elle shot her little sister a look so murderous that the ten-year-old snapped her mouth shut and went back to scrolling through her phone without a word.

Elle had read every article on writing the perfect college essay, but none of them had helped. It was an impossible task, full of high stakes and contradictions. Be confident but not cocky. Sincere but not sappy. Make it logical and intellectual, *and* emotional and vulnerable. Oh, and don't forget to be concise. Because you only have less than six-hundred-and-fifty words to somehow capture your *entire self* in an essay that will single-handedly make or break the next four years of your life.

"It's just your first draft, Elle." Her mom sighed. "You have months to get it right."

Elle rolled her eyes. Sure, she had months . . . months that would dwindle even faster than her summer vacation had, having been consumed by campus tours and summer projects and birthday parties and futile attempts to squeeze some fun into her final months of pre-adulthood life. Attempts like this vacation.

Her parents gave her the trip as a surprise for her seventeenth birthday. With the first day of senior year just around the corner, they thought a few days at her favorite theme park would be the perfect opportunity for family fun. Which made sense! After all, semi-annual trips had been their go-to way of celebrating special occasions for as long as Elle could remember. And even though her dad hadn't been able to take off work, the fact that it was a girls' trip — just the sisters and their mom — should've made it even more memorable.

Six-year-old Elle would've loved it. Heck, *sixteen-year-old* Elle would've loved it! But seventeen-year-old Elle didn't have time for it. Unfortunately, she also lacked the nerve to say that to her parents' enthusiastic, smiling faces. A choice she now regretted, since the car had nearly reached their hotel and she still had nothing to show for her efforts but a blank document, a killer headache, and an increasingly-foul mood.

"I'm already too far behind," Elle said. Just the thought made her heart beat faster. Her laptop jiggled as she bounced her knee anxiously. Purple and red street signs and cars full of happier tourists flashed past her window with dizzying speed. "All my friends wrote their essays over the summer. I don't even have a sentence!"

"Which is why you need a break to clear your head," her mom urged. Elle recognized that tone, low and slow as a lullaby, like the one used to soothe a fussy toddler. It was meant to calm Elle's nerves, although it always had the opposite effect. "Besides, it doesn't matter as much as you think —"

"Sure, it's not like my entire *future* is on the line," Elle snapped, her voice dripping with sarcasm. She locked eyes with her mom. "Oh wait. It is."

"Look!" Annie interrupted. "We're here!" Sure enough, the turrets of the theme park's signature castle peeked over the tree-tops. Normally, the sight would fill Elle with glee. This time, it triggered a spasm of anxiety. Her plan had backfired. Time was up.

So much for family fun.

As Elle's mom unloaded their luggage in the hotel room and Annie bounced around like a Chihuahua hyped up on caffeine, both wearing matching t-shirts, Elle sank onto the couch and shut her eyes. Although her laptop sat closed on the side table, the white glow of the screen remained imprinted on the inside of her eyelids. She flopped her head back, listening to her family bustle around her. Instead of the buzz of adrenaline and excitement, nervousness churned in her stomach. *How could she tell them?*

When it was built half a century ago, the hotel represented the pinnacle of futuristic modernity. But to Elle, it evoked nostalgia for the past instead. *Her* past. Ever since Elle was little, her family stayed at this hotel every time they visited the theme park. It had earned her family's loyalty because of its proximity to Elle's favorite park and a particularly fun restaurant where guests could party with characters while eating a festively-themed breakfast. And even when rooms were redecorated or amenities were updated, the hotel never changed . . . not really. But she had.

Elle's heart twisted as her mom tackled her jumping-bean sister and tugged a comb through her hair. Things had been so much easier at that age. Not like now, when she had responsibilities and worries and an essay that had to be written. She couldn't just go gallivanting off into a land where people never had to grow up.

No matter how much she wanted to.

It was a disconcerting sensation, to no longer fit in a place where you had always belonged.

"Mom?" Elle said in a small voice. "I was thinking . . ."

"Just a minute, sweetheart. Let me finish up here." Her mom adjusted Annie's sparkly headband, topped by two round circles and an oversized bow, until Annie squirmed away, barely able to contain her excitement. "Everyone, make sure you have your wallets, tickets, phones — Elle!" Her mom stopped ticking items off on her fingers when her scattered gaze landed on her older daughter. "You haven't changed yet?"

"I . . . I can't. I don't have —"

"Your shirt? Your head is certainly in the clouds today, isn't it. Don't worry, I'll get it for you." Elle's mom tossed a t-shirt — emblazoned with a castle, the current year written above it in a burst of fireworks — onto the couch. "Now hurry up. If we don't leave in five minutes, I think Annie is going to break down the door," she said with a laugh.

Elle fingered the t-shirt's cotton fabric. Some families charted their children's growth by measuring their heights on a wall. Elle's measured it in theme park photos. Frames lined the front hallway back home: photos of the three of them — then the four of them once Annie was born — standing in front of the castle, decked out in matching t-shirts and beaming grins. Elle couldn't help but smile at the memory, but then her smile faltered. Their girls trip photo would be missing a girl. But they all had to get used to that, didn't they? Once college started and she moved into a dorm, it would be the first of many.

She wrung the shirt in her hands. "I think it's better if I stay here. Work on my essay."

"Oh, come on, Cinder-Elle," her mom said, using Elle's childhood nickname. "Even hardworking princesses like yourself need to have fun sometimes —"

"I'm not a princess!" Elle shouted. Something about hearing her old nickname pricked a hole in her dam of emotions, and a pent-up mixture of frustration and guilt flooded out. "I'm practically an adult, okay? I can make my own decisions." Her voice softened. "Go have fun. For Annie. I'll just bring you down anyway."

Elle's mom sat beside her. "Don't be silly. How can we have any fun without you?"

"*I* won't have any fun until I get something done," Elle replied honestly. "I just need . . . if I don't write something . . ." Hot tears burned the corners of her eyes as her stomach clenched.

"How about a compromise?" Elle's mom stroked her cheek, her eyes worried. "I want you to enjoy yourself. And if that means taking today to get something accomplished, you should do what you need to do. But tomorrow, you come with us no matter how many words are in that document of yours. Deal?"

Elle nodded and wiped back her tears, forcing a smile to her face. "Deal." *Maybe.*

She maintained her phony smile as Annie yanked their mom out the door, the little girl's headband already askew. But as soon as the door clicked shut, Elle's lip quivered. "Stop being such a baby," she scolded herself in between sniffs. "This is what you wanted." She *couldn't* go to the theme park, not if it meant ruining her chances of writing her essay, which in turn would ruin her chances of getting into a good college, which would then ruin her entire life. But since when did getting what she wanted feel so lousy? Oh well. No one said that being a responsible adult was easy, but she'd have to get used to that, too.

For some reason, instead of providing motivation, the thought brought on a wracking sob. Elle flung herself onto the bed face-first, tears flowing freely now.

Ironically enough, this was a quintessential moment in nearly every princess movie. The moment when the princess — hopes dashed and consumed by overwhelming misery — flops onto the nearest surface and cries her eyes out. In movies, these moments of utter devastation were inevitably followed by assistance from an enchanted helper, be it a talking tea pot, a sea witch, a fairy godmother, or a squad of forest animals. Someone who would give you the solution to your problem and lead you to your happy ending.

But no amount of tears could summon someone to write Elle's essay for her. Perhaps it was because Elle didn't look nearly as graceful as most tearful princesses, with snot dripping from her nose, arms and legs akimbo, and cheeks growing pink from rubbing against scratchy hotel room sheets. But more likely, she reminded herself sternly, it was because real life wasn't a fairy tale. If she wanted her essay written, she had to do it herself.

Ten minutes later, Elle — her face scrubbed clean of tears, her lips set in a resolute line — sat at the desk in the hotel room, glaring at her laptop. Her finger hovered over the 'on' button. *Writer's block. My old enemy. We meet again.*

Her laptop glared back at her. Or rather, her own face glared back at her, reflected in the black screen. It looked annoyingly judgmental, as if it was criticizing her lack of courage. "Come on, Elle. Step One. Turn it on," Elle coached herself.

After a moment's pause, Elle pressed the button. As the laptop booted up, footsteps pounded down the hotel hallway, paired with raucous high-pitched giggles: the sound of another family running off to have fun at the theme park, just as her own family had done. Without her. *Like you asked them to, don't forget.* Elle shook her head and brought her attention back to the laptop. She took a deep breath. Then, with a deliberate click, she opened the document. Anxiety clawed its way up from her stomach into her throat as she stared at the blank white page.

"Just write a word," she said, the sound of her voice breaking the spell. "Any word." She flicked her fingers across the keyboard. A-n-y-space-w-o-r-d. Not exactly college material.

Elle wracked her brain for a witty pun, a heartfelt anecdote — any crumb of inspiration that could unclog her constipated creative well. Her gaze wandered along with her thoughts, absent-mindedly taking in the two queen-sized beds, the couch . . . until it landed on the big window on the other side of the room. Beyond sidewalks and parking lots, the castle sparkled in the distance. Sunlight glinted off its turrets. Elle traced the familiar silhouette with her eyes, feeling a rush of excitement despite herself. From this far away, it looked as tiny and perfect as a minia-ture inside a snow-globe. To the right of the castle, the landscape was dominated by a big white structure, home to one of Elle's favorite roller coasters. Annie had decided she was finally brave enough to try it this year, if Elle was there to hold her hand.

Abruptly, Elle stood up, stomped over to the window, and yanked the curtains shut.

Forget about being the most magical: this was the most *distracting* place on earth.

Elle settled back into the desk chair and closed her eyes. It was just her and her brain now. Nothing left to distract —

An obnoxious melody shattered the silence. Elle jerked her head up, torn between startled panic and resigned annoyance. She knew that ringtone. Elle tracked the sound to the floor in between the beds. Sure enough, there was Annie's phone, forgotten in her little sister's rush out the door. Responsible wasn't exactly a word that anyone would use to describe Annie. But prone-to-temper-tantrums was. Elle answered it, already predicting how the call would go.

"Yes, Mom, Annie's phone is here," she said bluntly. "I just found it."

"Oh thank goodness." Her mom's voice became fainter as she presumably turned away from her phone. "See? You left it in the room. That's why I told you to double-check . . . Yes, I reminded you right before we... No, of course I don't think you dropped it on purpose, but . . ." Her tone grew more strained. "Annie, honey, I know you want to take pictures on your own phone. But unless you want us to lose our place in line, you'll have to use . . ."

Elle moved the phone away from her ear, moments before Annie's familiar shriek would've pierced her eardrum. She waited a few seconds, just to be safe, before raising her own voice to be heard above the disaster-in-progress. "It's okay, Mom! I'll bring the phone to you."

"That's so sweet, but I don't want you to give up . . ." Her mom's voice faded again, switching from pleasant to sharp in one second flat. "Annie. If you can't calm yourself down, we're going to have to —"

Elle weighed the odds in her head. Dragging Annie out of line and all the way back to the hotel room would destroy any chance of salvaging the day for any of them. A half hour of staring at her laptop, versus coming to her family's rescue? There was no question which option won. Elle grabbed her own phone, her park ticket... and, after a moment of hesitation, her t-shirt. "I'll be there in fifteen minutes," Elle said firmly, already halfway out the door.

Elle didn't know why her head felt clearer the second she stepped onto the walkway that connected the hotel with the park entrance any more than she knew why she had stuffed her t-shirt into her bag. But regardless of the reason, it was a welcome change. As the warm Florida breeze played with her hair, her shoulders unhunched and her neck unkinked. Her head had felt like an overfilled balloon all day, all tense and pressured. But with every footstep, a little more air leaked out of it.

Maybe this half hour didn't have to be a *total* loss.

After all, Elle reasoned, half of a writer's work was done away from the keyboard. The best ideas drifted into an open mind when you least expected them . . . and her mind finally felt like it had a little room to spare.

Sure enough, as Elle walked down the familiar sidewalk — passing excited, smiley guests heading toward the park, and exhausted, sweat-drenched ones heading away from it — her mind began to wander . . . in the wrong direction. Tantalizing images of castles and fairy dust and ice cream and roller coasters and churros filled her head. Without meaning to, she began to walk faster, a new spring in her step.

With a concerted effort, Elle pulled her thoughts back to the subject at hand. This was no fun outing — it was an errand, nothing more. Once she dropped off Annie's phone, she'd head straight back to her laptop. But despite her best attempts, her feet didn't get the message. They pulled her down the sidewalk of their own accord, her steps so light she practically skipped.

Until she saw the long lines of guests snaking beyond the turnstiles at the park entrance.

Elle's speedy steps screeched to a halt. No wonder her mom didn't want to lose their spot in line. She sent a text, a sinking feeling in her stomach:

> Any chance you're still in line?

Elle waited for the three dots on her phone screen to turn into words. Finally, her mom's response appeared. Elle's heart deflated, just as her balloon head re-inflated.

> No, finally made it through. Are you here?

Her half hour round-trip estimate had just doubled, at the least. Elle sighed.

> Just getting in line now. Do a ride to keep Annie distracted: I'm gonna be a while.

After a twenty-minute wait that felt more like twenty hours, Elle finally reached the front of the line, scanned her ticket, and took off running. She swerved around grinning guests who posed for photos in front of a floral design, then bolted through the entrance tunnel at full tilt.

The outside world melted away.

Despite herself, Elle froze. Peppy melodies filled her ears, embracing her like a warm hug. A horse-drawn trolley jingled down the street. Near a flag pole, cartoon characters come-to-life greeted happy guests armed with autograph books and cameras. The turn-of-the-century buildings that surrounded her transported her back to a simpler time — one that never truly existed, except in the collective imaginations of the visionaries who built the park and the countless guests who passed this way before her. And at the end of the street, the castle rose up above it all: a majestic scene, ripped straight from the pages of a fairy tale.

For a brief, wonderful moment, all of Elle's stress melted away too. Nothing existed but this magical place, where the worries of the real world didn't apply.

And then the real world poked its head back in. She was just a delivery girl — one who was running way behind schedule.

Elle dodged the crowds as she worked her way down the street. She glowered at the revelers as she hurried by, one cranky face in a sea of gleeful ones. Their chatter, their smiles as they took family photos destined to hang in front hallways like her own . . . it just made her mood worse. Didn't they have responsibilities? What reasonable person would spend forty-five minutes in line to get their picture with a human-sized mouse? Or an hour for an eight-minute boat ride past a bunch of robots in pirate costumes? The whole thing was pointless. Even the castle seemed to have lost its shine.

It was all just plaster, paint, and pretend.

The sooner Elle could leave, the better.

'Now who's pretending?' her subconscious asked.

Elle typed up a text as she walked, glad for the excuse to keep her reddened eyes downcast. *Finally here. At the castle. Where are you?*

The three dots lingered on her screen for an ominously long time. Why did it have to take her mom so long to type up a simple response? Elle snarled at her phone, grouchier by the second.

> WHERE ARE YOU??

A whole paragraph appeared. Never a good sign.

> Hi, sweetheart! We're in line for Annie's favorite ride. The sign said 20 min wait but we got stuck behind a tour group. Probably still 15 min away from the boats. Meet you outside the ride exit in 30 min?? So sorry for the delay. Love you! <3 <3 <3

Elle resisted the urge to throw her phone into the castle moat. It was no surprise that Annie picked that ride. She was obsessed with the dolls' international costumes and the catchy theme song. What *was* surprising was the fact that they were still there, considering how quickly the line usually moved. Apparently, the universe was against her writing her essay. Elle stabbed at the screen. She'd remind her mother that *some* people had responsibilities waiting for them. That this was a lousy reward for sacrificing her time to do a favor for Annie . . . But wait — there was a better option. Elle just sent one word, letting the short, curt response carry the weight of her frustration for her.

Fine.

Annie's favorite ride was in the heart of the park's most fantastical area. It used to be Elle's favorite area too, but when one is in an extremely foul mood, the last thing one wants is to be surrounded by sparkles and joy that only remind you how cranky you are in comparison. Plan A was to sit on a bench near the attraction's exit. But, no surprise considering her luck, the seat was already taken. Plan B was to just stand there. But it didn't help Elle's mood to lurk on increasingly-sore feet and watch all the happy people leaving the ride. So she settled for Plan C: find a curb away from crowds, where she could sit and wait in peace. Elle found the ideal location outside a nearby restaurant, sandwiched between a bathroom and a fake brick turret that matched the castle.

Perfect. Nothing fun happened in a bathroom.

Elle settled onto the concrete curb. If she was stuck there, she might as well try to get some writing in. She begrudgingly opened the notes app on her phone.

High, twinkly music — instrumental versions of songs from iconic movies — drifted over from the carousel nearby. Elle started humming along before she could stop herself.

Balancing her phone on her lap to free up her hands, Elle covered both ears. Take that, distractions. The music became muffled and distant, though she could hear the throbbing of her own heartbeat instead, not unlike the pulse of her laptop cursor.

Elle stared down at her phone, the blank note no easier to fill than the blank document. Suddenly, her stomach grumbled. Elle shot it a dirty look. Even her own body was against her getting anything done. Although, she reconsidered, that might explain her mood. Her mom always said she got cranky when she was hungry. Elle pocketed her phone and went in search of a snack. The mature thing to do would be getting herself a sandwich, but a kiosk caught her eye first. Ice cream bars: a special kind, only available at the theme park. Her favorite vacation treat. Elle's mouth watered. It was an awfully hot day — surely the *more* mature thing to do would be getting something that cooled her down. Without hesitation, Elle pulled out a few crinkled bills from her pocket and rushed for the kiosk.

Elle brought the ice cream back to her curb, a mighty huntress returning with her prey. She eagerly ripped the plastic wrapper open and eyed the shiny chocolate coating, glistening with condensation, before taking a big bite. The flavor of melting chocolate and ice-cold vanilla exploded onto her tongue. Why did ice cream taste better when it was molded in the shape of three circles, dunked in chocolate, and put on a stick? Elle took another bite, and another. Soon the whole bar was gone. Her stomach wasn't the only thing that felt less grumbly now.

Elle licked chocolate smudges off her sticky fingers, feeling an energized buzz. The sugar's fault probably. She wiped her hands on her shorts. No more excuses. She picked up her phone with considerably less enthusiasm than she had tackled the ice cream.

The buzz faded away. Elle stared at her lock screen photo, a selfie of herself and Annie from their last trip, wearing matching headbands, matching t-shirts, and matching smiles. This theme park was her happy place. Or at least, it used to be.

Growing up was no fun.

Just then, the tinkling melody of one of her favorite songs drifted over from the carousel. Elle looked over at the attraction. The line was nearly deserted — it couldn't be more than a five-minute wait. As long as she was there, it couldn't hurt to do *one* ride . . . right?

Elle stuffed her phone into her pocket and ran to the carousel. Her steed — a white horse bedecked in a silver helmet and a red knight's shield — seemed to wink at her as she swung her leg over its back, a giddy smile on her face. She grabbed the golden pole. It felt cool in her grip, despite the Florida heat.

Maybe she didn't have to grow up all the way quite yet.

While she waited for her family to arrive, Elle relaxed on a bench in front of the castle, soaking in the cheerful music, the beautiful view of the castle . . . everything. The sunshine warmed her face as she bopped her head along with the melody, her phone stashed out of sight. She had put it away after sending one last text to her mom, right after her carousel ride finished: *Change of plans — meet me at the castle!*

Now, she scanned the faces all around her. Stranger after stranger walked past, until — there! Elle's family walked down the castle ramp. Her mom's gaze darted nervously across the crowd, her brow furrowed and her lips pressed tightly together. Elle giggled. Her mom clearly expected that Elle would be furious over the delay.

Elle stood up and waved enthusiastically. As Annie dashed over with grabby hands extended for her phone, her mom's face broke into a surprised smile. "What are you . . ."

"Wearing? I couldn't break tradition, now could I?" Elle gestured at the matching t-shirt that she had tugged over her tank top.

"What a wonderful surprise!" Elle's mom pulled her into a hug. "You haven't just made Annie's day. You've made mine too."

Elle smirked. "I know."

Her mom sniffed away happy tears.

"Don't cry." Elle laughed. "You don't want red eyes in our picture, do you?" She herded her family toward the nearest photographer.

Elle and her family lined up with the castle behind them, their arms wrapped around each other's shoulders. A warm feeling coursed through Elle's chest that had nothing to do with their sunbaked bodies pressing together. For the first time in weeks, she could actually breathe. Elle smiled for the camera with a big, toothy grin, nothing forced about it this time. Forget about plastic and paint — the park's magic lived in the hearts of the people who visited it.

Her smile grew even wider as an idea struck her.

As soon as the photographer finished, Elle yanked out of her family's grip. She darted over to a bench, grabbed her phone, and started typing furiously.

"Oh." Her mom's face fell. "Do you have to get back to work already?"

Elle nodded, barely listening.

"Can't it wait until you're back in the room?" her mom asked.

Elle shook her head.

"Really, Elle? The silent treatment? I thought that you —"

"Give me five minutes!" Elle barked, never taking her eyes off her phone. Elle's family waited as her thumbs jabbed at her screen with record speed. Annie, bored, took a dozen terrible selfies that were mostly nose and ear. Finally, her mom had enough. "I know you have to write today, but the two of us —"

"Okay, done!" Elle put her phone back in her pocket. "Sorry about that. Can we ride the roller coaster next?" Her feet were already pulling her toward the park's futuristic section, where her favorite ride awaited her.

"We?" Elle's mom said incredulously. "But I thought you had to work on your essay!"

Elle retrieved her phone and turned it so her mom could read the screen.

Fairy tales are full of magical items — glass slippers and pumpkin carriages, poisoned apples and cursed spindles. But in real life, magic isn't as easy to find. Wands are made of plastic, castles are just brick and mortar, and glass slippers? An impractical, uncomfortable foot wound waiting to happen. Compared to their storybook counterparts, even the most enchanting objects are ordinary and powerless . . . if one looks only with one's eyes. In the real world, magic isn't found in objects, but in the hearts and minds of those who seek it. The same is true of stories. Their power doesn't come from letters and words, but rather the imaginations of those who read and write them. And that's why I want to be an author.

"I am," Elle replied, feeling happier than she had in a long time. She grabbed Annie's hand and ran toward the roller coaster.

"Who's going to scream louder?" she teased.

"I'm not going to scream!" Annie said confidently . . . and incorrectly, Elle was certain. Her little sister was going to scream her head off.

And Elle wouldn't miss it for the world.

About Alexandra Z. Lazar

Alexandra Z. Lazar is an author, Disneyphile, animal lover, and fairy tale aficionado. She writes fiction for kids, middle-schoolers, and young adults, including some projects for Disney Publishing. Whether she's working on freelance projects or her own books, she adds a dash of pixie dust to stories for the young and young at heart! Her published works include *Aladdin: Beyond the Palace Walls* and the *Big Hero 6 Read-Along Storybook and CD* for Disney, and multiple stories in anthologies. She also contributed to Ridley Pearson's best-selling *Kingdom Keepers* series. Alexandra has an MFA in Creative Writing from Southern New Hampshire University. She lives in Vermont with her family and many pets, including her cats/mascots/overlords Zooey III and Oliver. She is currently working on her first original novel, a fairytale reimagining about the Fairy Godmother's sister.

Website: alexandrazlazar.com

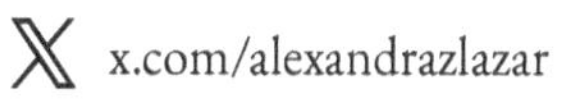 x.com/alexandrazlazar

Down the Blackened River

K. Psych

**Trigger Warnings* for mention of parental death, mention of diaspora, mention of colonization and slavery, mention of a monster, mention of blood, grief*

I have never deemed it possible to find myself consumed by the simplest of human emotions until today, the day of *her* arrival. Weariness. Distraught. Curiosity. A plethora of sensations I once assumed only inhabited the creatures known as mankind burst inside of me. The same beings who would dump anything and *everything* into me.

Once worshiped by charismatic and selfless people who praised and honored my waters. Who birthed stories around fires not far from my banks and gathered food and water from my body to survive, I, the Blackened River, have not found myself surrounded by compassionate souls since those times. Centuries it has been until *her*.

From every side of the riverbank, I have been detrimental to the creation of a village full of life and miracles, but alas the familiarity ceased once the tainted hands of unfamiliar visitors greedily settled and reclaimed the territory as their own. The strange menfolk from overseas paid no heed to the locals' rightful fury at their blatant disrespect and mistreatment towards me, the river, using my waters for nothing more than to invade and terrorize. If my waves and ringlets could split open and shape a mouth in place, I would gladly speak and scream my disapproval, my rage. Being reclaimed by foreigners and outsiders was not a choice of mine, but what else could I do other than sit by idly as time moved on? Trying to hinder their advancements and travel did very little.

So I laid there, growing and stretching from one tail end of the bank to another. I silently rested there as man rowed and paddled over me, using my body for their selfish gains. I painfully remained at the wayside as some of my old worshippers screamed and begged from below ships, kept in confinement to be taken to places I knew nothing of. I despise those memories most of all.

As time blossomed and withered, objects, belongings, and garbage left by egotistical and discourteous humans were discarded into me, not once treating my vessel as the handiwork of God or a gift given to them from Mother Nature. Not like the native dwellers before them. No, I, the Blackened River have been used for any means. Instead of gold and riches being lovingly fed into me, bodies have been dumped and plummeted to the bottom of my belly. Human blood has seeped into my wet veins. Flesh has been torn apart and disintegrated into me, blending in with the watery grave.

But I must admit. I look forward to the days where my heavy heart is lifted — confessional days. Humans are a befuddling and chaotic group, full of greed and deprivation, but if one looks close enough, there is a spark of mystery and desire hidden in the depths of their darkness. A basic need for companionship, connection, and love. I anticipate the days and nights when their hunger for attention and their thirst for belonging overwhelms so they seek me out. Sitting on my shore, secrets pour out of their mouths and fall into my waters. Some are tiny white lies. Some are words and tales filled with promises and glee. Oftentimes stories full of trauma and decay are told, followed by tears thickened with anguish, bitterness, sadness, and numbness. Tales spew from the mouths of men, women, and children praying for someone to hear their confessions on those dark or happy days.

Accounts and woes flow inside filling me. But on this day, I am sure that this newest confession will be one to remember for the rest of time before I am forsaken and forgotten, left to dry up and converted into a foundation or crossing more useful for humans.

Spring. The perfect season to cleanse the mind and soul. My favorite time of the year. Layers of fog float above my body. Chilling drops of rain fall from the heavens, possibly a sign of God's disappointment and frustration. The leaves on the trees near the river's edge waft with the current. Bits of branches, pinecones, and greenery lift from the ground and blow through the air, sometimes landing on me. Oh, how I welcome these moments. It is a stormy day satiated with clouds and frigid rain, strong enough to hide the tears and gut-wrenching screams I foresee.

I push my waves in anticipation of my newest confessor. Searching the riverbank, I finally spy dots. How strange. Black and white dots on a curvaceous object. It is not until the stranger approaches that I recognize the thing in their hand. An umbrella. Many of those have been left with me.

Trembling fingers curled around the umbrella is all I can make out. A face hidden by a mane of thick black curls. Keeping the window to their soul hidden, perhaps? Strange to do so in front of a body of water, but not unusual.

I shift my waves closer hoping to get a better peek at them. I take in her dress, the dark lace draped down her back, fabric so long the train threatens to dip into the water. Thick black boots poke out from underneath, soft yellow daisies tucked into the laces.

"I'm so sorry, Mama," the guest whispers, sobs caught in the back of their throat threatening to wrack their body. At the sound of such a soft and delicate voice, I prepare myself to listen and provide comfort. Comfort, a new skill for me. "I didn't think it was your time. Never in a million years did I think you'd leave me before Papa. Leave your daughter in a cruel unforgiving world." A gloved hand nudges the curtain of hair out of the way and through the storm I am greeted with chestnut, reddened skin, and though protected from the rain, tears glisten on her round cheeks.

Her voice cracks as she licks her lips as if to keep more sobs from stumbling out. I watch as a handkerchief is pulled from her coat pocket and the poor piece of cloth that had seen better days clutches tighter and tighter in her grip.

Heartache and sorrows dampen the fabric, adding another stain to the old ones already inhabiting it. I find myself wondering about the stories behind those stains left by not just the woman, but also her mother, her grandmother, her great-grandmother. How much generational pain, trauma, and grief does it hold? "This handkerchief, *your* kerchief . . . I do not deserve your precious cloth, I know, but I needed something to hold me together today. It's been rough. The guilt . . ." A strangled sob leaves her frame as more tears dribble from her eyes. "I didn't mean to harm you, Mama."

I calm myself, halting my waves, as I wait to hear her speak again. For the first time how, I wish to converse with someone. With *her*.

I decide to move closer to the mesmerizing and perplexing being at my bank, her boots already coated with mud. Immediately a hint of pine and vanilla hits my waters. An intoxicating mixture of her sadness and guilt knotted together like a child's blanket crudely, but lovingly knitted with accidental knots, like the one a mother tossed into me, her deceased son's favorite coverlet, after a burial. But why the guilt? I affiliate pine to be a scent that permeates from the worst of the worst: criminals, slave traders, murderers, thieves. What has happened to create such a tang from the young lady?

I gently force a wave in her direction. Her attention averts down as a splash of my body runs around her boots. A small smile blooms on her face. Grasping her dress in her hand, the mourning woman lifts the hem until it reaches past her thighs. Biting back a hiss of pain and exposing a bruised knee, she kneels in the mud.

"Hello there," she says. I still. No one has spoken directly to me in centuries. "Yes, I know all about you, Blackened River." Her gloved hand, a finger, dips into the water. I stir in reply.

"My mama told me all about you. For years she'd tell me the history behind you. Stories about how God and Mother Nature created you for us. I remember her bringing me here when I was a little thing. It was the first time we met."

I search my memories but cannot recollect them. I am quite positive I would have remembered someone as lovely as her.

She chuckles as my waves continue to splash around her knelt form and swim around her hand, soaking her gloves. "It's okay, darling. That was a long time ago. A very long time ago." A heavy sigh follows her words. "God, how I miss those days. I miss frolicking under the bare sun. I miss the smiles and laughter. I miss the innocence of it all."

I rest my movements and wait for her to continue, the tranquility of myself easing us both. Her eyes appear to glaze over as a sort of memory replays in her head. "Mama used to bring me here hoping you would ease my pain. She was right, but it was only temporary. Nothing could stop the nightmares that haunted me. Everywhere I went the godawful dreams and the things that haunted my vision were there. I wasn't always like this, a loner who'd walk along the woods talking to creatures and God's creations like you. I had better things to do with my time until I met *it*." The hiss that leaves her lips isn't missed.

I have heard many chronicles during my lifespan, and I believe that this story will be akin to the ones told by other past confessors who were clueless about my listening. But then again, those humans did not care or acknowledge my presence as much. Dumping their secrets in it as they did their waste was all that concerned them. So, in my eyes, this woman, this *human*, is disparate from any other.

"Mama didn't believe me when I told her about that day. She said I'd been listening to too many of her and Nana's tales. Said I didn't understand the difference between reality and truth, but I did. That *thing* was real, and it made me into the person I am today." She scoffs. "Believe me, River, that isn't saying much. I saw it in the dead of night. Not too far from here. Mama was too busy to bring me to you one afternoon. I understand now why she worked three jobs to take care of me and my brother, but as a little one, her absence left me hurt and wanting. Upset. *Angry* that she put work before me, so I went out on my own to search for you."

I acknowledge my new companion with another soft splash, yearning to alleviate the burden and anguish staining her. And it does if only for a moment; my friend sighs in harmony with the breeze hitting against her back and the overbearing trees in the distance before continuing. "Yes, I needed you and I vowed that I would find you all on my own. I searched and searched. My scrawny legs only took me so far, but then I had to come to terms with the fact that I was lost. I was nowhere near you. I wanted you but couldn't find you. I wanted my mama, but she was working and didn't know I had left the house. I couldn't do anything, so I did the same thing I'm doing now" — she gently wipes the tears from her face — "I cried. I don't know how long I sobbed. I laid down in the middle of the woods, curled my arms around myself, and wailed until my throat grew raw. Nothing answered me until I heard something. A scream."

I fall silent as she carries on, but it hurts. I despise the wretched noise of hurt in her speech. I scorn the fear lacing her words, but there isn't much I can do about it except attend and pacify.

"I didn't know what it was. I got up from the ground, not caring about the dirt and leaves stuck to my new dress Mama had saved up to buy me. I didn't care about the spanking I knew I would get when she saw it. I didn't care about anything when I got up because all I could focus on was the bright red eyes staring at me through the darkness."

Full of bereavement that still haunts her to this day as much as it did when she was a babe lost in the woods that surround me, staring down at her shaking fists, she sighs before shutting her eyes. "It growled at me, but it didn't move. I'm unsure if I wandered into its territory and it came to chase me off or if it was hunting its prey, but we stood there staring at one another. I'm not sure if it was hours that passed or only seconds, but before I could take a single step back, it lunged. I barely had time to think before I ran. I made it home somehow. I climbed up the raggedy ladder that I had hidden outside my window. I didn't even get undressed. I just jumped into bed and shut my eyes, thinking it was all a dream until I looked down when a sharp pain ran up my arm."

Hmm, now I find myself wondering what manner of beast had come upon this lady when she was nothing more than a child? I know them all well, for they drink from me and treat me far kinder than the humans have done.

Pulling her sleeve back and stretching out her arm, it is on display, and I cannot help the tremor wave I send at her feet. Three long faint scars mar her skin. Those are abnormal. Of course, when those who lived off the land had faced countless threats of mauling by bears and wolves, they would be met by claws and teeth, leaving with deadly wounds of similar fashion. But these . . . they appear to be . . . monstrous.

Dropping her arm, the sleeve droops down and returns as a veil to conceal from wandering eyes. She nods, a sniffle and cough follow. "I wasn't crazy. I showed Mama in the morning, and she was furious. Not at the marks, but at my ruined dress. I didn't realize it was almost shredded. I told her what happened, but she didn't believe me."

Unbeknown to her, the bowing of her head knocks a tear loose and into the stream. Into me and with that, pictures and sounds swim around, offering me an insight into what occurred between mother and daughter that fateful night.

"Katara, w-wh…" Her mother, exhausted after coming home from a thirteen-hour shift at the local nursing home, stuttered over her words as she towered over ten-year-old Katara. The brand-new dress she had spent countless hours sewing and stitching together — destroyed. Ruined. Almost in tatters. "H-how did this happen? What in the world … " She could barely form complete sentences as she fingered the gashes and tears clinging to her daughter's shivering frame. Her motherly hands and fingers still showcased punctures from the needles to prove her diligence and effort to craft her firstborn a dress for the upcoming Resurrection service at church. Yellow and soft pinks laced with daises and puppy designs, Katara's favorites. But by the look on her mother's face, Katara couldn't fathom the thoughts that brewed in her mama's head. Ungratefulness. Selfishness. Hurt. But that was far from the truth.

"I . . . I saw it, Mama." Katara finally uttered around the lump in her throat after finding the strength to wipe the tears still falling down her ripe, chubby face as she peered up at her mother.

"What? What did you do? Were you in the woods again? Dammit, Katara, I told you not to go there without me. You know the kinds of men who hunt in those copses. I —" She stopped as Katara shook her head at her words. "No? You weren't in the woods? Then where —"

Little Katara had no other choice, but to stop the tears and tell her mama what she saw. "It wasn't the white men from town, Mama, honest. It was the Creeper." She gasped out the name, unsure if her mother heard her over her blubbering, but she did. Mama froze for a moment, astonished at the urban legend nickname.

"No, no, no . . ."

"But M-mama —"

"I said no!"

Katara jumped at the sound of her mother's voice raised. That was not common in their household.

"It did this! I fell down lots running home a-and it k-kept coming and coming and coming and I didn't know what to do! I'm not lyin'!" Katara begged and pleaded for her to understand the truth that the Creeper was real. The story her Pop Pop and second Uncle and great Aunt had told her during a blackout as they all gathered in the living room with nothing but lit candles and spooky stories to keep them company two summers prior was real. But again, Katara's mama had had enough of hearing of the Creeper, and the Wolfman and the Stringless Lady.

"Katara . . ." Strange how her voice lowered, and though full of anger and annoyance, there was fatigue and fear. "I beg you; your uncle and Nana have begged you; please put your childish ways behind. I love your imagination, you know I do, but this...I've had enough. You've scared your baby brother half to death with this shit and I . . . I don't want to hear about it no more. Do you hear me, young lady? Done. You did this to your dress, the one your grand-mother and I worked so hard to make with the supplies we could barely afford, and you did this? It was no Creeper man or thing or whatever you want to call it!" The finality in her mama's words shook Katara more than the Creeper's long sinewy fingers grip around her leg.

I am brought back, no longer a witness to a cruel event that should not happen to anyone. "Mama said I was sleepwalking again, so I believed her until the next morning. My uncle woke me up asking me if I'd seen Mama and I told him not since that morning. He thought that was weird because she usually had breakfast on the table, and he was there to drive her to work. I followed him into her bedroom but she wasn't there. We searched house until he found her in the den in front of the tv on our busted old couch. Dead. It was my fault," she mumbles those last words before soft snivels follow.

I wish to shed tears of my own for her. To wash away her weeping and ache. To make it known that the death of her mother lies in no fault of her own, but mine. Where was I during her time of need? Was I deafened to her agonizing bellows and wails in the deep trees I call allies?

As if Katara can read in me what would be known as thoughts to her kind, she shakes her head. "It *was* my fault. There was so much blood. Claw marks like the ones on my arm were everywhere. It followed me home. If I hadn't left home and been in the woods, this never would've happened."

Such a sweet soul. Blame should be placed on *myself*. If not for me, then that little girl never would've left the comfort and safety of her home looking for me. It was not her fault, and Katara needs to understand that before the guilt consumes and swallows her whole.

"I don't blame you," Katara whispered to the river. "I've never blamed you. I envy you."

The winds blow harder. My currents sway stronger. A small smile rises on her tear-stained face. Her hand reaches out again, trickling along the top of my surging body. "Even after my mama's death, I wanted you. I wanted you to bring me comfort no one else could bring. Mama said where she was from, bodies of water are symbols of relief. You bring comfort in the darkest times. Your comfort reaches the blackened parts of people's souls."

I calm, the entire forest finds itself at a standstill, at her soft acclamation and watch as Katara finally rises to her feet, mud and water caked on her knees and clothes. I do nothing as she gently removes the coat from her body. "You see, Blackened River, I've been waiting for the day I could throw my secret into you. Today's the 20th anniversary of my mama's death, and all I could think were the stories she told me of you." Her speech never falters even as she slips the boots off her feet, ignoring the daisies in her laces falling out. I cannot help but part and form a small path as bare feet greet me. Stillness all around us. The winds do not blow. The birds do not chirp. My waters do not wave as she wanders within me, a majestic queen finding solace on her throne.

"I've waited for the day I could share my blackened soul with the blackened river and be at peace. So, with that, I thank you."

About K. Psych

Kapri Psych (K. Psych) is a Black, queer, and disabled writer of adult horror SFF and erotic literary fiction. With a bachelor's degree in Liberal Studies, a certificate in Web Design, and concentration in Literature, there are no limits to their creativity. Between 2024 and 2025, Kapri will be releasing their first erotic horror novella titled SLICE OF HEAVEN and an untitled religious horror chapbook while editing LAST ONE STANDING, a BIPOC final girl anthology, and opening FINDERS CREEPERS, an indie horror multimedia company.

When they aren't analyzing biblical lore and spinning it into their own monstrous creations full of blood, trauma, and complex feelings about morality, they can be found rotting in bed rewatching *Saw* or *Constantine* for the millionth time or designing a clothing line that'll never see the light of day.

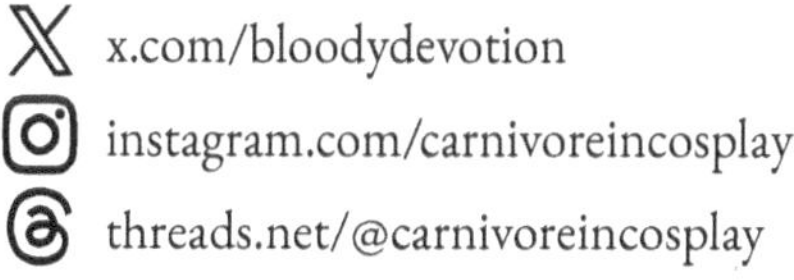

Party at Qoroth Station

Gerardo J. Mercado

***Trigger Warnings for violence, intoxication, and gore*

When her ship docked on the orbiting station Minerva became mesmerized by the broken planet though, she couldn't place why. It wasn't the shattered mantle, or the planet-wide chasm, nor the amorphous shadows of its surface. It wasn't the shower of red light from the old star, but something pulled her attention towards it, a strange undercurrent, even its vague forcefulness felt right, inviting. All tensions and anxieties seemed to melt. Maybe it was relief from ending the two-hundred-hour flight, or getting away from her family, or the end of her work-imposed hermitage, maybe all of it.

She wondered if Wilda had felt it too — this loosening. Probably not; her friend was wound up like a clock whenever she worked on something, anything. When she told Minerva she was going to spend a month organizing a party for the heiress Rilka Orsino — in some decommissioned research station — Minerva knew it might consume her. She'd been worried at first, but Wilda pulled through like she always did, she even got Minerva on the guest list right before preparations started. A little pit in her stomach opened thinking about all the people probably already inside. Minerva hadn't been to a party in ages and dug her nails into her palms hoping to ground herself. She needed an escape, even if just for a moment, and imagined the colossal gap was an inviting smile as she stepped into the station.

A certain desire quivered through the dead planet as it flowed, again, into the orbiting station. *It* had been too forceful before, too hungry, and those within the metal halls had fizzled into bloodless corpses before it could feast properly. Now, however, it would be different: those inside did not come to study its dead body, they came to be exquisite, euphoric, thrilled, and delighted in ceremony.

They came to be enraptured. They came to be roped in its light, air, and flesh; they came to give it life once more.

Looking out from the opened porthole in her room Wilda's mind flooded: schedules, supplies, guests, crew, music, activities, food, and drinks. Her tablet vibrated, again, and she looked at the security feed to see another small fleet of incoming guests anchoring to the station. Her eyes stung from checking the screen and she wished she could throw herself into the planet's chasm. It seemed so quiet and restful inside the giant mouth. She wanted a long warm shower and a stiff drink, but it wasn't time yet; Rilka *had* to love the party. Another payment like the last one meant no more working herself to exhaustion with multiple jobs, no more out-of-touch drama or wasteful tastes, and she could dance full-time.

It's like she'd told Minerva a few weeks ago, she just needed to hold out, like when Rilka made her study all those nonsense files so she could "arrange things properly" for an "aesthetic apotheosis," She doesn't ask a rich person "why?" she asked "what's the budget?" and do what she was hired to do, like arrange decorations, harmonize the rooms with flowers and trees, find room for Rilka's morbid sculptures, and incorporate all the cryptic imagery of ghosts, angels, and spells seamlessly. She was particularly proud of using classic LED lights for the magic symbols — lots of circles and loops. The idea had come to her in a dream.

It *had* been tiresome work, but composition *is* everything, like when people arrived, what would they see? Are the directions unobtrusive but clear enough? Parties, like anything, can take a life of their own, they simply need a clear path and be allowed to be whatever the moment needs. In fact, it was that feeling, that sensation, that energy in the atmosphere whenever people get together that got her into this line of work.

She lingered on her weariness as she watched the red light of the old star creep into the gray surface of the planet and into its shadowy abyss. She realized that had been the longest she'd stared at it alone. It was calm. Her mind emptied. The flooding had ceased, and she focused on the very center of the maw, where the light would not plunge into. Her head inched forward. Maybe there was something to what Rilka wanted, that aesthetic apotheosis; *she* was always looking at the planet. The planet swallowed her field of vision and her forehead tapped the viewing screen, she could almost make out a sound, a voice.

Then the tablet rang again. "Right," she said to herself, snapping back into her body. Minerva had arrived and the other guests had begun to filter in; the party was starting.

Stepping into the main hallway, Wilda heard the final testing sounds of the speakers echo through the corridors of the doughnut-shaped station. The music would start soon. She wondered if everything would go smoothly: the schedules, supplies, guests, crew, music, activities, food, and drinks. The station seemed to tremble a little and she wondered if she was going to survive the next few dozen hours.

Inside the metal body mutters and steps merged into a tempo-less harmony. Amassing around the entrances flesh-on-flesh grazed the walls. Their heat was *almost* succulent, but it all was so little. Qoroth's hunger wanted them to dance and move and sweat and run, it wanted to take all they could give. In the climax of those funneled throngs, it would be born properly, not in the tasteless gore of some prying minds recording the melody of its drifting corpse.

Through the shadows, between its atoms, it moved. It slipped into the rooms where the electric wires hummed just below the fake plastered walls, where the friction of hidden corners hissed. It pushed into all places, into closed windows and halls, it felt like an unbearable gray mist lift as it drank in the brewing energy. Its memories mixed with everything it passed and echoes of ancient throngs folded time and space. Ever so slightly, a shiver of expectation pulsed through the attendees. Ever so slightly, Qoroth's hunger edged the station closer to itself.

It ached to escape from its failed cocoon, that wasted corpse — still, it would be patient.

Rilka Orsino woke up from her nap; she had dreamed a great deal of things. She had dreamed of an angel in the metal shell, dancing around its old carcass, watching them prod and add to its body, to its soul. She had dreamed of a great snake coming from the planet's gaping wound and swallowing them whole.

She could hear her party, and the electric pulse of the machinery felt like a heartbeat with so many vessels inside the station, so many eyes, mouths, and bodies. She'd just finished the last sculpture for her celebration and had fallen asleep under it.

She saw Wilda's barrage of messages. It was time.

She sat on her chair, prayed to the angel, and went ahead with the schedule.

Minerva walked around the hall's low lights outlining the different passages and entrances. It wasn't exactly beautiful — the fake walls reminded her of an endless vestibule — but Wilda had told her this was miles away from the ship's original design with its odd practicality of equipment, fast fixes, and chewed-up surfaces. She started to feel the vibrations of the party in her feet. They called her to join in the mass celebration hiding every opulent craving you could think of.

She took a drink from a server and let it overtake her for a moment. Her neck and shoulders relaxed, her nervous hands and tapping feet stopped, her breathing evened out. She reminded herself she needed a break before life permanently got away from her, before she drowned. She wasn't her father's mother, she wasn't her sister's babysitter, and she certainly wasn't her boss's saving grace. She was gonna let loose and forget about everyone. She felt her body yearning for it. She would find herself stiffer drinks, a beautiful person, weren't there flowers in the ship somewhere? She would think about nothing and simply be present. Yes, she was gonna let her body take the lead.

Minerva vanished into the crowd as the face of a woman appeared on the monitors.

Rilka looked directly at the camera, appearing on every monitor along the station, eyes open wide, smiling, and arms stretched out. The image panned out and behind her a wall-sized glass appeared revealing the planet behind, appearing to be making a half-opened eye with its silhouette.

"Dear friends," Rilka began, "our fires are marching through themselves in self-revelation and ecstasy," the voice reverberated through the halls, "I'm so happy everyone's here to share in my joy, my grief, my healing. After Mom died, I'd stopped feeling everything: my art, my goals, my emotions. Ideas came and went without any heart or soul, without any sense of being. I traveled far. I met people, fell in and out of love a few times, but nothing ever *called* me back to myself. Can you imagine how awful it is to feel like you have everything and nothing at the same time? That's when I found this place, Qoroth, where fire and clarity found me."

Spread throughout the halls, as she spoke, some nodded, some cringed, some simply hoped she'd prepared smoking rooms. Some had already muted her speech and eagerly took their second, third, or fourth spirit. The ambiance called for it, the lighting was beautiful, with music and food all around. Others wondered where she was, sitting in that ornate chair under a spotlight. Others wondered if there were private beds somewhere — the smiling strangers around were all magnetic. Others didn't know Rilka, they were just plus ones enjoying the smell of lilies and roses.

"An ancient poet once said," Rilka continued, "Angels do not show themselves to us for their love would overwhelm us, but the truth is, I *want* to overwhelm you. I want to share *this* with you. *Live*, let go of your chains which do nothing but suppress your inner divine."

Minerva stood marveling at Rilka's humanoid statues, their suggested movement and unsymmetrical background inviting her to get lost in them. She wondered at their symbolism. One titled "The Tower" exposed its spine as it stretched like a dangling chain, its arms and chest reaching upwards to some impossible height; "The Crawler" on all four moved to some unknown end with bisected hands and feet and knees; "The Dancer" was stuck in an atrophied cartwheel while their skin fell to the sides.

"Dear friends, when you are ready, join me here, where I wait with more truth, and though your bodies will guide you soon enough for now I leave you with the voice I found, the voice of love."

Rilka pressed something out of frame and her image disappeared. All portholes around the station opened and the red light of the star flushed inside. Through small speakers, a muffled humming and scratching sound played beneath the disparate energies.

Qoroth's will swam through the intoxicated crowds. It wove through their sounds and motions, the blasting music and vivid dances, their cracking laughter and hushed voices in lonely corners. The crowd moved along with nothing but instinct, seeking more and more and more. A spasm of pleasure phased through all the bodies in the station and everything began to warm. The hunger grew with each taste, contracting, contorting, throbbing, craving.

The party had become a living world. The ocean of voices being drowned out by music and shouting. Guests with delirious eyes marveling at the lights and sculptures. Gesturing hands pointing to the planet in delight and confusion, a mass of shadows played in the red light. A room of people drinking began merging with another group drenched sweat from dancing on a platform. Some in the middle of seduction found their hands groping for more. Everything was coated in red as currents of people blurred from room to room like blood through veins.

All those minds and hearts were absorbed into themselves, but Wilda's head was killing her. After the earlier-than-planned speech, Rilka had told Wilda that she needed extra time for the final piece before her dance. That had been three hours ago, and all the while Wilda had moved and checked and corrected as she walked through the halls. Her clothes were soaked with sweat and stuck to her after circling the station a few times. She was tired. She was annoyed and thirsty. Her lips were dry, and vaguely salty. Her lower back ached. The constant background noise kept pounding. She scuttled to a corner and let a group pass as the recording played on and on and on ...

Then, in the corner, next to one of the speakers, Wilda

noticed one of the whiskey dispensers. The vibrations of the wall grabbed her by the chest. Her muscles ached; her hand moved by itself as she realized how bone-dry, like a barren desert her throat was. She filled a glass to the brim and downed it in three gulps. She let the warmness overtake her for a moment.

"Just one more for the road," she told herself just as Minerva's gorgeous mane of dreadlocks rushed by her while a torn face followed close behind her.

Rilka wondered what had kept the holy being trapped in a husk: Accident? Interference? Treason? What aborted its first birth from the planet below? Not that it mattered. She'd done everything it had conferred through her dreams, through her art; it's why she had been chosen as its oracle. She knew to trust her instincts, when to give in to the sublime. It was an artist's highest purpose. Just as her mother had taught her: you do not question God, you obey *willingly* and respond, if called, just as the planner had been called and had done as she was told. Rilka stood and contemplated what she'd accomplished.

When the angel had shown her the bodies hidden between the station's joints, she knew she'd been blessed. She would work with the most sacred medium of the soul: the body. Even as she gave form to the sculptures, she knew they were mere practice for the centerpiece altar in her workshop, her place of divination under a watchful eye, her room and sanctuary.

Through the looking glass Qoroth slowly grew, drawing them closer to its embrace. She took in the new life breathing through the station. She drew strength from knowing she had single-handedly made it happen.

She watched the crowds from her computer screen, their terrifying ecstasy fueling the air. She laughed at the fights breaking out, erratic dancers breaking the fake walls, her sculptures roaming the halls and shepherding bodies to her workshop. She thought she might join-in and began to dance.

People moved in clusters. Everything was wet with blood and sweat. Everything was going in circles. Minerva was dimly aware of her desire to stop moving. She could see Wilda from the corner of her eyes trying to get to her but being continually pulled and pushed by a being composed of a hundred faces with its impossible body contracting and expanding. Twisting itself, stretching out, reaching, and taking in more faces. Around and around the station Minerva moved, every time passing closer to the room with some tower inside. "Break the loop," she began telling herself.

Minerva had passed Wilda three times now, but her voice wouldn't work. A wave carried her away. Had she so little resistance? And when a stranger stumbled into her, she grabbed him from behind and rammed him against the wall. Once. Twice. He laughed and continued to head-butt the same place, again, and again, and again, until the wall and his face broke.

More people began slamming against the walls and pools of blood formed on the floor. She felt like crying, laughing, screaming all at once. Still, she continued to move. Why'd she come to this party?

All around her the fake walls started to come down. She swirled her hands above her head and around her frame. Circles, circles, circles. Her movement carried her away from those around her. Dance, her body demanded, take it all in.

She stomped her legs rhythmically, side to side, on a collision course to another dancer. Minerva recognized them: its skinless face, metal teeth, bolted joints, dragged sigils, and painted legs. It was one of the sculptures, The Dancer. They began to move around each other, jumping sideways, arms gesturing and making angles, chests popping up, down. The thing began to stomp rapidly in one spot, tearing its remaining flesh from its body, throwing it to the ground as it spun.

She reached for her own forearm and scratched. Pulled and scratched. Blood began dripping from her fingers.

Break the loop, her mind screamed.

She screamed.

Her body delivered itself to numbness as Wilda pulled her away from the dancing corpse.

Rilka danced below her columns of muscles, hearts, lungs, eyes, hands, and voiceless mouths. The air felt jagged and heavy, the gathering bodies around her swelling. She tripped under the mounting pressure. Where was the divine impulse? Her body awakening to the moment? Where was her moment? She had done everything; she had conceived the party. Why couldn't she feel? She had brought her art, she had made a temple.

The walls felt smaller. The tumble of twisting metal tripped her again. Red light veiled the looming planet as its colossal silhouette loomed ever closer. Her heart was beating fast, so fast. Had she been wrong? No, she hadn't been wrong. She had followed herself, her insight, her dreams — the angel. It was a test, yes, it's only just a test. She would trust the angel. She continued to jump as strangers gathered around her, all of them delirious, dancing, and dying. She raised her crimson hands pointing at their destination.

Desire ached around the starving dead planet as life drummed closer to it; its shell cracked as airless gusts commanded the ground; the hungry vessel cried and beckoned as its death began to die.

The whispers in the light promised Wilda such sweet things if only she'd finish the ceremony, but she carried onward to the docking station. Minerva, unconscious, twitched inside the box cart she'd been placed in, her limbs tensing one way or the other like puppet strings. Wilda carefully avoided the bodies melting into the walls near the neon sigils whenever she passed one. Some people limped or crawled on the floor towards Rilka's room, guided by the remaining two sculptures who simply bowed to her. Rilka re-played the same four lines over and over in her head, *"arrange things properly," "aesthetic apotheosis," "Why?", "What's the budget?"*

Her body knew the way after weeks of walking around, though it felt pulled in every direction but forward the closer she got to her destination. She looked out a window once but quickly went on her way.

"New flesh," the mouths of the columns said.

"Budding flesh," The Tower said as they raised Rilka's limp body.

"Flowering flesh," the crawler repeated as it slid through the puddles of blood and sweat bubbling through the station making new symbols on the floor.

A breath growled vast and deep, filling the station.

Garbled from the speakers, a terribly shrill voice said: "I am . . ." It echoed from the walls and the bodies within them, from the body that was the station now.

From the safety of the ship, Wilda and Minerva saw the station briefly wriggle like a red worm before being swallowed by the abysmal mouth. They lingered in their silence, half-expecting to see an eye, maybe an arm, maybe fangs sprout from it and into space, but nothing happened.

Minerva programmed the ship to take them to the nearest hub-station, and Wilda kept her eyes on the planet as it grew smaller and smaller. They stood still, numb, in the music of the transport, the electric humming of its wires, the hissings of its far-off corners, the friction of metals hidden from sight. Wilda cleaned and gauzed Minerva's wounds in the cramped space; it would be another three hours before the red light left them.

About Gerardo J. Mercado

Gerardo J. Mercado is a Puerto Rican poet and fiction writer, his work has been published in online magazines, such as **Three-Lobed Burning Eye Magazine** and in other anthologies Gerardo's work focuses on spirituality, self-identity, the Caribbean, nature, science, and symbols.

X x.com/OddToB

instagram.com/gery_jou

Pulp

J. Ophelia Vazquez

The perfume of the city carries notes of orange blossom and ozone. The whistle of hot wind is her voice, jaunty and wicked.

The earth is damp and cakes against my pant legs as I run. I want to wipe it off, but I don't stop. I can't stop because I need to leave. I'm sure he is dead, so I can't be here. I cannot be here when they wrench him out from under the felled tree, prying bits of him out like mislaid seedlings.

The empire laughs.

Three days ago, Martin called me into the office. After, not during, my shift. Company management says clocking out wastes too much time, so they save important meetings for when we're off the books. I was sure he was gonna fire me, but he did the exact opposite.

"Management wants you as a team lead," he had said.

I didn't know how to take it. I'd been begging for more hours since Nina and I moved in together, so I should've felt grateful. Instead, it felt belated. Remember your godmother finding out you liked Tony Hawk, and twelve years later she got you a skateboard too small to step on without snapping it in half? Felt like that.

But it didn't matter how I felt because Martin was already entering my new schedule on the team calendar. "You're not in school or anything right? It's full-time. Weekends."

Full-time. That meant more hours. That meant benefits. Health insurance. I'd already been without since my last birthday.

I licked my lips. "Yeah, man, when do I start?"

I got home at four in the morning and jiggered around with the thin wire we use to open the house's side gate. It shuddered open, and the passage led to the in-law unit where Nina and I stayed. Neighborhood dogs barked and howled as I walked in. I did my best not to wake Nina, but she slept light.

"Fucking dogs," she mumbled. Her frown was obvious. Bitter.

She needed her rest. Every morning, Nina rolled out of bed and followed the same route I took to get home, backwards. Down the 215, up the 10, both freeway-arteries running up the limbs of the Inland Empire, the place we called home. Those freeways carried passengers into the empire's crotch, on the east side, where goodies slide out of warehouses and other strange slits with the click of a mouse.

Nina says she likes driving through the Inland Empire at night. That the first time her parents drove into San Bernardino, it was night, too.

Pretty town, her mom had said while neon lights buzzed and the green gate of the city beckoned their Ford like open arms. Then dawn broke and the smog settled on the horizon.

Pretty when you don't look too close, said her dad.

Nina sat up and stretched, her knuckles knocking against the headboard. "Bah, I couldn't sleep, anyways. Martin's been on my back all month."

I kicked off my shoes and frowned. "Sucks."

It did suck. Our manager, the guy she rightfully bitched about regularly, was gonna be training me.

A car alarm went off. More dogs started howling; Nina's face twisted and she groaned. "Martin, this shitty job, the hours — they're gonna be the death of us." Then she looked up at me and the tension melted. "What'chu got going on? You look like you wanna tell me something."

"Got promoted to team lead," I answered.

"Oh. Good." She gave me a thoughtful — or maybe hopeful — look and combed her fingers through her hair. Black and thick and strong. "That come with a raise, or is it just more work for the same pay?"

I shrugged off my jacket and threw it on the ground. "Small raise. Not enough for you to quit yet."

Nina exhaled. "Damn." She said it all quiet-like, the way she does when she's got more to say and won't, so I left it alone. I reminded her to grab her inhaler. She crawled out of bed while I crawled in, settling into the spot of warmth she left behind.

I had time to kill when I woke up. So I drove. I drove by the old housing projects by the gorge and drove up the hills and mountains and edged along the Cajon Pass, where the burn scars of a fire season growing longer and longer remained blackened. Eventually, I headed south and made my way back to the northeast side of San Berdoo.

When I was a kid, my family lived in a mold-filled apartment out on the northern end of Waterman Avenue. Blacktop heat baked through my rubber-soled shoes when I stepped outside. I couldn't keep pace with my brothers; they ran too fast for me to keep up, and cursed under their breaths when I caught up, so I learned to stop chasing them and kept to myself.

I got to know San Berdoo and the rest of the Inland Empire

well in those days. There were fields back then. Rectangles of a hundred-thousand square feet of dry grass that rustled as the wind kicked up. Junk lots littered with shattered beer bottles that made the ground glitter like it was worth something. But the orchards? Those were my favorite. I remember biking to the edge of the city just to pedal through rows and rows of orange trees at sunset, when the world was washed with gold and the scent of citrus was heavy enough to get drunk on.

I grew up and grew old. So did the city. Nowadays, I drive by those same spots on four wheels instead of two. The fields are gone. In their place are walls of concrete, blindingly white. The warehouses.

You see, the city was founded on two industries: agriculture and shipping. Agriculture came first, and it came easy. Here, the summers were dry, the winters mild, the earth rich. Turns out fruit grows well here. The junction of all the big Southern California freeways and the geography allowed freight to make its home here.

Over time, shipping won out. The only fruit trees left are owned by people too stubborn or too rich to sell the land. Warehouses and diesel ruled.

I'd visit old friends if I could. The smart ones, the *really* smart ones left; there's no work out here for them. The smart-ish ones choke on gas fumes all along the 210 or 10 or 60 all day, commuting to places where you don't need to break your spirit or back to earn minimum wage. Everyone else, the ones who couldn't leave, take odd jobs at odder hours to make ends meet.

It made for a lonely life. But I had Nina.

Our schedules didn't match up, but she had a gap between shifts she used as a lunch break. So we met up at one of the Mexican joints with the red and yellow striped roofs and a name starting with "Al" and shared a wet burrito and thick-cut fries.

We talked about nothing special: shows to torrent, plans to move out of the in-law we were renting from her step-dad. I responded, and I listened absently while the hot wind kicked up a shivering miniature tornado of dead leaves and trash. A common sight in early October. Santa Ana winds and all that. But I thought I'd point it out anyway.

"Jesus Christ, you see that? It's, like . . . like, witchcraft or some shit," I said to her.

"Goddamn. Berdoo's cursed. Or is doing the cursing." She laughed.

Then the laughs turned into coughs. Rough, mannish coughing. Coughing that was gonna leave her hoarse later, because she was absolutely *hacking* up a lung. She put her face to the crook of her elbow and waved me away when I tried to smack her back, because she hates it when I do that, but she gladly accepted the inhaler when I put that to her mouth.

"You good?" I asked.

She punched me in the shoulder, and the corner of her lip curled into a smirk. A good sign, but not good enough.

She's had that mystery cough for a while. Maybe it's allergies, desert dirt and pollen and heat scraping lungs raw. Maybe it was the Los Angeles smog, swept into the Empire's valley by the wind and trapped here by the mountains. Could've been the diesel fumes from the trucks backing in and out of the logistics facilities. Or asthma: that's common here, mostly because of the fumes.

Or maybe she just fucking had cancer, and we didn't know because the company wouldn't give her benefits.

Nina rested her head on her flat palm and stared at me, her eyes big and brown and shimmering. "Babe. I'm tired of working there."

Now that I think about it, I brushed her off. I didn't give her advice, didn't bitch about the company to make her feel better, none of that. You know what I said? "Baby, we gotta pay rent."

She looked like she wanted to say more. Instead, she just got quiet. "I know. Just saying."

All I did was pay her tab, then give her a peck on the lips and a smack on the ass. But she did smile at that.

"Did you see the way they stacked the pallets? Put the heavier shit on top. It was leaning. Fuckin' animals," Martin said.

Martin and I were shooting the shit after our shift, sitting on the bed of my truck. By then, he'd been training me for two days. The work I'd was doing was pretty much the same crap I'd been doing before, but now I had to micromanage a dozen people in addition to that. I wasn't liking the feeling of being a professional snitch, and Martin could tell, so that night he pulled out a bougie six-pack from some microbrewery he claimed to know the owner of.

It was my Friday night, and no bars were open, so I obliged him.

He waggled one of the empty cans in my face and cracked a grin. "Good to piss in during a busy shift, eh?" He'd started slurring his words.

Lightweight, I thought. I faked a laugh, but the sound of it was lost in the breeze.

"Can't drive home like this." He burped. "Let's fuckin' walk, man."

We went to the edge of the parking lot and started edging our way into the old orange groves. The company had bought hundreds of acres of land, and while most of that had been built on, there were still undeveloped pockets here or there. The grove Martin chose to trudge through had been bought years back but hadn't been cleared out. Or tended to, for that matter.

Instead of neat rows of trees, wild weeds crisscrossed along what used to be furrows. The space reeked of piss and fermented citrus. It looked more like a forest than anything intentional. All the while, the leaves rustled and tree branches creaked.

I rubbed the slight chill out of my arms while Martin continued blustering. I mostly ignored him until he started muttering names. "Jordan, Joseph, and Nina."

It caught me off-guard. Nina and I don't shit where we eat.

None of our coworkers know we live together — or even know each other. I almost thought Martin was testing me, until I remembered he was too stupid to do that.

So I played dumb. "What about them?"

"Gotta get rid of 'em, that's what. They cost too much to keep." A stupid smile spread on his face. "That's something you'll need to do as a Team Lead. Fire people. I'll show you how next week."

I stopped walking. I had to; I couldn't hear myself think, the blood was rushing so furiously through my ears. Yeah, I'd heard rumors that the company got rid of people who'd been working there too long. But rumor manifesting into reality like that?

"I didn't know that was something we actually did." I said it to myself, but Martin didn't get the memo.

He replied, "Well, sure. On paper, seniority means raises, more hours. That shit. But the overhead on that ain't sustainable. It makes employee turnover necessary."

Nina'd been there for almost a year. And she was damn good at packing, at sorting, at reminding the girls on her crew what their rights were. She deserved more than she got.

I remembered her wheezing coughs from the day before and felt my fists balling up tighter and tighter, my nails digging burning crescents into the flesh of my palms. But I controlled myself. "Wouldn't unemployment be a problem?"

"My mistake. You aren't firing 'em. You're getting 'em to quit," he corrected. "Cut their hours, give them shifts they can't take. Make their lives hell. Then you don't gotta worry about severance or any of that."

Trees creaked and groaned around us. A branch, heavily splintered, fell directly in my path.

I couldn't conceal how tight my tone had gotten. "That ain't legal, right? Won't they sue?"

Martin looked at me like I was stupid. "You think anyone here has the money to sue?"

I thought about Nina, scrabbling for an expired inhaler. No. No one does.

I heard the squelch of Martin's shoes on rotting fruit and squinted against harsh-blowing air.

It wasn't right. Anyone could see that. Shit, anyone could *smell* that, feel it scraping the inside of their lungs.

The sound of groaning tree trunks interrupted me. I barely registered the noise through the rest of the twitchy movements of the foliage, but there was a tree ahead of Martin, swaying. Splintering. It was about to fall, not on but ahead of him. Move him a few feet ahead and . . .

Maybe I imagined it, but I swore I heard the wind whispering. *Do it.*

I sucked in a breath. A roiling gust of wind tickled the sweat on my brow and snapped the tree ahead of Martin in half. I jumped ahead one, two, three steps.

Pushing a drunk was easy.

I hunch over on my knees at the edge of the parking lot, expecting nausea to make me throw up, but it never comes. I'm just standing like an idiot over my sneakers, so I decide to weigh the options. Someone normal would have called the cops, so I do. Their whirling sirens arrive. Assess the damage. Take a report I stammer through.

The cop smells the liquor on my breath and zips up his windbreaker with a grimace. "Fucking drunks," I hear him murmur as he and his partner drive away.

I sit in my car for a long time after that. It's just me and the empire. I feel stupid for doing it, but I . . . I start talking. To the empire. To no one. "Are you fucking proud?"

Proud of yourself? Proud of me?

I don't know.

When the bubbly sensation leaves my bloodstream, I make my way back home.

I don't talk to Nina for a while.

She understands.

As I gear up to go to work a few days later, I realize I haven't heard her cough once since the accident. Maybe it's the witchcraft of the city, of the Inland Empire. Or maybe it's nothing. I pull up to the company.

The parking lot smells like oranges.

About J. Ofelia Vazquez

J. Ofelia Vazquez is a Mexican-American born and raised in and around the Inland Empire, which is where their investment in the social determinants of health — the air we breathe, the food we eat, the environment we grow up in — began. You can find them at @ofeliawrites on most platforms.

A Dark and Lovely Wood

Casie Bazay

***Trigger Warnings for mention of suicide, death, and alcoholism*

Spring

One early May afternoon, Stella sat upon a fallen tree, eyes fixed upon a sprawling spider clinging to the center of its web. Surely, a fly would happen along at any moment and become entangled in the snare. Stella didn't want to miss the event when it occurred.

"Come on insects, where are you?" She tore her gaze away from the spider in search of would-be prey. No flies to be found, but she did spot a bright green grasshopper near her feet. "Aha!" Perhaps the *design of darkness* Robert Frost spoke of was in need of some help.

Stella carefully plucked the small insect from between blades of grass and tossed it into the web. The spider scrambled toward its free meal and, within seconds, was spinning a shiny cocoon of white around the grasshopper. *Assorted characters of death and blight* on display before her very eyes! Two spindly legs trembled as the spider continued to encase the insect's body, and soon enough, Stella could see no part of the grasshopper at all, nothing to indicate there was a living (or more accurately, dying) creature inside the cocoon.

But like air from a punctured balloon, Stella's initial curiosity fizzled right out. She'd wanted to see the spider *eat* the grasshopper, not wrap it inside a miniature coffin. She looked away as the shape of a real-sized coffin came to mind. This one was baby blue and sealed tight, hiding away death's mysterious claim on her mother.

They didn't even have a viewing before the funeral, which Stella knew was customary. They'd had one with Great-grandma Pearl after all. Also with Uncle Jimmy. But when Mother died, Stella heard the mortician tell Father that some people were better remembered in life than in their final tragic moments. Of course, that didn't keep Stella from imagining all kinds of things freezing river water could do to body — especially one that had been in there for four days.

While Stella mourned her mother, there was also a different kind of sadness. Over the last few months of her life, Mother had somehow forgotten she had two children — not just the son who went off to war two years ago and never came back. Stella heard mumblings of *POW* and *MIA*, but all she knew was that she'd likely never see her big brother again. And now, it was just her and her father in a new house she refused to call home, Stella's only solace, these lovely nearby woods.

Overhead, a songbird trilled, pulling her attention to the treetops. If she really listened, dozens of songs all played at once, a sound her brain had somehow tuned out until this moment.

"I hear you, birdies," she called before trying to mimic one of the tunes. Ernie hadn't taught her much, but he had shown her how to whistle before he buzzed off his long hair and joined the armed forces.

Stella walked as she whistled, her feet following a faint path probably worn by coyotes or some other kind of wild creature. She wasn't particularly afraid of wild creatures; most of them only came out at night and wouldn't bother a person unless provoked. The books Stella had read made her quite certain of this.

Supple leaves whispered in the breeze and birds serenaded her as she strolled. Stella had a sudden urge to be up there among all that green, to see what the birds could see. What she needed was a good climbing tree.

After surveying at least two dozen, she found one with a nice low split in its trunk, a place where she could wedge a foot and grab hold of a branch to hoist herself up. It wasn't nearly as easy as climbing the small pear tree in her old front yard, but soon enough, Stella was cradled within a V provided by two sturdy branches, a good twenty feet above ground. The view was a heady thing, temporarily dissolving all the sorrow she'd endured in her twelve short years. Stella reached out, pulling a diamond-shaped leaf from the tree and tucking it inside the band of her ponytail.

"You may call me Stella of the Trees," she said in her most dignified voice, one Stella had used to recite poetry to Mother as she arranged flowers for the dining room table or ironed Father's shirts.

"We will," a voice whispered back, so soft that Stella almost missed it.

For the first time in months, she smiled.

Summer

One July morning, the most dreadful stench drew Stella into a part of the woods she had yet to explore. Wearing knee-high rubber boots and a red romper she'd nearly outgrown, she waded through tall grass, determined to find the source of the smell. In one hand, she held a stick like a royal scepter, using it to push back any brambles or branches that dared to stand in her way. A yellow butterfly drifted past, wings seemingly too delicate to carry its weight. But just like that butterfly, Stella was stronger than she looked.

"Stella of the Trees coming through," she proclaimed. "Please stay back." She whacked at a dangling vine with her scepter. The stench grew stronger, enough to make Stella's stomach turn. Undeterred, she pinched her nose between two fingers and continued on. Exactly fifteen footsteps later, she spotted it: the gray corpse of a rotting armadillo. Stella had never seen one in real life, but somehow she knew that's what the decaying thing was. She inched closer, pinching her nose tighter, though the putrid air now seeped into her lungs. Flies buzzed in circles around the dead animal, and several beetles crawled along its back. Or was it a shell? She wasn't quite sure what to call it. Stella poked at the armadillo with her scepter, squealing when what remained of its head fell away.

"You are absolutely disgusting," she told the unhearing animal. Yet, she couldn't look away. *This is what happened to Mother,* she thought, and not for the first time. Maybe Ernie, too, wherever he was. Stella wasn't sure how to feel about that.

She poked at the dead thing again, rolling it over. Maggots squirmed and dropped from the underbelly of the armadillo. Stella let out a scream loud enough to clear the stench from her lungs. After a moment, she forced herself to look closer.

"Earth's recyclers," she reminded herself. That's all maggots were. Mrs. Johnson, her fifth grade teacher from the city, had taught her that. Though the smell of death hadn't abated, Stella was growing somewhat accustomed to it, enough so that she un-pinched her nose and drew in a deep breath. Her mind searched for adjectives to describe the air particles settling inside her nostrils: *Pungent. Acrid. Malodorous.* Mrs. Johnson would be pleased.

"I wonder how it all ended for you," she said, peering down at the armadillo with more sympathy now. "Was it a fox? Perhaps a badger? A pack of wild dogs?" Another thought occurred to her. Maybe the armadillo had simply died of old age. "No matter the cause of death, I think you deserve a proper burial, even half-rotted as you are. I'll go fetch a shovel and give you that honor." Stella started away, but soon paused, turning to speak over her shoulder. "Now don't you go anywhere!" She nearly burst into a fit of giggles at the ridiculous command.

The small backyard shed turned up a rake, a pile of old boards, and several small gardening tools, none of them shovel-like.

"Hmm." Stella lifted a finger into the air. "I have another idea."

The screen door smacked closed as she entered the house and marched straight to the kitchen, with its ugly yellow-painted walls and pea green Frigidaire. Rummaging through a drawer, Stella found the biggest serving spoon they owned — one Mother once used to scoop generous helpings of her famous casseroles or mashed potatoes and gravy. It would have to do.

Back on the front porch, spoon in hand, she paused again. Poor Ernie deserved a proper burial, too. In the spare bedroom, she pulled the cardboard box full of family photos from beneath the bed, digging through them until she found her brother's senior portrait, the one where he wore stylish plaid slacks and a brown button-down shirt and didn't look at all like the type of boy who'd swap his nice clothing for that ugly green army uniform.

With the scepter, spoon, and photo, Stella was finally ready to return to the woods. "I'm coming, Mr. Armadillo!" she called.

The carcass was easier to find the second time around, and Stella didn't bother to pinch her nose at all. She found a bare patch of earth not far from the armadillo and began scooping away the dirt. It was tedious work, thanks to the tangles of roots that kept getting in her way. At one point, a prickly, white root wrapped right around her spoon, tugging it from her grasp. Stella blinked and frowned down at the hole. She grabbed the spoon with both hands and yanked hard, the root finally snapping to set her tool free.

"How odd," she remarked, but continued on with her task.

The hole changed shape, becoming more narrow than wide, and she finally cleared enough dirt to make space for the body.

Swiping sweat from her brow, Stella sat back to admire the burial site. Her wrists ached from all the work, but the armadillo deserved it. Ernie, too. Using her scepter, she pushed the corpse, maggots and all, inside the hole. The tail bent at an odd angle and made a crackling noise as she pushed it down to fit.

"Oops! Sorry, Mr. Armadillo!"

Next came Ernie's portrait, far more pleasant to look at than the dead animal. Stella realized that she should say a prayer; a proper burial called for that. But all she knew were poems, so she chose "Do Not Stand at My Grave and Weep" by Mary Elizabeth Frye. Afterward, she used the spoon to cover Ernie and the armadillo, and once the earth had been tamped down, Stella searched for wildflowers to place upon the grave. It didn't take long to secure a small bouquet, and the fragrance greatly improved upon the lingering stench.

"Farewell, Mr. Armadillo and Ernie." Stella stood and wiped the dirt from her knees. "I'm off to have a snack."

Fall

One October afternoon, when Father was in an especially sour mood, Stella retrieved her favorite poetry book and took to the woods once more. She had hopes of reading to the armadillo and Ernie, but now that the leaves had turned copper and the summer grass was golden, the gravesite was nowhere to be found. Some type of marker would have been nice — a small pile of rocks as a headstone at the very least. Stella chided herself for not thinking of such, but for today, her climbing tree would do. She clambered up to the familiar V and read aloud *The Raven and Other Poems* by Edgar Allan Poe. When the crows cawed with appreciation, Stella took a small bow.

However, by poem number twenty-nine, her eyelids had grown droopy as her body softened into that trancelike state between wakefulness and sleep. The crows had flown away, and only the raspy rustle of leaves remained.

"Sleep, dear Stella," they seemed to say.

Her breathing fell into a slow and steady rhythm as she rested her head against one side of the V. Stella felt the tug of darkness, but it wasn't a completely unwelcome sensation. She allowed the blackness to pull her under its spell.

Stella's eyes flashed open as her fingernails dug into the hard flesh of the tree. Inside her chest, her heart beat like a woodpecker's frantic pecking. She pulled herself upright before peering down at the ground so far below where her poetry book lay, pages fluttering in the breeze.

"How absolutely idiotic of me! I could have fallen to my death." Limbs trembling, she climbed down from the tree.

Scavenging for oyster mushrooms seemed a safer choice, and one that would likely please Father as well. Stella hummed as she searched, relishing the sensation of crunching leaves and cool dirt beneath her bare feet. She knelt to peek beneath fallen trees and closely examined the trunks of standing ones. When she finally discovered a fan-shaped cluster of oysters, she carefully pried them from the bark using the front of Ernie's too-big Beatles T-shirt as a makeshift basket. Then she hurried toward the house to show Father.

Her yard was in sight when something pierced Stella's heel, stinging with the force of a hundred bees. Maybe even a thousand. She screamed and dropped her collection of mushrooms. The culprit lay there unashamed: a small thorny branch from a honey locust. *Devil trees.* The burn in her heel sharpened, and tears slipped down Stella's cheeks as she hobbled toward the house.

"Father!" she called, though she knew it was unlikely he would hear. Her tears flowed more freely and Stella soon found it impossible to place any weight on her injured foot. She wanted to examine the puncture but was afraid that if she sat down, she'd never be able to get back up. So she hopped like a one-legged frog across the lawn and up the sagging porch steps, yanking open the door and crashing onto the sticky linoleum floor. That got Father's attention.

He scooped her up and carried her to the kitchen sink where he washed her foot with soap and warm water. The wound was a tiny thing. Stella wasn't sure Father understood just how badly it hurt, but she wiped her tears away and pushed her mouth into a smile. This was the nicest thing Father had done for her in ages.

Winter

Father had taken to the bottle. At least that's what Grandma Mary said at Thanksgiving dinner. Things had gotten worse after that. Grandma and Father had argued, which involved a fair amount of cursing on Father's part before he seemed to remember Stella sitting there at the table.

"Go wait in the car," he had told her.

They didn't speak on the drive home. In fact, Father hadn't said much of anything to her since that day. Now they were in the throes of December, and winter had never felt so dark and lonely.

Driven by sorrow or maybe something else, Stella grew determined to locate the final resting spot of the armadillo and Ernie. Thanks to the honey locust, she still walked with a limp and had begrudgingly begun wearing her rubber boots again. Today, her woolen socks kept slipping down inside them, adding to her dismal mood.

The air had a cruel bite to it, numbing Stella's nose and prying its way into the fingertips of her gloves, but she much preferred this kind of cold to Father's chilly disposition. She wasn't sure if he loved her at all anymore; perhaps he was plotting to leave like Mother did.

"Mr. Armadillo, Ernie," she called, if only to break the unbearable silence. "Please tell me where you are."

No birds sang today. They'd probably all flown south for the winter. Stella paused, hoping the dead might speak to her the way the trees sometimes did.

Frigid stillness echoed all around her.

With heavy legs, she trudged onward. Everything was gray: The sky. The trees. The grass. She thought some color might return to the world if she could just find Mr. Armadillo and Ernie. Maybe that rainbow of wildflowers would still lay scattered across the grave, dried but mildly fragrant.

Just then, a single ray of sunlight peeked through the clouds, and as if by magic, a stick the size of a scepter appeared. It could have been *her* scepter, for all she knew. She hadn't used it since summer. Stella snatched it up and waved it around like a wand.

"Lead me to Mr. Armadillo and Ernie," she ordered. The wand pointed left and Stella hurried in that direction. Ahead, a brown and leafless vine hung from a tree like a limp rope. Stella's eyes crinkled around the edges. This *was* the right direction; she could feel it in her gut. The wand led her on. In a small clearing, something silver glinted in the dull light. The serving spoon! Stella had left a marker after all.

She fell to her knees, happy tears springing forth. They glided down her cheeks like tiny ice cubes. But now that she was here, merely seeing the grave didn't feel like enough. Stella tore off her gloves, digging her nails into the hard dirt. She scraped at the earth until her fingertips burned, but her eyes widened with excitement when Ernie's crumpled photo appeared. She grabbed for it, but part of the photo clung to the armadillo shell, and it ripped in half when she tried to tug it free.

"No!" she yelled. More icy tears came, and her nose began to run. Stella tossed the photo piece aside, determined to be more careful with the armadillo. When she finally pried the shell from the ground, the rest of the small skeleton lay intact beneath.

"Mr. Armadillo!" she cried. "I'm sorry I abandoned you for so long." Stella retrieved a handful of bones and held them to her chest. Curling herself into a tight ball, she clutched the bones like a treasured pearl inside a clam and rocked back and forth.

Everything turns to bones, she thought. Ernie. Mother. The armadillo. Father will too.

Stella rocked and rocked.

After a while, she sang a silly bedtime song Mother used to sing to her. Then she recited "Stopping by Woods on a Snowy Evening" before growing quiet again, thinking.

"I don't want to turn to bones," she whispered. "I'd rather be a spider or a tree."

"Stella of the Trees . . ." She wasn't sure if the woods were talking again or if the voice was only in her head. She uncurled a little and turned her head to one side, listening.

The wind picked up, rustling dry branches overhead. Stella peeked over her elbow, discovering that darkness had settled upon the woods. Had she really been out here that long?

She wiped at her face before depositing all but one rib bone back into the hole. Both halves of Ernie's portrait, too. She pushed dirt back over the grave and stood, her body aching and tired and so very cold.

Something small and sharp pinged against her forehead. Then another. And another. Angry ice pellets.

Stella turned and stumbled in the direction of her house just as the evening air was pierced by a sad and distant howl. She shivered and hugged her arms tight across her chest.

"Stella?" a voice called.

Was it Father or the trees?

Her teeth chattered. "I- I-I'm coming."

The ice pellets pinged harder, attacking her face and bouncing off her peacoat. She needed shelter. And quickly.

"Here," the voice called, a little louder this time.

Stella turned toward the sound, discovering a tree with a girl-sized hole in its trunk. It looked like the tree where she'd found the oyster mushrooms a few months back, though she didn't remember the hole.

Using the rib bone, Stella scraped away a cobweb and then wedged herself inside. She sank to the ground and pulled her knees to her chest. Outside, the ice pellets danced over the forest floor, and the coyotes howled again. Hopefully, they would find shelter, too. Stella felt strangely safe inside her tree. Cozy even. But the longer she sat there, listening to the icy rain, the smaller the girl-sized hole seemed to shrink. Stella blinked curiously and reached a finger out to trace the diminishing shape. She wasn't particularly alarmed, even as it shriveled to a squirrel-sized hole. Nor when it closed completely and darkness enveloped her.

The woods are lovely, dark and deep, she recalled.

And Stella had no promises to keep.

About Casie Bazay

Casie Bazay is the author of the YA novel, *Not Our Summer* (Running Press Teens, 2021). After leaving the teaching profession 13 years ago, she has worked mainly as a freelance writer, specializing in equine health and care, but Casie also offers editing services and tutors kids in reading. She has hundreds of articles published with various companies and publications such as *The Horse, Country Extra, Natural Horse Magazine, Oklahoma Horses Magazine* and more. Casie's other full-time job is mothering two wonderful but headstrong children and many (less headstrong) four-legged pets.

Website: casiebazay.com

About the Editor

Lauren T. Davila is a Pushcart-nominated, Latina author, anthologist, and editor. She has edited multiple short story anthologies, including:

As We Convene: An Anthology of Time and Place (Inked In Gray Press; June 2024)

To Root Somewhere Beautiful: An Anthology of Reclamation (Outland Entertainment; March 2024)

When Other People Saw Us, They Saw the Dead (Haunt Publishing, May 2022; Outland Entertainment, May 2023)

Her poetry and short fiction has appeared online at Granada Magazine, The Paragon Journal, Ghost Heart Literary Magazine, Peach Velvet Mag, Voyage Journal, Second Chance Magazine, Headcanon Magazine, In Parentheses, and Poets Reading the News. She is currently editing her debut adult novel, as well as working on poetry and short story collections.

Lauren has an MA in English from Claremont Graduate University and an MFA in Fiction Writing from George Mason University. Besides her personal creative work, she is the Acquisitions Editor at Inked In Gray Press and is actively acquiring genre fiction from historically marginalized writers. She is also the Assistant Director at PocketMFA, an online writing and mentorship program.

She lives in the greater Los Angeles area where you can find her swimming, walking her golden retriever, and drinking one too many lattes.

She is represented by Susan Velazquez Colmant at JABberwocky Literary Agency.

Also by Inked in Gray

Thank you so much for reading As We Convene! We hope you enjoyed it! We'd love for you to leave a review on any retail and review platforms such as Inked in Gray product page, Bookshop.org, IndieStoryGeek, Goodreads, or Amazon.com

If you enjoyed this anthology, please check out our other anthologies or buy another book by one of our authors!

Inked in Gray Anthologies:

The First Stain

What Remains

We Deserve to Exist